EVERYTHING BEGAN
AT HOME

I hope this gives
you a Christmas giggle
or two Rosemary –
Laurie Oxsen
Dec. 20, 2011

EVERYTHING BEGAN AT HOME

One of an Interior Design Enthusiast's
Quirky Dreams

A Novel

Laurie Oxsen

iUniverse, Inc.
New York Lincoln Shanghai

Everything Began at Home
One of an Interior Design Enthusiast's Quirky Dreams

Copyright © 2008 by Laurie Oxsen

iUniverse books may be ordered through booksellers or by contacting:

iUniverse
2021 Pine Lake Road, Suite 100
Lincoln, NE 68512
www.iuniverse.com
1-800-Authors (1-800-288-4677)

Because of the dynamic nature of the Internet, any Web addresses or links contained in this book may have changed since publication and may no longer be valid.

This is a work of fiction. All of the characters, names, incidents, places, organizations, and dialogue in this novel are either the products of the author's imagination or are used fictitiously.

ISBN: 978-0-595-49415-6 (pbk)
ISBN: 978-0-595-49238-1 (cloth)
ISBN: 978-0-595-61091-4 (ebk)

Printed in the United States of America

God has been very kind to me and bestowed me with many blessings. I would like to dedicate this book to two of them, the love of my life and my soul mate, Anthony Oxsen, and my best friend and a sister in my heart, Karen March.

CHAPTER 1

Lady Shelby Whitethorn Abbott closed her front door on the last mourner and stood not moving. Dressed in a simply tailored black dress, she pressed her forehead against the door and let the tears she'd been holding back flow unchecked. She knew if she left the spot, turned and walked away, that the reality of Sam's death would broadside her again. Once again she would have to walk through their home, lovingly created over the past twenty years, and face that her first and only love was gone. "My God" she uttered, "I had always heard that people didn't know what to say when someone passes, but, my God! How awful reality is." Still crying, she picked up the simple carving Sam bought for her on their first date. She had been visiting from England and bumped into Sam in a little antique shop. She never knew she would be so blessed; Sam had wanted the carving too and when he found out she was visiting, bought it for her and took her to lunch to discuss "visiting" rights. Shelby never went home and the twenty years since had been a rich bond of love she was sure would never be repeated.

What had Dorothy James said? Oh yes, "Don't worry Shelby; with your looks I'm sure you won't be alone for long." How crass. True, she was very pretty, tall, slim and with beautiful auburn hair and that famous English complexion. There was another reason for her radiance though. Sam and Shelby had postponed having children so that they could build their home, travel as they wanted and then "nest" when they had done all those things that children didn't allow for. Now at 45, Shelby was two and a half months pregnant and the grief over Sam's sudden death touched her inner core, her soul, with a raw rupture she was sure she would never repair. Why didn't Sam see the doctor as she asked? Headaches, especially migraine headaches, were never an element in his life. The aneurism might have been found, he might have been alive to see his child grow.

The caterer stopped short upon seeing Shelby when she entered. Edith had never seen such monumental grief show on a face at any of the funeral receptions she had ever catered. "Excuse me Mrs. Abbott. I have finished cleaning up the refreshments and stored the food in containers for you. I know you don't feel like eating, but I do hope you'll try. Is there anything at all I can do for you before I leave? Would you like to try a cup of tea or coffee?"

"No thank you Edith. You did a wonderful service today and I want to thank you for going above and beyond a caterer's job. How did you manage to know when I needed you to ask me for something?"

"I've been a caterer for 35 years and I can prepare food and serve it in my sleep. I love helping folks when they need my talents, but it does leave me with an acute hearing ability for comments of those who "mean well" towards my clients that are grieving. I know an insensitive guest that needs to be moved to an area where they will fill their mouths with food—effectively shutting them up—when I hear one."

Edith heard a small lift in her voice when she replied "well, you saved me from making a spectacle of myself nonetheless. Let me walk you out, I have a little something for you in the foyer." Shelby grabbed one of two envelopes with Edith's name on it and handed it to her with a hug. "This is more than you quoted, but I want you to pick up something delightful, non-necessary, and that just tickles you inside—I want you to know a piece of the man you helped us say goodbye to today."

"Oh, Mrs. Abbott, now I'm going to cry." Edith put on her coat and left. Shelby turned once again and attempted to walk directly to their bedroom and change out of the heels pinching her feet and into something she could lounge in. She wasn't going to look around as she usually did as she went through their home. Their beautiful home; it always made her anxious to come back at the end of a day. She loved her little boutique, but here, she felt so serene, so much in a world that was only for Sam and her—and they had hoped their child. The minute they had found out she was pregnant; they had put together a nursery. It had been fun to go to the baby stores and pick out a theme room. They hadn't told anyone she was pregnant yet; at 45 she knew not to cross the forbidden rule of not waiting until the first trimester ended. But inside, she knew this child was meant to be and that all was well. Wisely, she had closed the nursery door before the funeral. Unfortunately, not before her brother, Lord David Whitethorn had arrived and found her out. He wanted her to move back to England immediately, before the pregnancy became advanced, and stay at Whitethorn Castle. He was only partly correct in what Shelby had decided she would do for herself and her baby.

David had been a blessing. They had always been close—even after her marriage and life in the United States—but she didn't belong at Whitethorn Castle anymore. Sometimes Shelby wondered if David hadn't been so entrenched with duty if he would have stayed there and continued the "line". Well, it was something they never discussed and he had finally agreed to help her look at real estate here in Keddie. The unusual city with its seaside charm and rich farmlands was centrally located between San Francisco and Sacramento. Shelby never knew a city could be described as a "quaint" community. The mix of small artisan shops and gated residences with their front porches didn't allow for one to notice the freeways and malls interspersed throughout the city. California had become her home and she wanted her child to grow up where Sam did. This was such a small part she could give this child of a father never to be known; that and her memories. Shelby needed a new home, smaller and something created just for her and her baby. A home that wouldn't hit her soul with crippling pain each time she looked around and realized with fresh awareness what she had lost. She needed a home that would push her to her future and heal her quickly to a space where she could treasure this unexpected moment and honor a blessed past.

Shelby finished her bath and wandered into the kitchen. Suddenly Edith's idea of tea, herbal of course, sounded like something that might soothe her so she could sleep. David was coming at 9:00 in the morning to start the tour of homes with the real estate agent and she desperately needed to rest. She was touched by Edith again when she found a note on the counter letting her know some minestrone soup was on "warm" in the oven and her hopes that Shelby would at least try some. Feeling as if she had been hugged, Lady Shelby Whitethorn Abbot did just that as she watched a late September twilight dapple over the Chinese Pistache trees in the backyard.

CHAPTER 2

Lord David Whitethorn heard the shrill ring of the phone and forced himself awake. He was bone tired. First, the call from his sister bringing him on the flight from home, then all of the paper, attorneys, funeral arrangements and endless details. As if that wasn't enough, the shock of her pregnancy and then her wrestling his promise to help her relocate here, in California, of all things! Well, he loved her and envied her. David could only wish that his entry down the marriage path had been as rich and full. He stopped his thoughts—enough of that awful memory. It was 5:00 in the morning and he was meeting Shelby and her realtor at 9:00 sharp. He wanted to catch his children at a good time for them—after lunch and before their afternoon exercise was best. So, tired he was, but he thanked the operator for her wake up call, took care of those early morning necessities and dialed home. He looked around the opulent pent-house suite as he waited for the connection and thought of Whitethorn. It was home, had always been his home and was now his children's home. Funny, but the suite really didn't make him feel the need to hurry back home—only his children did.

His housekeeper Emily answered the phone and happily heard her employer's voice. "Oh hello, Lord David, I'm glad to hear from you and how is Lady Shelby holding up?"

"Hello Emily, she's doing as well as can be expected given the shock. How are my children and are they about that I can speak with them?"

"Yes, of course, sir. They just finished their lunch with Nanny and were about to go outside for a bit. I'll get them for you right away."

David could hear the laughing in the background as the children came to the phone. "Hello papa! Are you coming home today?" Catherine eagerly asked. "My dolly has a bad broken leg and I need you to fix it."

Stifling laughter David replied "No Cat, I have to finish some things with your Aunt Shelby and I may be a few more days yet. How did your dolly break her leg?"

"She was stuck in her bed and didn't bend it when I pulled her out."

"Oh, well I'll fix her when I get home. Ask Nanny if she will bandage it for me to keep the leg still."

"She did that already papa after I said she couldn't fix dolly. I need you to fix her—you know how to fix anything. Tim, stop touching me. You'll have a turn when I'm ready!"

"Cat, let me say hello to your brother. I know you were going outside and I want to speak with him too."

"Hello papa, I have a kite! Nanny said the wind is good today and I can try to fly it!"

"That sounds like fun, Tim. I wish I could be there to see that. Did you and Nanny make your kite?"

"Yes. It was too hard for me and Nanny fixed it with some glue and string."

"That sounds fine Tim. I miss you and Cat very much and I will be home in a few days. Let me speak with Nanny and then you and Cat can try your kite."

Nanny Gwendolyn had been standing holding Catherine's hand so that Timothy could talk to his father. When the phone suddenly was thrust at her as he ran, she assumed Lord David wanted to talk with her. "Yes sir, Nanny here."

"Hello Gwen. I wanted to thank you for the extra care you are giving the children while I am away and ask how they are doing in my absence. I will be at least a few more days with Lady Shelby, possibly up to a week."

"They are doing fine sir. Of course the little ones miss you, but your calls have helped. At six and four they don't really understand a funeral or what has happened to their uncle, but they know their aunt is sad and needs your help. I have been keeping them busy when they are awake and answering any questions with as much as I think they can understand. They will get by and be more than ready for your return."

"Very good Gwen, I am sure you are handling the situation with your usual talent. I know you haven't been able to see your grandchildren while I've been gone. When I return, please feel free to schedule a week off to go for a long visit with them."

"Thank you sir, I will."

David could hear the children begging Nanny to let them go fly the kite and hurriedly said his goodbyes just as he heard gentle knocking on his door. He knew it was his man, Henry, before he heard his voice calling for entry. "Good morning sir. I trust you slept well."

"Good morning Henry, as well as can be expected when traveling thank you. What have we for breakfast today?"

"There is some fresh fruit from what they call their "farmers market" along with two eggs, poached, and a muffin with jams. I agreed to try some pomegranate juice, but I have orange if you would rather. The paper is here and the weather is quite fine today. You have your choice of coffee or tea, both are prepared, and I will confirm arrangements for the car for 8:45 if there has been no change of plans with Lady Shelby."

"That is perfect Henry. I am still due at Lady Shelby's house at 9:00 to meet her realtor and begin the tour of homes. If the weather is going to be as warm as yesterday I would appreciate your preparing my summer suit to wear. My black was stifling in this climate. Bit different from home isn't it?"

"Yes sir. I am surprised Lady Shelby wants to stay here. The autumn trees are beautiful but I would have hoped for more of a chill in the morning and with no family near her I would have expected her to return to Whitethorn. I'll prepare your suit while you eat. Will you be working on your drawings for the new building this morning?"

"Thank you Henry, but no, I haven't heard back from the client about the last changes for me to proceed. No need for you to trouble yourself with getting the drafts out."

David didn't reply to Henry's comment about family. Shelby was still early in her pregnancy and she hadn't told anyone about the "blessed event" yet. He didn't know why, but this was definitely her decision and he would honor it. He smelled his breakfast and found himself very hungry in spite of his exhaustion. The juice was new to him and surprisingly, he liked it. Breakfast done, he finished his dress and met the waiting car in the lobby. He was anxious to get the day started and didn't notice the women turning their heads as he walked through. Lord David had long since given up caring whether women found him handsome or not. At forty-eight he had chosen his life and was not thinking of changing anything at all.

Shelby's home was impressive in the autumn morning. He rang the bell and was surprised at how quickly the door was answered. Shelby had been on the other side saying goodbye to her housekeeper. "Oh, hello David, right on time, I just need a moment. Please come in and make yourself comfortable in the living room. There is some coffee in the kitchen if you want some. Turning, she continued with her housekeeper. "Thank you for all of your help Mary. Now remember, take some time off and spend my gift exactly as I asked you to." Mary held the envelope and shook Shelby's hand. "I will Mrs. Abbott and thank you for remembering me at such a time. You and Mr. Abbott have always been a joy to serve. Will you need my services in your new home?"

"I don't know Mary. I am hoping to get something smaller and I may be able to keep it up myself. I am going to have to see how it all works out. I may not have as much time as I think with the holiday season starting at the boutique. I am still going to need you as usual until the new house is found and escrow has closed. Why don't we wait and see what the future brings?" Shelby didn't want to tell her she was going to be staying home once her baby was born. She didn't want to have to deal with one more reason for someone to tell her an expression of either congratulations or sympathy.

"Oh, you're right. We are really getting ahead of ourselves. Oh course we will keep things as is and change my services as need be."

Shelby returned to the kitchen and found David with coffee cup in hand introducing himself to her realtor, Jeannie Lawson. "Jeannie and David, I am so sorry to keep you waiting. I trust you two have finished the introductions?"

"Yes Shelby, Jeannie was just showing me her list of properties for us to tour today. Since she has fifteen on the list, I agree with her that we should get started right away."

"Oh, yes, of course. Jeannie, do you want to give me an overview in the car on the way?"

"Yes Shelby I think that would be smart and save us some time. Finding a smaller home with the details you gave me in an established area that will make you feel as comfortable as Piedmont Estates is a challenge. I think we have some good prospects and there is one in particular that I think might be perfect. Just in case you don't agree I think we need to be prepared to see them all."

"Let's get started then."

David had never been so bored in his life. The homes that Jeannie had shown him so far had all been nice, but nothing compared to the one Shelby already owned. He saw nothing of character or promise in any of the five homes they had already toured and he was beginning to doubt that the realtor really had a "perfect" choice planned in the day. They were advancing on a little bricked cottage type home, number six on their list, as he looked at his sister. Shelby had a forlorn look on her face through the last two homes and as he saw her face suddenly brighten, he looked out the car in the direction of her gaze. The house was in the middle of three homes on a courtyard, but it drew you in. An established magnolia tree in the front shielded the old brick courtyard. Primroses and bougainvilleas on climbing vines over lush greenery lead to a door surrounded by pottery and a "friends welcome" sign. Well the outside was promising he thought. Jeannie broke into their thoughts "this is the house I thought would be perfect for you. It looks small from the front but it is actually 2,300 square feet. A little larger than you asked for Shelby, but I think when you see the inside you will consider it the right downsize for you. You may end up surprised by how 5,000 matches up to 2,000 square feet."

Stepping out of the car, the three walked up a stepping-stone pathway and rang the bell. Of course it was a formality to verify no one was home. Jeannie opened the lock box and took the key to open the door, then stepped aside to let Shelby and David enter first. They entered and looked up, and in, and around, and then at each other with stunned faces. It was as if divine intervention had answered Shelby's every wish. Jeannie was right, this was "the home" and this was also where new lives would begin for them all.

CHAPTER 3

Laurel Andrews rose immediately with the 4:45 am alarm. She and Greg had argued until 10:00 the previous evening and she didn't feel like doing any morning cuddling with him thank you very much. Greg gave a polite "good morning" and rose too. While Greg was showering to get ready for his commute to work, Laurel was anxious to dress for her run and be gone before his shower ended. She was still too angry to want to kiss him goodbye and a strong run would help her get over her anger. That didn't stop her from appreciating the sight of him in his shower before she left.

She turned on the lights so she could see to lock the door and turned to enter the street. Starting slow to stretch her muscles naturally, she let her mind wander as she usually did. She couldn't believe Greg's gall. They had sold their house, a miracle in a buyer's market, but it was the package the buyer wanted that both delighted and terrified her. She knew the move was inevitable and had hoped that in this market it would take some time so she could adjust. Unfortunately the strong minded widow bought their home in the first week and with one showing! As if that wasn't enough to wrap her mind around, the package included the house "as is"—all the furnishings, handmade drapes, pictures—everything that wasn't a personal belonging/keepsake, which was to be listed and approved by her, and she wanted a four week escrow. Laurel was delighted to know that someone appreciated her talents in the home decorating arena and a long held dream of a career in interior design sparked once again. She and Greg could never really afford for her to take the chance of her own business and with nothing but a portfolio of friends homes she had done and no formal schooling in design, an established firm would never hire her. "So how do I say what is personal?" she wondered. "How do I say, the mosaic dresser is a keepsake because it was my first project and I love it when I could very well do another? How do I say I handpicked the pussy willows in their array of gold, red and green and then dried them before arranging them in pots? Or the stenciled cornices?"

Greg was thrilled with the offer—especially since the buyer had added $100,000.00 to the asking price for all of Laurel's furnishings when he expected to be lucky if the selling price covered their existing mortgage and a down payment on a new house down south. He had already signed the papers with their realtor before she got home from grocery shopping after work last night. The realtor was there and if he saw her face, he ignored it. This was a great deal and he needed it. His finances were running well under his earnings of the last few years and he hadn't finished preparing for the slump when it hit. So looking at Greg's face, she buckled to the pressure and signed the documents. Now she had four weeks to give notice at her job and start finding a new home and job down south. At least she didn't have to worry about a lot of boxing—all they were really taking was their clothing, bathroom and kitchen textiles and a few keepsakes. She knew once she found her new home she could draft out a new design in no time and have what she needed within a few weeks of moving in. When she and Greg had built their home before, Laurel had it basically as it was today within three weeks of moving in. She had carefully planned each room, the colors of the home and the furnishings she would need to accomplish her vision. And she had done it. She found the sofas, sewed the draperies, stenciled, arranged, painted and completed the courtyard. Greg always did the yard. Since he was taking his time about flowers, Laurel had picked up some when she was out one day and they had their first fight in their new home. Greg couldn't stand that Laurel had to do everything "right now". He didn't understand that this was "her courtyard", her place outside for chats with friends or reading in the afternoon sun. His feeling was that they had all the time in the world and she was chastising him by not trusting him with the yard.

Greg never understood her excitement and the adrenaline rush she got each time a design hit her. Her need for art and design had always been there—even as a child. Unfortunately her parents didn't feel art was necessary, especially when her intelligence was disclosed to them when she was in the first grade. From then on, if it wasn't academic, it wasn't pursued. Every time one of her drawings or sketches was discovered within her homework, a lecture about wasted time always followed. It hurt so much to have her pages of ideas thrown away. She felt so free when she left for college—so young. She made sure she went far away so she didn't have her parents dictating how she spent her time. Yes, she loved to read and the library was special, but to be able to go to an art museum was heaven. When Laurel's dad died and she had to leave college to help support the family was devastating in more ways than one. She adored her dad in spite of his backing the curriculum plan. He was always the quiet one when the drawings went away—it was her mom who was adamant that they go in the garbage. She remembered the last conversation she had with him. It confused her at the time because he suddenly wanted to make sure she was happy and living her life "taking time to smell the roses and look at the daisies." She decided he knew something was wrong and listened to his last lesson in life. How ironic that for all her academics she had become a secretary/bookkeeper when she left college. It was the one job she could get and use her math and computer knowledge to make enough money for everyone.

Left foot, right foot, only four more miles were left. Laurel's entry into marathon running had been a godsend. She never knew what a run could do for stress management or for rounding out her ideas. As a bonus, at forty she was still as slim as she was at eighteen.

Laurel snapped out of her thoughts for just a moment to check her route. Damn! She hadn't meant to ignore which route she was taking, she was just preoccupied with getting rid of the anger. A run-in with a nut a few years before had taught her to change her route every day. Never make a pattern for someone to follow easily. OK, she had gone to the road on the right of the fork at the park yesterday; she would take the road on the left at the fork today.

Left foot, right foot, she was running well and her rhythmic footfalls resonated in the pre-dawn hour. Mind back to wandering she continued on. The fact that it was dark certainly didn't help lift her mood. Laurel loved this time of year and long runs on Saturdays. She could run forever in the crisp morning air and look at the gorgeous colors in the trees surrounding her. She could also wear her walkman and go even further—her mind off of her body and into the songs of her favorite singers.

She couldn't believe what Greg wanted her to do now. The one thing of importance they hadn't accomplished in their marriage was have a child. Oh, it wasn't that they didn't want a baby it was that Laurel probably wouldn't conceive. After a year of trying and a lack of success, the doctor had found that fibroids had completely blocked one of her fallopian tubes and seriously hampered the other. Greg didn't want to adopt a child, he felt they should sacrifice to save and try alternatives to have their own. So, they lived like they were still in college and tried artificial insemination and anything else the doctor suggested again and again. When they finally gave up, they didn't have the money to support a child. Adoption was no longer on the table; they were now thirty and would have to go out of the country.

Greg was still so high after the realtor left that he decided to tell her about the rest of his plan. Since they had come out so far ahead with the sale of their home, he wanted her to go with him to a new doctor and try again to have a child. She couldn't believe he was serious. She was forty for God's sake. He was so excited about some articles he had read about grandmothers getting pregnant that he was sure there was something new they could do to finally have their child. Laurel tried to tell him that she didn't think she could go through shots and sterile tubes and timed sex again. When she suggested that they take some of the windfall and adopt, Greg's face closed. He wanted the experience of pregnancy and their child. "I can't believe it!" she murmured. "He is completely ignoring who will be going through most of the discomfort. He doesn't get it that he won't be the one to go for more than just the nine months of pregnancy with the associated morning sickness, weight gain and sleepless nights. I could be another year just trying to get pregnant. And what about the risks involved with pregnancy at forty—both to me and the child?" She never knew she could be so mad at him or that he would ever be so incredibly insensitive.

Laurel ran on and while her anger calmed with her exertion, she still hadn't decided on how to make Greg understand why she didn't want to try any scientific method for pregnancy. If God blessed them, great and if not, we accept his will. She decided she would make something he really loved for dinner to help their anger dissipate and hopefully open the way for discussion—and resolution.

That settled, Laurel could see her house up ahead. As usual, she smiled as she neared her home. Lord how was she ever going to let the house go? She heard a car coming up behind her and moved closer to the sidewalk in front of their community mailbox. The van was slowing down right next to her. Neighbors probably forgot to get their mail last night, she thought. She glanced to her left and saw the van door slide open and an arm come out in her direction. Then she didn't see anything at all.

CHAPTER 4

Scott Gregory finished putting on the khaki uniform of the overnight delivery company he worked for and headed for the door. He didn't make coffee in his kitchen or look around as he left. The apartment was only a temporary place to sleep. His mind was already on his day as a part of his goal to win Angie back. She had told him just last week that she thought they should see other people. She wasn't sure that Scott was "the one" she could spend her life with. He knew it was his job and bank account. Angie wanted a house and kids. She wanted to stay home and devote herself to her family. She was right about one thing, his hourly wage and paying off credit cards didn't pay for any of the things she wanted. Scott didn't get a chance to tell her that he had been working for the last couple of months towards becoming a Supervisor. It would mean a lot more money and a step towards going up the management ladder. All she saw was his sparse apartment. Their cheap dates left her feeling short-changed. She didn't know he was saving for her; he had wanted to surprise her in a few months. Now he'd waited too long and he had spent a sleepless night wondering what else he could do to speed up a promotion and get her back.

The competition had put out some jazzy commercials that were really taking off and cutting into his company's business. All of the deliverymen had been in weekly update meetings for the past two months to get ideas for what they could do on their routes to drum up business. The bosses also encouraged the guys to speak up with any ideas they might have. Scott listened to all of the lessons from his boss and had implemented every one of them. He never volunteered his ideas though. He didn't want any of the guys to shine more than he did. That promotion was his! Since the meetings began, Scott started his plan. He made a point to organize his packages so that he could make the business deliveries by 9:00 and hopefully finish the residential ones by 1:00 or so in the afternoon. It meant he was going in early, but if it got him noticed who cared? He also made a point to learn the names of all of the customers on his route. He had to come up with some silly rhymes to remember some of them—he was never very good at names—but it was worth it. Now his customers remembered him and he always managed to mention the time so they realized they were getting their delivery early. Every one of his customers thought they were the only one getting special treatment. Genius! The early hours and customer services were working in his favor and to tip the scales further he made sure he helped with fence gates that somehow became unlatched allowing little Sparky to get loose; bent sprinkler sprockets turned facing away from gardens and lawns; noticing "jumping house" deliveries for Tommy's birthday party needing the electric cord plugged in, and on and on it went.

Two weeks ago he was featured at the beginning of the weekly meeting as an example management wanted all their deliverymen to emulate. As Scott smiled and shook his boss' hand, the Senior Manager deflated his moment by telling them they were still trailing the competition and leaving more work for them to do.

Scott was more determined than ever to get that promotion and even though his latest idea was unethical and possibly illegal, getting Angie back made him throw caution right out the delivery truck's side door. He hadn't gone to college and barely passed high school. He had to man up to whatever it took to beat out the competition. So, when he went to make a delivery, if there was one of the competition's yellow notices about an attempted delivery on the door, he took it. He had been careful to look around so he hadn't been caught—yet. Since he was finishing his deliveries early on his new schedule, he always circled back to houses he had left "no signature required" deliveries at "just to make sure you got your package Mrs. Carter" and check out his route one more time. His customers were noticing that they always got their packages from Scott with no trouble. One couple told him that when they order from mail order catalogs now they actually were requesting his company for delivery!

Scott finished his last business delivery earlier than usual and started his residential route. He had a smile on his face when he saw the first delivery—Mrs. Andrews in Green Glenn. Scott started whistling as he drove and thought about the possibility of her being home. He thought she had started working an 8 to 5 but he wasn't sure. If she was home, she would open the door; not only would he get to see a beautiful woman, he'd also get to see her home. The first time he delivered a package to her, he couldn't stop his jaw from dropping when she opened the door. He was drawn to the large green eyes set in her very pretty face, then past her when he glanced down the entry-way. What he saw made him want to just walk in, pass her by and look in every room he could.

"Mrs. Andrews?"

"Yes."

"I have a package here for Greg Andrews from Cabellas."

"Why thank you. My husband always looks forward to his favorite treat!" Laurel took in the look on his face mistaking it for some sort of problem. "Is something wrong? Do you need a glass of water?"

"No ma'am. I just couldn't help but notice your beautiful home. I always liked the outside of it; I just never knew the inside would be so fine."

"You've made my day! Would you like to see the rest of the house, er …?"

"Scott. I would but company policy is that we cannot enter any home. I guess I'll just have to settle for a slice of the pie this time."

"I understand Scott. Thanks again for the package and so early! Have a nice day."

Someday he was going to get Angie and a house. He was going to see if Mrs. Andrews would help him decorate it. She seemed really nice. I wonder if she would ask a lot of money. He swore he would never use a credit card again, but he wanted the best for Angie and he was going to get it no matter what it cost.

As he drove up to the Andrews' front yard he could see a yellow tag on her door. Shit! He turned into the back of the truck and picked her package off the shelf. He noticed it was from a paint company and required her signature. The Andrews' house was in the center of a court. When Scott turned to exit the truck, he quickly scanned the court looking for anyone out and about. Thank God he was early! It was light, but the sun still hadn't fully lit the houses through the autumn leaves. He was just past the kids leaving for school and their parent's rush hour drive to work but before the stay at homes started any errands. As he started up the stepping stones he glanced behind the truck—no cars coming into the court. As Scott reached the door, his right hand raised and grabbed the yellow slip on the way to ring the doorbell and keep arcing right into his left shirt pocket. He waited the customary minute and for once he was glad Mrs. Andrews wasn't home. He filled out his company's white "attempted delivery" slip, slapped it on the door and headed back to his truck. Hopping in, he placed the package on the return shelf and gunned the motor.

Scott nervously checked the street again as he drove away. Satisfied no one had seen him, he made the turn out of the court and pulled the yellow slip from his pocket. Holding the steering wheel with his knees, he tore the slip into bits and tossed it into the van's garbage bag along with all the others. Unfortunately, Scott never read the slips, if he saw yellow, he reacted as he'd planned.

They say every criminal makes one stupid mistake. Scott drove along on his route. Calm again and whistling along with the radio to his favorite tune, Scott never knew he had just been extremely stupid.

CHAPTER 5

Lord David Whitethorn sat brooding in the soft leather seat of his chair listening to the quiet hum of his plane and tried to digest what he had done. His gaze rested on the beautiful passenger sleeping across from him as he contemplated the possible repercussions for his actions. He'd had plenty of time to think and rehearse an explanation to her for when she woke up and he was fervently praying that would be soon. They only had an hour left until landing at Whitethorn and he wanted to make sure she was not only aware he intended her no harm, but also agreed to his request for her services. He couldn't ask Henry how much longer she would be out since they both had been given one of his shots specifically designed to produce sleep. David never guessed he would be happy for Henry's fear of flying. The only way Henry could accompany David on his many business trips was to be in oblivion directly after take-off and then straight through to their landing.

My God! Kidnapping! He still couldn't quite believe it. He knew the moment he and Shelby entered Laurel's home that he needed to hire her decorator. Imagine his surprise when Jeannie informed him that Laurel was the decorator, the house had predominately been done in three weeks time, and that it was her "hobby." He should have known. He had never seen anything like her home or felt anything like her home. Every room had a comfort that drew you in and made you feel at ease as if in slippered feet looking for your favorite chair. Her home emanated the feel one gets only from well worn furniture and yet everything was flawless and only marked if intended by design. Each room had touches of nature and as one turned from here to there a surprise just waited to delight the eye. One room, it appeared to be a guest or grown child's room, was done with the feel of the ocean. Seashells, a sea blue and mist green color scheme and one wall painted in the stripe of the drapes. Knobby baskets and then the surprise: a pop of red, in a throw over the green wicker chair and on a mosaic piece centered in the room. The mosaic had a harlequin design on top in the blue, green and red colors acting as a canopy on the three shelved case. He could actually feel the ocean in the room and matching seashell bathroom. He couldn't help but notice the cattails and pussy willows strategically placed in the entry way and the formal living area in all of its autumn glory. The surprises in there were floating shelves with glass vases catching the sun here and there in an opening to the family room. The vaulted ceilings had small upper windows that held more glass sending shards of color over the room. One wall had a Tuscan paint treatment done in a mossy green embracing windows draped in tapestry from stenciled cornices. What was that? Was it glass beads in the parted drapes? Marvelous! The kitchen echoed Tuscany again. Rich cabinetry and a bricked floor were accented with grape leaves and a rather nice wine collection. Rounding a corner there was another bedroom that he thought might belong to a daughter. She must be younger he thought, there was a little brass plaque on the door that said "The Morgan Room." What a delight—all done in puppy dogs and butterflies to capture Pindar's *Odes of Condolence*. The surprise was the colors—not pinks and purples, but browns and creams accented by gold. And near the end was the master suite. He actually heard Shelby catch her breath. It was the most unusual combination of male and female. The large bed was done in forest greens, burnt oranges and reds, but the dressers and tables were in a creamy white. Were they both hunters? The sitting area walls were covered with Bev Doolittle prints and Mountain Man memorabilia. Yet the shelves held little wooden quail between the books and a hummingbird light as air in a brightly feathered body. They entered the master bath through an arched doorway and immediately felt as if they had happened upon a country path. Ivy vines were painted over the arched doorways and green towels peaked out from feather covered baskets. And there, at the end of her vanity were beautiful, lush plants in various pots of the same hues as the jetted tub's floral arrangement. They hadn't even made it to the home gym and David knew Shelby would want this house and why she would want it "as is." No one would be able to recreate the combination of texture, color and warmth permeating their senses. He also knew he would hire this woman to give his children the home he had always wanted for them.

Henry groggily walked up the aisle and glanced down at Laurel. "She's still sound asleep sir."

"I know Henry. Now that you're awake do you think you can help rouse her? I want matters settled before we land at Whitethorn."

"I'll try sir. She should be coming around. I've never given a shot to someone else, but she seems to be about my weight. Oh, there, I think she's starting to come out of it. I'll go get some water for her."

"Henry you just want to leave me alone to explain. Sit down across the aisle immediately."

David grasped the seat arms tightly as he watched Laurel come awake. He was so stunned by the large green eyes in front of him he was unprepared for the shrieking, whirling dervish appearing instantaneously.

Laurel worked to open her heavy lids and wake up. When she did, her heart went through the roof as she saw one man leaning over her and another on her right reaching out at her. She heard "you're safe, you're safe" and "no harm will come to you" but she couldn't help instinctively trying to get her legs under her and get away from these people.

Something held her and through her fog she took in not only that there was a seat belt across her lap, but that there was sky out the window. They were on a plane! The calming male voice cantered again and Laurel was finally able to realize no one had moved to hurt her. She regained her focus and stopped her screaming. She sat wide-eyed; stunned; her nostrils flaring with her heavy breaths; and, finally, willed herself to sit still. She looked at the men, one to the other until the bigger one stopped his litany and spoke to her.

"I'm Lord David Whitethorn and I am very sorry to have scared you. As I said, you are safe and we mean you no harm. We will be landing at my home in about forty-five minutes and I would like your agreement to listen to me until I have finished what I have to say."

Laurel looked at the tall, auburn haired man. He sat watching as she took his measure. He had a nice face, kind even. He was obviously a wealthy man; his suit was perfectly tailored to fit his slim physique flawlessly. Still silent, she moved on to the other man. Smaller, she mused that she was probably taller than he. Dark haired and fair skinned, he appeared to be having trouble with his conscience—his brow furrowed over his eyes.

Laurels husky voice took both men by surprise. "How kind of you to ask my permission to listen to you since it is quite obvious to me that I really have no choice in the matter. While I realize I've been drugged, I am coherent enough to deduce I am on a plane and seem to be without a parachute in my back pocket. So please, get on with your story, especially the part where you prove "no harm" and tell me how quickly you can turn around and get me home."

David suppressed a smile and tried to control his reaction to her sarcasm. He didn't know why he should be surprised by her wit since there hadn't been one usual characteristic about her person he had yet to find. The pictures in her home didn't do her justice. They couldn't though; you just had to feel the sparks from those eyes. Even without makeup she was perfect. She had a renaissance look about her—the perfect skin and a mouth that was just a bit small. She reminded him of pictures of angels he had seen growing up. When Henry took off her hat and golden curls tumbled through his hands it seemed to confirm all the pieces to be exactly right in her facial canvas.

"As I told you I am Lord David Whitethorn and we are about to land at my home, Whitethorn Castle in Northumberland."

"NORTHUM..!"

"Shush! You agreed to listen until I finished. Now then, you are here because I recently went through your home with my sister, Shelby. She is the widow that purchased your home—completely as is. Just as my sister knew a gem when she saw one, I knew an answer to prayers for my children. You see, for reasons I prefer to keep private, I am a single father to Catherine Elizabeth, age six, and Timothy William, age four. I am a good father and I love my children above anything else. Whitethorn Castle has been our ancestral home for generations. I am an architect that specializes in either restoring castles, or updating castles throughout England and Scotland. Whitethorn was the first castle I ever remodeled into a modern home. While I may be able to produce a structure that is in keeping with time and a client's desires, I am not able to come close to the magic you are capable of in the creation of its interior spaces. And that is what I want you to do for my children. I want you to use your talent to make Whitethorn Castle a home. I want my children to feel the comfort you generate and make their room a personalized, individual delight for them to grow in."

"Castle? Did you say a..."

"Damn it woman, shush!" David's eagerness to finish his tale and deal with his fate was feeding the anxiety in his stomach and his shout startled Laurel into submission. "Again, please hear me out. I had intended to extend my stay with my sister so that I could take time to convince you to take on Whitethorn and come to England. Unfortunately, my daughter broke her arm flying a kite the day after we toured your home requiring my return home immediately. There isn't anything I wouldn't do to give my children the home you can create for them. For the same reasons I am a single parent, I have also been living a solitary life on our considerable property. Circumstances being what they are, I took uncharacteristically drastic measures. I have a staff of five, including my man Henry, to see to our needs. So; that said, my sister's realtor informed us that you were able to finish your basic home in three weeks time. I am asking that you allow me to employ you for six weeks while you work your magic on Whitethorn. You will have workman and materials at your disposal and complete reign over the interior design. I am prepared to pay you one million dollars, reference your name in client requests and return you home safely. There is one caveat; I need you to promise not to upset my children or staff during your stay. My staff is very loyal to me and would be distressed if they thought you would do me harm. They are under the impression that you are a friend of Shelby's and agreed to leave with me suddenly when you heard of Cat's arm and that I would be providing for your needs upon arrival at Whitethorn. Because of that impression, you will not be allowed to contact anyone outside of Whitethorn."

David could see the tops of Whitethorn's north tower looming in the distance. They would be landing at his airstrip very soon. He leaned in towards Laurel and brusquely uttered, "Do you agree to my proposal?"

Laurel's mind had been spinning at just hearing about the castle. A castle! She kept pinching her legs and arms just to make sure this wasn't an insane dream and she had really heard Lord Whitethorn say six weeks, a million dollars and complete control over her design. Then she felt the plane going down, heard the wheels drop, and looked out the window. There it was—Whitethorn Castle. Pinching her arm, her face lit up causing the men to look at the window for sunlight. But it was the sheer joy of getting a chance to immerse herself in something she so loved to do. She turned back to the two men sitting still as statues and shocked them to their core by countering Lord David's generous offer.

"I will agree to this assignment, but I do have some conditions of my own. First and foremost, I must contact my husband. Your staff has the advantage of knowing of my arrival but my husband is going to an empty home with no explanations. Second, while I can appreciate your desire for seclusion and the need to keep your reasons private, I am now going to be out of employment I recently began when I return home. Therefore, in six weeks I want the million, the referrals, and I want you to allow any reputable architectural magazine of your choice to send a photo-journalist and produce an article on our joint collaboration. I will give you complete control for how our partnership came to be but I want to make sure I end up with a business when I return to the United States."

David looked at Henry and felt the wheels touch the ground. Henry nodded and David put out his hand to shake Laurel's. "Agreed. By the way, you don't have to worry about your husband, I left him a note."

CHAPTER 6

Greg Andrews was on the last ten miles of his miserable trip home. His usually smiling face was set hard—grave almost—as he traversed the highway. He had managed not to face what he'd said to Laurel last night all day long. First he'd prioritized his day down to every minute detail on the commute to work. Then, he stayed very, very busy by doing every task with tremendous detail until quitting time. The day done and a long commute home, however, left him with nothing to stop the inevitable—what the 'h-e-double l' he was going to do. "Christ!" he thought. "I cannot believe I was such an ass last night. I shouldn't have rushed her, I should have explained instead of just charging in. I can't blame her for leaving without saying goodbye this morning. If she had hit me with a demand out of the blue the way I did her and then threatened, threatened!, I'm not sure I'd have stayed the night. My God, I won't have to ask her for hints for the confession box this week. Damn! I'm going to get this straightened out before dinner. Once she knows everything going on at my work she's going to agree to try a pregnancy again and be as excited as she should have been last night."

Greg and Laurel had been hit hard by the housing slump. Construction companies were actually shutting down. When Greg had a bad feeling his firm was going to close, Laurel took an administrative job to make sure they had insurance coverage and some outside income. He didn't know why she panicked; he had always supported her so she could pursue her little hobby for God's sake. But, she was scared and in hindsight, he had to admit that she was right this time. There was no way they could have known that a commercial company was going to pick him up out of hundreds of resumes, better his salary and offer full family insurance coverage. But they had, and what Laurel didn't know was that his new project was going to benefit them more than just financially.

The first week into the project, Greg was introduced to the team of doctors whose practice he was building. This was going to be a "design build" job where the architect, owners and construction management met regularly to control the project. Greg loved building like this. There weren't going to be the thousands of change orders or structural differences with the architect like a traditional build. Since he could take the plans and give the architect the construction side of the business, there weren't any parts of the building that hadn't been reviewed—from what structural materials would produce the design on the plans and where costs savings would enhance the building without sacrificing safety or style.

Meeting the owners was the icing on the cake for Greg. These guys were fertility specialists and their practice was strictly for people like Greg and Laurel. Good people whom wanted to be parents, would be terrific parents providing an established, loving home and who just needed some help taming Mother Nature. One of the doctors had a real interest in building and he and Greg had become friends. When Greg told him about his and Laurel's problem conceiving, he told Greg about all of the advancements that he felt would offer them a really good chance of getting pregnant. He even offered to treat Laurel without charge—it was obvious to him how much Greg loved his wife and family character shone through in every facet of his being—these were two people with a great deal of love for one another and theirs would be a lucky child. He also told him that he had seen a lot of successful families using surrogacy as a final option and that he and Laurel should consider that alternative too.

Greg was more convinced than ever that this project and their child were meant to be when he met Joy, the cement subcontractor. Joy was 38 and so much like Greg's little sister. She had worked in construction for so long; she really was just 'one of the guys'. She was friendly with everyone and joined the crew at day's end for a beer and was never singled out until some guy in the place would come over to get her to dance. Then they all had a great time teasing her about make believe warts on the guy's head or one ear being bigger than the other. She could take it and she loved it. Since Greg was the superintendent on the project, he and Joy talked more than the others and a real friendship had sprung. Laurel had met her and she knew they really were just co-workers and good friends, but Greg had only found out how good last week. After Joy finished her concrete pour one morning, they went out to lunch and talked about some pretty personal stuff. Joy confessed that she had wanted to marry and have a family ten years before, but she never met a guy that was anything more than a friend. She had wanted to wait for the one man she couldn't live without, but that hadn't happened. Now she was considering artificial insemination and raising a child on her own. Greg shared his and Laurel's story and Joy had tears in her eyes when he finished. This was the kind of relationship she had wanted for herself. Joy stopped by Greg's office two days later and told Greg that if the new treatment program didn't succeed in a pregnancy for them, she would be a surrogate if they wanted to try that route. Joy knew Greg and Laurel would be terrific parents. She had to believe that as modern parents, knowing the bond she would feel with their baby, they would let her be a part of his or her life. This is what a baby should have, she had said, two parents that love him and each other. She also said that's what she felt a family is all about; something she was hoping to have for herself one day. The new advances Greg told her about made her feel like she had more time and options than she realized, allowing her hope for that "someday" dream to stay alive for herself.

Greg loved Laurel so much, he always had since the first time he met her. He couldn't imagine not having a baby with her, and only her. They had met in college and Greg still chuckled to himself whenever he thought of the young, naive girl she had been. She was beautiful then and she was beautiful now. But she seemed so fragile and he found she was too trusting. It never occurred to Laurel that there might be someone who would want to hurt her. Greg thought he was just looking out for her and tried to convince himself he was going to remain a bachelor until after college. But then they clicked. Both catholic, both had quick wits and a slightly bawdy sense of humor. While they both loved movies, Laurel's taste leaned towards "chick flicks." She couldn't stomach Greg's favorite—murder mysteries. He'd actually lost her at a drive-in when he tried one with her on their third date. When the blood ruptured at the first killing, she excused herself to "go to the ladies room" and never came back. She actually called a taxi to take her home and vowed she couldn't go out with him again—she was sure he had a violent streak! Bachelor until after college—yeah, right. He begged like a dog for his chewy and married her six months later. When Laurel's dad died, they returned home and Laurel went to work to help support her mom and finished putting Greg through school. It was such a shock when Laurel's mom passed away. Greg thought she would go back to school, but she really didn't mind working and she wanted to study art. Art wouldn't pay their bills and Greg never really got that part of her any-way—until now.

Laurel wanted and needed to create as much as Greg wanted and needed to have a child. "God, I'm an ass!" he uttered aloud. He knew Laurel wanted children and she would be such a great mom. He had watched her over the years first with their nephew, Tyler, and then with their friend's daughter, Morgan. Aunt Laurel had always been Tyler's favorite and after high school, scholarship in hand, he lived with them while he went to the college—a college that happened to be close to Keddie. He turned out so great. Married now, he took a beginning job in Philadelphia doing broadcast journalism. He'd married last year and now he and his wife visited twice a year, at least, to see his folks up north and Greg and Laurel in Keddie. Their guest room was designed with Tyler and Jillian in mind. They both loved the ocean.

Morgan was one of God's blessings in their lives. Laurel made friends with all of their neighbors before they had even unpacked. Morgan's mom, Leslie, had become an instant friend and Morgan became their favorite guest. Whenever Leslie traveled on business or had a date, Morgan stayed with them. Laurel and Morgan shared their love of art and always did that homework first. They baked and giggled and Greg got to be the man in both their lives and he loved it. "I know she's going to be a fantastic mom, Greg thought as he pulled into their driveway. Now I just have to prove it's possible to her."

Their English springer spaniel, Callie, ambled over to Greg as the garage door opened. Walking around Laurel's car and reaching down to stroke her silky ears, Greg whispered into her ear, "Where's your mom, huh girl? Is she still really mad?" Loving brown eyes stared back at him and with a final pat, Greg entered their home.

"Wow" he thought, it's really quiet. Taking off his shoes in the mud room, he hollered out "Honey? I'm home. I really want us to talk but I have to shower off—I'm mud from head to toe." Without waiting for her to answer, he headed for the master bath.

Coming out of the shower, Greg couldn't help but notice how quiet the house was. He had been so centered on talking with Laurel that he failed to notice that the lights weren't on and that he didn't smell dinner coming from the kitchen. Wrapping a towel around his middle, Greg walked out of the master suite and headed for the kitchen.

"Honey—you home?" he said looking around. There was no answer of course, and she wasn't home. "She must have gone over to Leslie's and forgotten the time," he thought. Walking towards the phone in the kitchen, he noticed the blinking message light and hit the button for play. "This is Agnes calling for Laurel. Everyone here is hoping that all is well since we didn't hear from her regarding her absence today. Laurel, I was able to cover your desk today, but I would appreciate your contacting me at home this evening to let me know when you'll be back. My number is 589-5027 and I'm usually up until 10. I hate to tell you this, but as a new employee you haven't accrued any sick leave yet. I can talk to you about some options when I hear from you. Please call me as soon as possible."

Greg stood transfixed, not believing what he had just heard. He played the message again and felt his chest tighten with fear. Laurel was mad, yes, but he knew she would never just leave him. For one thing, she'd blow up at him with classic style first; secondly, she just didn't have an irresponsible bone in her body. Clenching his teeth to stop the chattering from the autumn chill, Greg dialed the phone. First he dialed Leslie; no answer. Next, he tried their friend Karen. She had known Laurel since high school and had been Maid of Honor at their wedding.

Karen answered on the second ring. "Hey Greg, what's up?"

"Karen, have you heard from Laurel today?"

"No I haven't, why?"

Greg quickly filled her in on the message from Agnes and, omitting their argument from the previous night, only recounted his leaving for work this morning and coming home to her car in the garage and no sign of her having been there all day.

"OK, Greg. Let's not panic. I'm coming over right now and you should start calling hospitals. Maybe she did one of those graceful flights she's famous for on the sidewalk and had more than just a bump this time. She could be in the hospital wrapped up in forms and tests you know."

Greg exhaled loudly. "That's it—you're right, Karen. I'll start calling around and then you and I can come up with the speech from Hell we're going to give her when we pick her up. Man, I was scared to death! I think the few brown hairs left on my head just turned grey. I'll leave the front door open for when you get here."

"OK, great. I'll be there in twenty minutes."

Greg quickly went to toss on some clothes and turn up the heat. Back at the phone, he pulled out the phonebook and dialed the closest hospital.

"Memorial Hospital, how may I direct your call?"

By the time Karen arrived twenty minutes later, Greg had tried all the hospital and urgent care centers in the book without any luck Wide eyed, their next call was to the police.

CHAPTER 7

The minute the agreement was struck and the plane's wheels touched the ground, Laurel was up out of her seat, grabbing the handles of aisle seats from row to row, all the while dipping to look out and see the castle as much as possible. She was like an excited child on Christmas morning ignoring everything and everyone in a hunt for her present from Santa.

The plane's hangar was at the rear of the property, behind a truly beautiful garden. All she could see of Whitethorn were the tops of the turrets and walls above the greenery of a central maze. As she watched, two adorable redheads with excited freckled faces erupted from a gateway, shouting and laughing at the top of their lungs. Behind them, four very proper looking adults tried to catch their little hands.

As the plane stopped, Henry went to open the door and David stepped aside for Laurel to exit first. "No, you need to go first and see to those two little ones. It appears, for some reason I cannot fathom, they miss you terribly."

Henry immediately took his eyes up to the ceiling and coughed to hide his laughter as an amused David sarcastically replied, "Thank you, I appreciate your understanding. They must be too young to realize my countless flaws. Henry will assist you down the steps."

"Perfect."

"Papa! Papa! You're home!" Tim cried as he ran with arms outstretched. Catherine was trying to keep up, but her cast made her gait uneven.

David whisked Tim high in the air, then hugged him back down against his chest while answering "Yes, Tim, I'm home. So what did you do to your sister that she's wearing funny jewelry?"

Cat smiled a toothy grin as she hugged her father hello and buried her face in his stomach.

Tim was still smiling and replied "I didn't do it Papa! Cat was watching my kite and not the ground. There was a hole and she fell down."

"Papa I broke my arm, and it really hurt, and the nurse said you can sign my cast, and will you do it now …"

"Cat! Slow down! Let me get my kiss hello and take a look at your arm. I think I can say hello to everyone while we walk in and you need to meet our guest."

With that the children and the staff looked around David to where Laurel and Henry were exiting the plane. The children took one look at her and scooted around their father to the pretty lady coming towards them.

"Hello! Are you the lady that's going to make a special room just for me?" Tim excitedly asked. Not to be outdone, Cat grasped one of Laurel's hands and shyly asked "Me too?"

Laurel had never seen two more adorable children in her life. Leaning down to their level she said, "My so many questions and I haven't even been properly introduced! Over the children's giggles she continued "My name is Laurel Andrews, I would like you to call me Laurel, and yes, Tim, and yes, Cat, I am going to do something very special for you two. I'm also going to do something special to the inside of your castle."

"What are you going to do? When are you going to start? Can my room be blue?" Tim was going to bust he was so thrilled about his special room. Both children were now holding Laurel's hands and had leaned into her while they spoke. David was surprised how quickly they took to her—his children were usually shy and withdrawn with strangers.

Standing up and keeping the children next to her, Laurel started walking towards the staff gathered in front of David while Henry, still smiling, trailed them.

"Laurel, allow me to introduce you to my staff." As an elderly couple with kind, smiling faces stepped forward, David continued. "Emily and Thomas, may I introduce you to Laurel Andrews. Laurel Emily is housekeeper here at Whitethorn and her husband, Thomas, is the gamekeeper and groundskeeper."

"How do you do?" the warm couple said in unison as they shook her hand. Emily was staring at the beautiful woman, "I'll be taking you inside to your room so you can freshen up and get settled."

"Thank you, Emily that would be wonderful. I was out on my morning run when Lord David caught me with the emergency about Cat's arm. He assured me that you would prepare literally everything for me. With a note to my husband, we boarded for Whitethorn immediately."

Looking at the remaining staff advancing, Laurel issued a polite warning, "Maybe you should all let me stand upwind while we continue the introductions? Did I mention I had run six miles when these two caught up with me?"

David's jaw dropped, Henry was looking up again, and the remaining adults just laughed at her charm while doing as she requested. The children, however, hadn't budged. Staring at Laurel with smiles and adoration, they appeared to be quite comfortable just as they were.

David closed his mouth and tried to continue as if nothing out of the ordinary was happening. This was just an everyday occurrence having a visitor drop in smelling like day-old garbage and expecting everything at the ready. "Yes, well then. Roger, Gwen, please allow me to introduce you so we can all move inside and Laurel can refresh herself. Laurel, Roger is the castle schoolmaster and Gwen is our nanny."

Laurel was surprised by Roger. Every other staff person could have been David and Laurel's parents. Roger was close in age and a handsome man. She liked the laughter and warmth that showed in his brown eyes. Gwen was a delightful, spry woman with curiosity shining everywhere about her. "Oh, how do you do?" she said, briefly rescuing her hands from the children to shake theirs. Introductions over, Cat and Tim reclaimed her hands and everyone started following David toward the rear entrance to the castle.

David was trying to keep the fatigue out of his voice as they made their way through the maze of the gardens and spoke with an authoritarian tone. "Laurel, you may remember I mentioned that I held our flight until 10:00 yesterday morning so that you could sleep on the plane and not have your days and nights mixed up in the time change. I am going to take a rest and I have asked Emily and Gwen to show you around Whitethorn after your bath so that you can get started with the makeover as soon as you're ready. Emily, I will meet with you all one hour before dinner to show Laurel the towers so I can review any correspondence. Cat, I'll sign your cast before you and Tim go with Master Roger back to your studies."

Laurel caught the story of their "earlier" conversation and tried not to salute while answering him. "Yes, David, that would work out perfectly." The close staff eyed one another with surprise. They were lucky to have worked in an informal atmosphere as if part of the family, but they had never referred to their employer as "David"

Since Laurel was busily turning her head this way and that to see all she could, she missed the surprised expression on David's face at the use of his surname, along with the staff's faces biting their cheeks and looking intently at the ground as they walked on.

Exiting the maze, everyone entered a rose garden surrounding a large fountain. Beyond that, Laurel could see stone—first in steps leading to an entryway, then up, and up, and up again. Stopped with craned neck, Laurel thought the castle's center must be forty feet high—she could count windows for four stories. There were two stone "wings," one on each side of the center. "Beautiful," she whispered. Everyone caught the reverence in her soft voice and just as the children were drawn to her, so were the staff. Her open, beautiful face and appreciation for Lord David's home won them over. In an instant, everything Lady Shelby had told them about Californians proved true—this was a woman who would respect where she was, and where she had come from.

"Very well, then, Cat come with me and I'll sign that cast. Tim you may come along too and Master Roger will take you both back with him to your school room." The children were reluctant to leave Laurel and didn't move right away. Catching David's stern look, she bent down low again and kissed them both on their cheeks.

"Listen you two. I need to clean up and have Emily and Nanny show me your rooms. I'm going to need you to do all of your lessons as soon as you can so we can talk. You see, I'm going to have to ask you lots and lots of questions."

"Why?" Cat and Tim asked simultaneously.

"Because to do a special room, I need to know everything there is about what makes you special. That means I need to know if you want worms or balls, pink flowers or …"

The children's laughter cut her off. "Oh! This is so much fun!" Tim said as he moved off. Cat hung back and pulled on the bottom of Laurel's shirt. "Can I ask you a question?" she said.

"Of course, Cat, what is it?"

"Are you an angel?"

Surprised, Laurel laughed and bent to whisper in her ear, said "No sweetheart, I'm not even close." Cat smiled wide and joined her father, brother and the school master.

"OK, Emily and Gwen, I'm all yours."

Thomas waved the women off as he headed back out into the grounds and Henry followed David, the children and Roger into the right wing. Laurel wanted a bath more than chocolate, but she was so excited to see the inside of the castle she thought she might wait. She was still pinching herself every now and then—something both Emily and Gwen noticed causing them to smile again as they deduced why.

Emily and Gwen took them in by way of the rear center doorway. As they entered, Emily did most of the talking. "Now then, this is actually the central keep. The keep is four stories high and the walls are as thick as my Thomas is tall. The keep, towers and gateway are all that remain of the original castle. The floors in the center are also made up of original stone. This is one of two cloak rooms, you'll find proper outerwear in case of rain over there," she said pointing to a beautifully carved oak closet. "Through here we enter a hallway going left which brings you past the kitchen and on to the formal dining room and further into the main keep. Toward the right there is one door to your left that holds the laundry facilities. Now then, we'll go through the kitchen and formal dining room into the great hall and then I'll take you to the left off of the hall. We will be going to the third floor where your guest room has been prepared.

As they entered the great room, Laurel had to stop, spin and gape upward. The center was entirely open all the way up the four stories and beautiful, huge, stained glass skylights streamed colors of light down on their heads and onto the stone walls. Continuing on, Gwen took over the tour.

"The wings of the castle are actually a single floor and the wing to our left contains a salon, a library, an indoor swimming pool, an exercise room and showering facilities. The wing on the opposite side houses the private family rooms. There is a private sitting room, a private dining room, a study, four children's sleeping rooms, my private room, and finally, the Lady Whitethorn's and Lord Whitethorn's private rooms. There are also private bathrooms for each of them."

Laurel followed along in a daze as the ladies walked them into the castle. She was quite comfortable with Gwen and Emily and didn't hide her surprise when they approached stone stairs leading up the side walls of the castle and ended up skirting around them instead. Just as she was about to ask why, she was ushered into an elevator that was hidden by a stone front. Smiling with delight, she stepped in and they moved silently upward. The elevator was glass so Laurel was able to see more as the ride went skyward.

Emily exited first and touched Laurel's elbow to move around the stone false front. Laurel could see doors to at least ten rooms around the outer stone walls. There was a railing of sorts all around the hallways made of what appeared to be cobblestone. At the second door, the women stopped and opened it up for Laurel to enter. Emily entered the room behind her and opened up a door on their left. Laurel stood still, looking at the beautiful space. The ceiling had more carved wood, oak she thought, and the walls were more of the grey silky stone. The windows were tall and arched and had heavy drapes hanging from wrought iron rods and opened onto tie backs on either side. Laurel noticed the large canopied bed and seating area, while pretty, were too heavy in their red and blue velvets to balance all of the stone. Through the windows, Laurel had a view of the grounds to the front. A gateway led to the central front of the keep and she could see more stone in a fence surrounding the property. There were a lot of oak trees on the property edges and she noticed they were near the ocean from the plane. There was so much green and lavender—everywhere. "Emily, what is all of the lavender I'm looking at?"

"Why that's heather ma'am, haven't you ever seen it?"

"Please ladies, if I can call you by your first names I insist you call me by mine, and no, Emily, I've only seen heather as a color choice in my winter clothing catalog." Both women smiled and continued around the quarters.

"Laurel, Lord David told me to pick up everything you would need for a six week stay. I had Gwen help me as I didn't know much about cosmetics not having used them in my life. You will find day clothing in the large wardrobe here in the sleeping area, and the smaller wardrobe in the private bath has your night things."

They had moved into the bath as Emily talked and Laurel was no longer pinching herself. She had a profound faith in her maker and she decided right then and there that if this was a dream, it was God given and she was going to enjoy every minute of it. She had her first thought of Greg as she looked at the bath. She so wished he could be there so they could fill it up and enjoy one of their famous bubble baths together. The ladies noticed her face when she thought of Greg and moved closer. "Laurel, are you well? Do you need to rest?" Gwen asked anxiously.

"No, Gwen, I'm fine. I was just missing my husband. He builds houses and he would so love to see this castle. It's going to be a long six weeks without him." Laurel missed the look exchanged by the two women. "Oh, what am I moping for? she wondered aloud. "If I am going to finish this project in six weeks, I'll be too busy to think of anything but the project and Greg is probably delighted to have complete control of our house and the television remote control for awhile—he won't even miss me!" Emily and Gwen highly doubted that, but if it made her feel better, they nodded agreement, smiled, and carried on.

"Now then, you will find towels in here, Emily said while pointing to a cabinet next to the enormous, raised, marble bathtub. The soaps and cosmetics are in the vanity under the sink. We will leave you alone now to freshen up. Do you think you remember how to get back to the kitchen?"

"Yes, I'm sure I do."

"Fine, then take your time and when you're ready, meet us there and we'll take you through the rest of the castle."

Walking them to the door, Laurel thanked them and turned to examine her domain for the next six weeks more closely. The sitting area of the bedroom had an adorable desk, but it looked small for her to sketch out her ideas. The bathroom was large and spacious. She certainly could do without the huge mirrors in both of the rooms. She had the same feeling as when she went to try on swimsuits at Macy's and had to face her derriere from every possible angle. Looking in the "day" wardrobe, she was very surprised to find clothing, including bras and panties, in her size. The clothes were perfect in every way. Whoever had picked these had chosen colors and styles that she would have, given the chance. "Well, well, well, Laurel said to herself. I can't wait to ask *Lord David* exactly how he managed to relay all my statistics to his very proper staff!" Laughing, she went into the bath and continued with her very pleasant dream.

CHAPTER 8

Outside the bedroom, Emily and Gwen couldn't wait to get into the elevator and share the thoughts they'd been holding in. Pressing the downward button, Gwen started, "Em, what did you think?"

"I think she's gorgeous, smart and going to knock the master right off his rocker!"

Laughing, Gwen held her sides and volleyed back "Yes! Exactly! Oh, I can't wait to see what she plans for the castle. If it's anything like Lady Shelby and Lord David said her house looked like it's going to be so grand. Do you think she's got any plans for our rooms, Em?"

"Oh, how I wish, Gwen. I was told she was going to be working on the interior, but how could she possibly do our rooms too in such a short amount of time?"

"Oh, you're right, I'm sure. I'm going to enjoy her stay all the same though. She's has a real spirit to her don't you think?"

"Yes, I do. I'm not surprised she has a husband, but I'm sorry that she does."

"Why is that Gwen?"

"Because she suits this house and the children, and if I'm not mistaken by the looks Lord David was giving her, our master too!"

Sighing, Emily agreed. "Yes, it would be so nice to have a Lady in the castle. Do you suppose the master will tell her about Lady Elizabeth?"

"Oh, don't be silly Emily! I know he said Laurel was a friend of Lady Shelby's, but she is a recent acquaintance to him. He would never risk the children finding out the truth about their mother."

"Yes, yes, quite right Gwen. Well, let's enjoy some tea while we wait for Laurel to finish her bath."

Exactly one hour later, a stunning vision entered the kitchen and took the women off guard by saying "Well, you two have had an hour to share your thoughts about this project, so come on; start talking!" As much as they wanted to do as requested, they just couldn't accommodate her right away. Both women thought she was pretty before, but with some softly applied makeup and fresh hair she was just too pretty for words. The skirt and sweater set flattered her figure and set off a great pair of legs. Clearing her throat, Emily spoke up. "Laurel you look wonderful! And you are correct, Gwen and I have been friends for six years now and we are trying to imagine what you are going to do to Whitethorn. You'll only be doing the main rooms, of course, but it's exciting all the same."

"Why ever would you think I would only do the main rooms? David gave me design control of the complete interior and I'm looking forward to doing just that. Now, please, show me the rest of the castle so I can determine if my ideas will work and get this project started."

Just as they started to leave on their tour, the children raced into the kitchen with Roger chasing from behind.

"Catherine and Timothy, get back here. You can't bother Laurel, Emily and Nanny right now."

Both children stopped short when they saw Laurel. Roger grabbed them from behind just as Timothy blurted out "You're pretty."

"Why thank you Tim." Grabbing both children's hands, Laurel looked at Roger. "Roger, would you mind letting the children join us? We're going to be seeing their rooms and I would really like to get an idea of their personalities so I can begin some drafts. I believe the most lived in rooms should be done first. That means I will be starting with the kitchen, main hall and the private rooms."

Roger couldn't help but agree to her request and appreciate how she looked—and smelled. "Certainly, and if you don't mind, I'll join you to help keep them in hand."

Looking at the two eager faces, she said "Shall we get started then?"

They had finished the lower three floors of the keep and both wings when it was time to meet Lord David. He had also bathed and changed into some casual clothing. As he rounded the stone face of the elevator on the third floor and saw Laurel across the way, he backed around the wall again for a moment. "How am I ever going to make it through six weeks with her looking like that?" he asked himself. Regaining his composure, he went out and joined the group.

"Good afternoon, everyone." He was getting rather irritated that his children didn't run over to him again, instead choosing to stay with Laurel. "I can see you've shown Laurel everything but the upper floor and the towers. I'll take over and then we'll join you for dinner in the large dining room."

Catherine fixed her large eyes on her father. "Papa, may we come with you?"

"No Cat, you know I don't like you and Tim in the towers. We'll be down for dinner very soon."

Emily and Gwen took the children in hand and Roger led the way to the elevator.

"Laurel, if you don't mind, I would like to start with the towers and the roof first before we lose too much daylight."

"Good idea. Let's go."

As the elevator rose, Laurel couldn't stop from asking the questions about the castle structure that she'd been holding in for hours. She sensed her more personal questions would not meet with satisfactory answers yet. "How did you get electricity and modern plumbing into the original castle keep?"

Pointing out the elevator as they neared the top, he said "I think if you look out there, part of your question will answer itself."

Looking in the direction he indicated, she smiled. There, hidden by the four towers were solar panels. The "ceiling" of the central keep was actually lower than the top of the towers by ten feet or so. Along the wings, the stone had been built up at the walls edge to conceal more panels. "How wonderful and practical! And the plumbing?"

"That was more difficult since the original walls are so thick. When the wings were built, while we made sure that the stone matches, it is merely a façade over stuccoed walls. I ran plumbing lines in the stucco walls, just as you would in a new home, and we only had to dig out the bottom floor of the keep. When the stones were replaced, only a thin layer was placed on top of a modern concrete foundation."

"And the stained glass skylights?"

"I saw those on a trip abroad and couldn't resist them. I added them in on a whim."

"A whim? They're beautiful and I can't wait to use them in my design."

As they entered the elevator to look at the fourth floor, he couldn't believe what she had just said. "Your design, already? You have some ideas for me then?"

"Well, you are partially correct, David. I have my designs but I won't be sharing them."

"Won't be sharing...."

Breaking in with, "What was that someone said to me recently? Oh yes, shush! Let me finish. You gave me complete reign over the interior of Whitethorn Castle and six weeks to complete the project, correct?"

Exasperated and intrigued, he answered gruffly, "yes."

"Aha, well then, what I have for you is a list supplies that I'll need and their schedule of necessity; your permission to send Gwen on a two week vacation; permission for Cat and Tim to bunk in with me; your availability schedule for a structural meeting; and, a need for workmen to arrive promptly at 9:00 in the morning, ready to work."

An awed and smiling Lord David Whitethorn escorted Laurel through the fourth floor. He could literally see racing thoughts on her face as she viewed the conservatory and ballroom. In reality all was quiet as she toured the rooms, but if the noise of her thoughts was audible, it would be deafening. Returning to the elevator, he asked dryly "And have you any other questions?"

"Why yes, thank you. As you know, I am a runner. I saw the running clothes in the wardrobe, but different shoes than I normally wear. I'll need to know a six mile course, fourteen for my long run on Saturday, where I might find a cd player and cd's, and who will be with me and at what pace?"

"Roger and I will be running with you. Both of us were cross country runners while at university. Your shoes are cross country runners which you will need in this terrain. We men will be carrying weapons as the course will go through our forest lands and we need to prepare for that. Six miles did you say? A 10K?"

"Yes, for now. As I get closer to my eighteen mile mark, I would like to increase it to eight miles, five days a week."

"Well, that's a bit further than we usually run, but I believe we can accommodate you. If you give me a day for the cd player, you will have a chance to ask me the other questions I know are running through that pretty head of yours."

"Why, thank you! If you're going to answer all of my questions, we might need to slow my usual pace a bit."

"What is your usual pace?"

"Depending on the music, it can be a little faster or slower than nine minute miles."

Blue eyes stared at green, "Of course. Shall we say 6:00 am at the castle rear entrance?"

Satisfied, Laurel looked at her watch and moved toward the elevator while answering David's pained expression. "Perfect. I can smell something delicious all the way up here. Shall we go down to dinner?"

Completely caught up in her curious spell, David merely nodded and followed along while making a mental note to have Emily secure some pain medication immediately.

Emily and Gwen exchanged a glance as they entered the dining room. Yes, it would have been so nice if she hadn't been married. Lord David was smiling again.

CHAPTER 9

Detective Phil Peters and his partner, Matt Johnson pulled up to the Andrews' home just past 8:00 in the evening. Neither one of the men felt like talking on the drive over from the station. Both of them were lost in thoughts and still seeing therapists to help them get over the nightmares from their last case that had started out just like the call this evening.

The porch light was turned on as they entered the courtyard. A pale, worried, Greg Andrews ushered the men in.

Detective Peters put out his hand "Mr. Andrews?"

Shaking his hand, Greg replied "Yes." Greg stood aside and nodded toward Karen, "and this is our good friend, Karen Vincent. She's been helping me with the phone calls and the search for Laurel."

"How do you do? I'm Phil Peters and this is my partner, Matt Johnson. Nodding to Greg, "we're here in response to a call that you suspect your wife is missing?"

Running his hands through his hair, Greg recounted his evening since arriving home to the two men. In his agitated state, he failed to notice that both men were eyeing the home's rooms with more than idle curiosity.

"Do you mind if we take a look around?"

"No, please, do whatever you need to. Just help me find my wife."

Both men immediately went from room to room looking at entryways and windows for intrusion. They also checked for any signs of foul play, all the while wishing anyone else had been assigned this call. Everything was too familiar, too fresh. They desperately needed this case to have a happy ending—for the husband to love his wife as he appeared to. Finding nothing amiss, the men joined Greg and Karen again in the living room where they had left them.

"Can you show me your wife's purse?" Phil asked.

"Sure, it's in our closet. I'll get it for you."

Matt walked with him while he went to retrieve the purse, giving his partner "alone time" with the friend.

"How long have you known Laurel and Greg Andrews, Karen?"

Clutching her hands together, Karen softly answered "I've been best friends with Laurel ever since we met in high school and with Greg ever since their courtship twenty years ago."

"Did you feel they were having any problems recently? Anything Laurel said about something being wrong?"

"No. I write travel books for group tours and I've been especially busy lately. I have never seen Greg and Laurel anything but happy and, well, normal. They have had their rough spots as in any marriage, but they are devoted to one another. I'm sure if anything had been wrong, Laurel would have told me."

Matt and Greg came back with Laurel's purse just as Karen finished talking. She and Greg exchanged a look and Phil started looking through Laurel's purse.

"Well, I can see your wife wasn't planning on going anywhere. Her driver's license, cell phone, wallet with $50.00, and her passport are in here. You say there was a message that she never went to work today?"

"Yes. I didn't erase it so you can listen to it if you need to."

"I do and I would like to—now."

Detective Peters took some notes while he listened to the message, mainly Agnes' name and phone number. He wanted to call her for himself and find out if Laurel had been acting strangely at work, or mentioned any personal problems she was having.

Returning to the living room, Detective Peters continued with his process. "Now, Mr. Andrews, I have to ask you some personal questions and I want you to understand that this is routine."

Greg nodded quickly, "I understand. Ask whatever you like."

Detective Johnson stood behind his seated partner watching Karen and Greg's faces as Phil asked his questions and he took notes.

"Have you and your wife had any problems or unusual stress lately?"

Greg put his head in his hands as he answered. "We had a doozy of an argument just last night. I'll be honest with you, I was a complete ass. I met someone at work that can help Laurel and I with some infertility problems and I completely blew my approach with her. We were unsuccessful ten years ago in what proved to be a horrendous process for Laurel. I was so excited about what the doctor told me, I pretty much demanded that Laurel try again. She was really pissed. I had intended to straighten things out tonight."

Karen and the detectives were watching Greg closely. Karen could just imagine Laurel's response to Greg's ultimatum—she remembered many nights of pain that they sat through together the last time she and Greg tried for a baby. She didn't appear alarmed though; she would never believe Greg capable of harming Laurel.

The two detectives cringed inside. "Here we go again," Phil lamented silently. "Mr. Andrews, do you think your wife was upset enough to leave you?"

"No, and why if she were leaving me wouldn't she have taken her car, or money...."

"Yes, that's true," he said interrupting him. "Have you noticed any strangers around your house or did your wife mention anything unusual?"

"No. Laurel is popular with just about anyone who's ever met her."

Karen lit up suddenly. "Greg, when I got here this evening, I pulled this slip about a missed delivery off of your door. I completely forgot in all of the excitement." She pulled the slip out of her pocket and handed it to the detectives.

"We'll have to check this out in the morning. Maybe the delivery guy saw something that might be helpful. What about your neighbors, Mr. Andrews, did they see anything?"

"We talked to everyone that was home in the court. No one said they saw anything unusual."

"You said your wife run's at 5:00 in the morning? Is this everyday and what about her route?"

"Laurel is a marathon runner. I think she's running about six miles a day right now. She does her long runs on Saturdays. Sunday's we attend church and she uses that as her "rest day." The one thing I do know about her route is that it changes every day. Laurel had a nut try to run her down with a bicycle a year or so ago and ever since then, she never runs the same course two days in a row."

"I see. Mr. Andrew's, it's obvious to me that you have money. I'm looking at several art pieces that look like you've traveled, and your house has obviously been decorated at some expense. Has anyone approached you about a loan recently and did you turn them down?"

Karen had perked up at the art pieces, she was just about to tell them they were gifts from her when Greg cut in. "You're way off base. Karen gave us most of the pieces you're talking about from her travels and this house was entirely decorated by my wife—it's her hobby. No one would have asked us for money or thought we had money right now. Everyone knew I was in danger of losing my job with the construction industry taking a hit right now."

"I see. One last question, please, Mr. Andrews. We can ask Ms. Vincent to leave the room if you would rather answer out of her presence."

Karen looked at Greg with questioning, yet understanding, eyes. "No, I have nothing to hide from Karen or anyone else. As long as your questions will help in finding my wife, you can ask me whatever you want for however long you want."

"All right then, Mr. Andrews, with the recent employment stresses and your disagreements over medical treatments, have you had or are you having an affair?"

Greg was totally taken off guard. "Do I honestly appear to be a cad?" he thought. Aloud, his voice loud, he rebutted with "No! I have been in love with my wife since the first time I saw her. We have always been faithful to one another and always will be—I'd stake my life on that. The only "other woman" that could turn up in my life recently is Joy Stewart. She's a subcontractor on my job and a friend to both of us. She also happens to be a woman who volunteered just today to be a surrogate if we wanted her to. That's part of what I wanted to tell my wife tonight too."

Karen and the detectives couldn't help but look at Greg. "Good God! Could the man be so oblivious to how this all sounds?" Matt wondered.

Phil continued, "Now, now, Mr. Andrews, you must know we have to ask all of these questions?"

Calming himself, Greg answered with a glare in the detective's direction, "I'm sure you do, but it is insulting nonetheless."

"I have to inform you that technically the law states that your wife isn't missing until twenty-four hours have passed. It is very clear to me, however, that she is missing and I want to escalate any and all options the department has to find her as quickly as possible. That said; I would like you to agree to a wire tap on your telephone in case she has been taken for ransom; circulate a recent picture of her; and, finally, your permission for a crime team to search your home for any clues we may have missed."

Both Karen and Greg looked stricken at the detective's last comments. The gravity of the situation wasn't lost as Greg answered the requests with a nod—his voice had left him in his fear for Laurel.

"I'll make some calls and set things in motion. I need to know where I can reach you if we have more questions."

Crossing to a side table, Greg picked up the picture frame and removed Laurel's picture. Handing the picture to Phil, he cleared his throat and said "I called my boss to let him know what's happened. He isn't expecting me in until Laurel is found. Laurel had this picture taken for me as an anniversary present last July."

"Thank you. We'll head out then. Please don't use your phone or touch doors and windows until after the crime team is finished. If there are any prints at all, the team will find them. Also, you could both help Laurel by not contacting anyone else—let us handle that. If Laurel has been kidnapped, we don't want to make it too difficult for the kidnapper to get to Greg."

Tears started in Greg's eyes when he heard that. Karen turned and started crying on his shoulder, too overcome to say anything at all. Clearing his throat again, Greg answered for both of them. "Just tell us what you want us to do. Just bring her home."

Phil and Matt looked at one another and as Phil rose to walk to the door, Matt asked one more question. "Mr. Andrews, do we have your permission to search your company vehicle as well?"

The light dawned on Greg's sad face. This bastard thought he had something to do with Laurel's disappearance—that he had hurt her! Moving angrily into Matt's face, he answered "You creep! I repeat. I have nothing, nothing to hide! You look anywhere your pea brain can think of and find my wife!"

Phil held Matt's arm and Karen had grabbed the back of Greg's shirt as the tension rose. "Matt, come on, let's go. Mr. Andrews I'm sorry for upsetting you further. We'll be in touch in the morning." Phil closed the front door as soon as he and Matt were over the doorsill. Silent until they were seat belted in the car, he started the motor and looked at his partner. "Shit, Matt! Why did you ask him about his truck like that?"

"Why are you so bent out of shape? Jesus H. Christ, Phil, it's the same story as last time all over again. When we check with his work and find out he wasn't even there today, that he had called in sick; then is it going to click for you, huh? They're fighting, he's having job trouble, oh and let's not forget "Joy." A surrogate my ass. She's his mistress and Laurel is dead. And I'll tell you something else, I wouldn't be surprised if there isn't something between he and Karen too—they sure looked comfortable sitting together on the couch."

Phil looked sadly into the court as he pulled away from the curb. "I think you're wrong, Matt. Couldn't you feel the love in that house? That wasn't something that happened overnight. No, these two have a well-bonded, loving relationship. I can feel it. I can also feel that Karen is like a sister to Greg, there was nothing sexual happening there. I also felt the husband is truly worried and frantic this time. That was raw emotion that erupted over you asking about searching his truck. Let's not forget, it wasn't "Joy" who called to tell us about her existence in their lives, Greg volunteered the information. He spilled his guts about their argument. No, this man has opened himself to complete vulnerability. He's not stupid and he's not lying. I'm telling you, Matt, this is a real mystery."

"I sure as hell hope you're right, Phil. I don't agree with you, I think he's dirty, but I'm going to pray you're wrong."

"Pray, Matt? When's the last time you did that?"

"After we got those two to confess to murder and found that poor woman's body in our last missing persons' case. I prayed that God would never put me, or anyone else, through something like that again."

"And if He does?"

"Then I'm quitting the force. I just can't have nightmares for the rest of my life."

CHAPTER 10

Karen hung up after talking with her editor. She had tremendous trouble getting through the call—she still couldn't believe this was happening. She had cancelled her flight to India and requested a clear calendar for a few weeks time. The editor could hear her crying as Karen told her of a "family emergency" and didn't question her further. Karen barely heard the editor's closing remarks, the standard, "call me if there is anything I can do or if you just need to talk."

Fresh box of tissues in hand, she started to get things together for a stay at Greg and Laurel's while the search for Laurel continued. She watered the plants; arranged for her mail to be held; and, the newspaper to stop delivery indefinitely. As she packed some clothes, memories of all the years floated through her thoughts. She laughed over the outlandish stunts and she cried over the shared sorrows. The years had been so full. "Please God, she prayed, don't let anything have happened to Laurel. I need her; she's the only sister I have ever had."

Karen glanced at her watch—she was supposed to meet Greg at Kinko's at 8:00. While the cops were searching Greg and Laurel's home and cars, she and Greg were going to have posters and flyers printed to put up around the area. Fresh tears sprang as she thought about their day. "Come on Karen, get a grip, she talked to herself through tears. "How are you supposed to help Greg to find Laurel if you keep falling apart all the time? Taking a deep breath, she continued to lecture herself. "Okay, I am going to sit and cry for five minutes, then I'm going to get my ass up and out that door, and we are going to find her damn it!"

Greg had contacted his widowed neighbor, Brenda, and asked if she had seen anything yesterday. Brenda was really good about watching out in their neighborhood, partly out of fear now that she was alone, partly because she was genuinely a caring neighbor. Sad and alarmed, she had told Greg she hadn't seen anything before leaving for the market and suggested they get their neighbors together and put up some posters. After Karen and Greg finished at Kinko's, they were going to Brenda's, using her home as a "command post" for the day. Greg wanted to help get the posters and flyers out, but he also wanted to be near home to help the cops with anything they may need.

Just as Karen's five minute, hissy fit time ended, her doorbell rang. She was surprised to find Detective Matt Johnson on her doorstep.

"Good morning, Ms. Vincent. I'm sorry to bother you, but I wanted to ask you some questions outside of Mr. Andrews presence."

She looked at him suspiciously as he moved to come through the doorway. She answered more calmly than she actually felt. "Of course, Detective Johnson, come in." Karen hadn't failed to notice the detective's look of disgust during the previous evening's discussion. She knew he didn't believe Greg.

Eyeing the luggage in the entryway, Matt could tell Karen had been crying. "Please call me Matt. Nodding toward the bags, he asked "taking a trip?"

"Well, I was supposed to be heading for India; I'm going to be writing a travel book on the country, but I cancelled my flight. I will be staying at Greg and Laurel's while we find out what happened to her and bring her home." After all the traveling Karen had under her belt, she had become very good at reading people. While Matt tried to hide what he actually thought about Karen's staying with Greg, she read his features and deduced what he was really thinking about her. "What a frickin' idiot!" she thought.

"Ah, yes, I've read some of your work. I took a trip to Sweden a few years back. Your suggestions on looking up family history were right on. I've already been by the Andrews' home; the team is trying to move as quickly as possible on this. It is critical that we find her within seventy-two hours; after that, the incidence of foul play goes up astronomically." He noticed fresh tears in her eyes as she quickly walked over to the coffee table, grabbed a tissue and began wiping her face. "I hate to bother you when you are so obviously upset, but as Laurel's best friend, you may have information that would be very helpful without realizing it."

Sitting down and motioning for Matt to be seated across from her, she released a slight hiccup before answering. "I understand. I can't imagine what more I could tell you than I did last night. My plan is to help in any way I can to help find Laurel. I'm due to meet Greg at Kinko's to get some posters and flyers printed."

"Yes, he told us that when he let us in the house this morning. Tell me, Ms. Vincent."

"Please, call me Karen."

"Yes, Karen, are you absolutely sure that you have had no indication of any trouble between Greg and Laurel? She never had a funny bruise she didn't quite explain, or, cry on your shoulder that she thought Greg was having an affair..?"

Karen angrily broke into his questioning. "You really are an idiot aren't you? No! Just as I told Detective Peters last night, I have never seen Laurel and Greg as anything but a solid, happy couple. How can you think he would hurt her? Didn't you see how distraught he was last night? Do you have any idea how hard it was for him to tell you about their fertility problems? Do you really think he would tell you about Joy if he had something to hide? Damn you, if everyone had a marriage like those two, there would be no need for divorce." Fuming, she sat glaring at Matt as he shot back at her with a very cocky tone.

"So sure of your friends, are you? Well, what if I told you that when I checked with Greg's work this morning, and they did verify he was at work yesterday, but that he arrived about an hour late? Or, how about my conversation with Joy where she admitted she had agreed to be a surrogate, but just to be "honest", that she did feel some regret about it when she realized she had more than just sisterly feelings for Greg?"

Karen shot to her feet and clinched her hands into fists at her sides. "So, that makes him a murderer? Did you bother to ask Greg why he was late, or if he was aware of Joy's feelings? Oh, don't even answer, you odious man, I can see that you didn't. You've already tried and convicted him haven't you?"

Annoyed that Matt had lost his temper, he tried to apologize. "Ms. Vincent, I'm sorry I've upset you further, it was not my intention. While I do have some suspicions about Greg, my real goal is to find out the truth as fast as I can. Please, let's both calm down and see if we can't work on anything you may know that could help in this case. Did you know that it is almost always a family member or close acquaintance that is the perpetrator in a disappearance of this type?"

Karen had turned her back on Matt after unleashing her temper at him. Taking deep breaths, she turned again and sat back down facing this ass of a man squarely. "Fine; of course I don't know anything about what is "usual" in this case, I've never, ever been through anything like this and *my occupation* does not involve crime," she remarked sarcastically.

Still smarting from her superior attitude, he decided to continue as if nothing had happened and he was completing a routine investigation interview. "Let's get started then so you can get going. Greg said that he had just sprung the attempt at pregnancy talk at Laurel the evening before she disappeared. Think back; are you sure she never mentioned him pressuring her about this prior to then?"

Karen wrinkled her brow as she studied the carpet, trying to remember anything Laurel might have mentioned on the topic. Shaking her head, putting her hands out upward and slapping down on her thighs in exasperation, she answered him. "No, there's nothing. I'm sure Greg's telling the truth on that. Even when I travel, Laurel and I email each other almost daily. If this had come up between them, there is no way she would have missed contacting me immediately. I'm sure he's dead right about how she reacted; she was a complete wreck by the time they gave up all treatment on the last go around. Matt, I'm not kidding, Laurel and I are extremely close and she is literally like a sister to me. If there was anything at all amiss, I'd be the one she would run to."

Matt studied her face as she spoke, satisfied she believed every word she was saying. "What about an affair? Do you think it's possible that Greg might have slipped? Are you sure that if he had and Laurel found out about it that she would tell you? Even in families, sometimes the most embarrassing stories remain hidden."

Once again Karen thought before answering. "I would have real trouble believing Greg capable of having an affair or Laurel capable of hiding that knowledge from anyone." Sighing loudly, she looked Matt directly in the eye. "Greg is in construction now, but did you know that he was a member of a Search and Rescue Team? This guy risked his life several times and it just tore him up when bad things happened to good people. Greg's a big, tough looking guy, Matt, but he does the most romantic things with Laurel. He surprises her with getaway trips for no reason and flowers just because he thinks of her when he sees them. I wouldn't be surprised if he is oblivious to Joy's feelings; he loves his wife. As far as Laurel goes, even if she wanted to keep trouble to herself, it would be impossible for her. You've seen her picture. Those enormous eyes of hers hide nothing about what she's feeling—joy or sorrow. Neither one of them are liars, they were both raised Catholic and have lived a moral life." She finished and looked to see if she had gotten anything through to him. Sadly, she didn't see anything different about him than she had in the past fifteen minutes.

"Well, thank you for your insight Ms. Vincent. I'll let you get back on your way. The posters and flyers are a good idea. Here's my card. If you hear anything at all from Laurel, I would appreciate you contacting me right away—before you contact Greg. And of course, if you think of anything you feel we should know, you can call me at any time."

"You're welcome, detective and I promise, if I think of anything, I will. I hope you've listened to what I've said so you can focus your energy somewhere other than on Greg. I know he's not involved in her disappearance and that you're wasting time trying to prove otherwise." She reached to shake his hand as she let him out the front door and then held on to it. "Please, verify Greg's reason for being late yesterday; find out if he is aware of Joy's feelings, and I'm betting he's not, and then move on. Use all of your resources to find her."

Releasing his hand from hers, he turned his head casually towards his car and back towards her before answering her. "Ms. Vincent, I assure you that I've listened to everything you've told me and hope you realize that I am doing everything possible, and within my realm of experience, to get Laurel home safely. You've asked me to move off of my prime suspect based on your friendship. I'm asking you to go back over what I've shared with you just now and do the same. Remove your feelings about friendship with Greg and re-examine whether you find anything at all that would cause you to suspect the possibility that those two may have had more than just an argument; that some previously unknown emotional temperament of Greg's may have escalated into a physical reaction. Do that; then call me if and when you realize that I may just be right about Greg and not wasting any time at all." With that he turned, leaving Karen standing there, mouth agape, trembling and fearing that what he just said could possibly be true.

Matt dialed Phil on his cell phone from the car as he was leaving. "Hey Phil, how's it going at the house?"

As Matt listened to Phil's answer, he wanted to turn the car around and get right in that know-it-all Karen's face. "Ha! Wonder what she would say to hearing that Greg stands to gain four hundred grand in equity off the sale of their house, and he is sole beneficiary on a million dollar life insurance policy taken out on his wife six months ago?" he sadly said aloud.

CHAPTER 11

Laurel woke to the delicious pleasure of two little redheads snuggled on each side of her. Nothing made this experience more real than these two children. David had no problem agreeing to their bunking in with her since he had promised Gwen some time off when he returned. Thinking about the rooms she was beginning today; the kitchen, the children's and Gwen's, she barely heard the light tap on her door. Regrettably, kissing the two sleeping children's cheeks, she left the snug haven to greet Emily at her door.

"Good morning Laurel. I'll stay here with my knitting while you do your run. Did you sleep well?" she whispered.

Whispering back so as not to wake Cat and Tim, "Yes Emily, I did. It was later than I expected it to be when David and I finished our 'meeting of the minds' in his room last night." She noticed Emily's wide eyes, realized what she had just said, and hurried to repair the poor woman's thoughts. "I mean, I had no idea my plans would take so long to convey to someone else. I've never consulted with anyone on a project before, I just did it."

Lowering her eyebrows back down to their proper place, Emily smiled. "Did Lord David give you much trouble over what you want to do?"

"Surprisingly, no," she answered with a smile. One of the children turned over and sighed. Laurel drew Emily over to the sitting area to continue their conversation. "There was only one part of the total design he was adamantly opposed to. I want to turn his room into one space for both Lord and Lady, and convert the existing Lady's room on the other side of the connecting bath into a nursery. He finally agreed when I pointed out that this design is a home for generations to come. I'm afraid I have to confess that I got a little loud in convincing him. I shouldn't be surprised, though, my ideas and "projects" have literally driven my husband nuts! I have these terrific ideas that pop into my head and I'm oblivious to the work that goes into accomplishing the vision. Since I don't have workmen at my disposal, my husband has had to do some very detailed carpentry to help me out." Laughing together, Laurel confessed. "Every time I say "Honey, I have an idea," the man tends to run from the room!"

Emily was laughing at the picture and leaned in closer to Laurel. "If he wasn't complaining over that, I bet just like all men he'd find something else to go on about!"

"That's the truth, isn't it? I better hurry now and get ready to run. I don't want to leave David and Roger waiting too long. They may go without me."

"No, Laurel, I'm sure you'll be downstairs before they are. Just between us, those two aren't quite as used to running as you are."

"What do you mean? David told me that while they don't usually run as far as I do, they do run daily."

"It's the word run, Laurel. I think a more accurate description might be that they jog daily."

Green eyes lit up. "Oh, Emily! I am going to have some fun this morning aren't I?" Winking she went off to the bathroom to gear up.

Lost in her thoughts, Laurel smiled as she dressed. She had already been excited about the castle project, but after her meeting with David, she was so excited to get started that if it hadn't been for her two little guests last night, she may not have made it to bed. Greg had always seemed mostly amused by her projects and only pitched in to help her if she asked him to. Watching David as she explained what she wanted to do structurally and what supplies she required was like watching a rose blossom before her eyes in mere minutes. As an architect, David was easily able to envision her renovation, and as a home-owner on a mission, thirsty enough to catch on to where her design was heading. She didn't have to ask him for help, he actually volunteered for the trickiest part for her. Laurel had many artistic talents, but painting murals wasn't one of them. The sheer delight David felt when she revealed her need for a painter with just such talents for the children's rooms was written all over his face. David happily revealed he had turned Lady Elizabeth's private room into a studio for his hobby—painting. He was thrilled to be able to contribute so intimately to his children's rooms. Declining to say anything more about Lady Elizabeth, they continued to review plans and her supplies list. Laurel had a brief, bittersweet moment when she remembered the early days with Greg and how they used to communicate in a unique language all their own. Shaking her head back into the present, she tied her shoes and waved goodbye to Emily on her way to meet the two men.

It's a good thing the men didn't see the devilish grin cn Laurel's face as the elevator descended. While her anger towards David had evaporated with understanding upon meeting his children, Laurel's love for a good prank spurred her mind towards a plan of sweet revenge.

Emily had been wrong; both men were waiting at the rear entrance when she arrived five minutes early. She hid her smile as she watched them preening with their "stretching" before their start. David looked up and acted as if he hadn't noticed she was there.

With a casual "Good morning, Laurel. Glad you could make it. Roger and I are almost done with our stretching but we would be happy to wait for a few minutes if you would like to stretch."

"Morning Roger, David," she replied nodding towards both men. "My coach always had us use the first two miles for loosening up. We add two minutes to our race pace and then move up to pace after the two miles. If any stretching is necessary, I will do it at the end of the run. You know, David, you did say I could talk to you with my personal questions while we ran. Maybe you could try running, just for today, using this training method and we would be able to talk a little easier?"

Still trying to look the part of seasoned runners, the men nodded first to one another and then to Laurel.

"Fine, fine Laurel," David said. "Roger, why don't you take the first watch for unwanted company and I'll take the second. I'm sure Laurel will have finished her questions by then. Laurel, go ahead and start directly to your right out of the garden. We'll match your pace and I'll signal directions as we go."

Too bad David wasn't a little more astute at watching Laurel's eyes. He would have noticed the gleam of pure devilment in the green orbs and proceeded with more caution.

Laurel took off running at about a ten minute pace in the direction David had indicated.

"Didn't you say you were going to add two minutes to the pace for the first two miles?" David tried to ask with an even voice.

Laurel didn't miss the alarm he tried to hide. Reigning in her grin, she innocently replied. "Oh, am I going too fast? Sorry, I'm just so used to running. I'll slow it down for you two."

Not to be outdone, David smiled his response while he had the breath "No, no, don't do that, I just thought you said you wanted nine minute miles and very soon we'll be at eight if we don't slow it down a bit."

"Oh, that's right, I did agree to nine minute miles, didn't I?"

With that comment, David realized he'd been had. Looking over at Roger, the men exchanged a look that clearly labeled Laurel a "damn vixen."

Deciding she better get her questions in before David couldn't get the breath to answer them, Laurel slacked off the pace a bit.

"David, how were you able to get me out of the United States? I don't have my passport with me."

"About ten years ago, President Clinton and Vice President Gore visited England for some talks with Queen Elizabeth. I was with an architectural firm as a partner at the time and had been instituting power and pollution saving efforts in all of my work. Both men were interested in implementing some of my designs in the United States when a day tour took them through some examples of modern English architecture that included one of my projects. As a Lord, I was given diplomatic immunity to travel more easily between our countries while I oversaw a housing project in Washington."

"But you would still have the problem of people noticing a passed out woman with you, I would think. However did you explain that?"

God how he wished he didn't have to answer this question. "Well, you see, Laurel, well, ah, you were in a trunk...."

"You put me in a trunk? Did you say a trunk?" Laurel, eyes blazing, started to run a bit faster.

"Please," David said, trying to keep his sentences short. "I hadn't had time to think things through when I got the call about Cat's accident. I told you I was sorry, I know it was wrong to just kidnap you off the street, but you've met my children, I would have done anything to do the project we're about to start and I had to leave for home."

"That doesn't make it right, David."

David noticed Roger was starting to favor his right leg. "I know, but I can't change what's already been done. Ask me your next question."

"You said you left my husband a note. Why can't I call him or email him then? Why haven't I seen any phones or computers inside?"

"I did leave your husband a note, Laurel. You can't contact your family for the same reason you didn't see any phones or computers inside. I told you on the plane, we live a solitary life and you are going to have to trust me that it is for my children's sake. By the glitter of the ring on your finger, I know your husband loves you very much. Think about him and your children, if there was no other way for you to grant them the home you can create, wouldn't you have done anything to give them that?"

"My children—what children? Greg and I weren't able to have children."

"When Shelby and I toured your home, two of the rooms appeared to be for children."

"Oh, no, sadly I'm afraid that's not the case." David could hear the sadness in her voice as she explained about Tyler and Morgan. After seeing her with his children, he felt saddened that life had played such an evil card.

"Oh, I'm so sorry to hear that. I can tell you would be a terrific mother just by watching you with Cat and Tim. Tell me, will it be horrible for you to be away from your husband for six weeks?"

"Well, I'll miss him, that's for sure. We're a strong couple though and I know Greg will understand my wanting to tackle the castle. He just started working with a new firm and is still having long days adjusting to changing locations and buildings. He was a superintendent for residential housing, but with the current slump, he was fortunate to find work in the commercial arena. It's a whole new world for him. I'm betting he's planning on taking advantage of the time to assimilate the job duties and gloat over not having to help me on this!" she said laughing and spreading her arms to include their proximity. "What do you do in case of an emergency and how do you order everything if you don't have phones or computers?"

The sweating Lord David, feeling guilt raise up its ugly head, tried not to pant as he formed his answer. He easily remembered the note he and Henry hurriedly scratched in the predawn hour. Greg had no idea she was gone on a "project"; she was simply gone for six weeks. "I didn't say we don't have them, just that they aren't available. I have cell phones. When I have to travel, I leave one with the staff so I can contact them, and they me. I also have a laptop computer. If there's a real emergency, there is a horn in the north tower that the staff knows how to signal different emergency responses with." Trying to buy some time to conserve his dwindling energy, he asked very quickly "Tell me about you and your husband. How did you meet? By your master bedroom theme I gather you are both hunters?"

David nodded to Roger and patted his gun to signal he would take the watch as Laurel started to answer. She wanted to take pity on him and slow the pace so he could breathe, but remembering he locked her in a trunk cancelled the thought. "You seem to remember the master bedroom so well. By any chance did you take a very detailed look in our closet too? Is that how you knew what size clothing I would need?

"Yes, I admit I did. At the time, I wasn't thinking of abducting you, I was just curious about the woman that created the home. I have a very good memory for details."

As it dawned on him that there was some very personal clothing in her closet, an obviously embarrassed David stammered "What I mean is, I noticed you wore a size eight dress and size nine shoes. I had Emily and Gwen manufacture the finer details."

Laurel knew she should take pity on the man but she was having way too much fun.

David moved her back onto his question. "So, how did you meet?"

"We met in college, the same way countless others have, I guess. At first, I thought we would be just friends. There was something about him, though. We didn't even realize how we talked differently than everyone else in our conversations until my sister-in-law, Cheri, brought it up. Greg has a very quick wit and it hits my competitive nature just enough to want to best him. This usually causes a ridiculous conversation of complete nonsense and pure fun. When we married, we were your typical poor students. This ring is a design I did and Greg had made for our tenth anniversary. I had never hunted before meeting Greg. I can handle the pheasant hunting, but I draw the line at Bambi. Greg competed in some Mountain Man competitions when he was young and some of the artworks were awards won in those meets. I love to camp, but I'm not exactly into Annie Oakley. Since we both love the outdoors, I combined rustic nature with those awards to make a room for both of us. We're both Catholic and not being able to have children hit us hard. Right now, our relationship is strained."

Working for the wind to breathe, David asked with surprise "Strained how?"

Laurel couldn't believe she was sharing something so personal, but something about David told her she should. "Greg and I had tried medical intervention about ten years ago when we found out I probably wouldn't get pregnant otherwise. It was the hardest thing I've ever done. First I had to take all of these pills to make my body produce eggs and prepare the womb. The hormonal side effects were horrible and I only continued because I wanted our baby so bad. Then, every month, I went through the worst depression whenever we found out it didn't work. For a year, I wasn't even me anymore. I was praying, ranting, crying or hurting before I finally couldn't take it anymore. I thought we had made peace with just having Tyler and Morgan in our lives, but I was wrong. Greg surprised me just the night before you grabbed me that he wants us to try again. I could tell something was up with him for awhile, I just never imagined it was that. I honestly don't know how we're going to resolve this. Maybe God was intervening by giving us the six weeks to think on it huh?"

David had flinched when she said "grabbed me." While Laurel was lost in her recital, David had felt cramping in both his legs and slowed his pace a little without her noticing. He checked Roger's red face and he was glad they only had two miles left to the run. "Shit!" he thought, "how are we supposed to do this again tomorrow?" As he answered Laurel, he made a mental note to check on the pain medication he had asked Emily to get. "I can understand why you wouldn't want to go through that again. Is Greg a runner too?"

"No, he's terrific support at all of my marathons though. Running is my thing and hunting is his. It's brought some great adventures to the table."

"I bet it has." Suddenly, the runners noticed some shrubbery moving and heard loud squealing. "It's a boar, Roger, get Laurel behind that tree!"

Roger propelled Laurel forward and around the tree just as the wild boar charged through the brush. David pulled his gun, aimed, and shot. The boar dropped in its tracks; the shot squarely hitting between the beady eyes.

David looked up at Roger and Laurel returning from behind the tree. "Looks like I better have Thomas get the truck out when we get back. Laurel, are you fond of pork?"

Staring wide-eyed, she stammered "What, uh, yes I am."

"Good. We'll roast him for dinner then."

Both men fell in as if nothing had happened and the kill gave them a much-needed rush of energy. "David, does this happen often?" Laurel asked.

David was smiling through the pain. "I'm sorry to say the answer is no. As you may recall, I did tell you the forest had wild game and that we would be bringing guns. This is the second time in eighteen months we've been waylaid by a visitor." He failed to mention that this was also the second time in that period that he and Roger and attempted to run a six mile course.

"Yes, you did." Laurel was still stunned and became somewhat quiet. "If you two don't mind, I'd like to take advantage of the opportunity for some cross-training while I'm here. Tomorrow, instead of running, I like to do a lap swim in the pool. What do you say to a run every other day and I'll do my long run alone on Saturday's? You did say I'd be doing that on a road to town with Henry following by car, didn't you David?"

"That's correct. If you do that, your music player should arrive before your next run. Will cross training enhance or hamper your training?"

"Enhance it—all of my muscles, including my core muscles, will become strong. I should run even faster before long."

A fresh, barely winded Laurel blurted that out with glee just as the three entered the back edge of the castle's gardens. Roger and David were both trying to keep their legs moving. "Oh, David, one last question please. I changed my route everyday for my runs. How did you and Henry know where to find me and when?"

"Laurel you may change your route, but you always start and end at the same place. I noticed the marathon pictures and medals in your gym. Long distance runners always run in the early morning."

Smiling at his resourcefulness, Laurel took the lead and raced ahead to greet Emily, Thomas, Henry and the children waiting on the castle's back steps.

Thomas asked David about the shot as Laurel raced up the steps to the children. "Run into some trouble sir?"

"No trouble Thomas—dinner! Bring the truck around and the three of us will go bring it in."

Just as Thomas was leaving to get the truck, David stopped him as Laurel bounded inside with the children. Gathering his staff close, he issued one terse order to them all. "I am expecting a lot of deliveries to start today and to go on for at least four weeks. One of the packages in the next day or so is going to be from a music store. Whoever finds it, I expect it placed in my room immediately without comment to Laurel. Is that understood?"

Roger said "You don't have to ask me twice" knowing that he would have to run even faster than he had today if Laurel got her hands on some music. As Roger and David left to get a drink before going with Thomas for the bore, David stopped at the entry and turned towards Emily. "Emily, where are the pain pills I requested?"

"Follow me, sir. I'll take you to them right away."

Roger and David limped away following Emily. Henry turned to Thomas and was barely able to hold his laughter until they were out of earshot to say "What do you make of that Thomas?"

Thomas didn't bother to hold back the thick, barrel laughter as he slapped Henry's back. "I think Emily and Gwen are right—she's going to knock him off his rocker!"

CHAPTER 12

Greg and Karen were sitting quietly having a somber breakfast, each lost in their own thoughts over the past few days' events. It was the day after the meeting with the neighbors at Brenda's. Everyone for three blocks turned out; they all knew and liked Laurel. She had helped many of them move into their homes and "dressed" them up. It was impossible for everyone to ignore the "crime scene" tape placed across the Andrews' door while the home search was going on. The previous kidnap and murder in Keddie was too fresh in everyone's memories. The closest neighbors that had become Greg and Laurel's friends were forcing themselves to believe that Greg would never harm Laurel. Every time Greg was summoned by an officer at the door with a question, nervous looks passed across those waiting for directions inside Brenda's home.

The neighbors broke up into four groups. Leslie and her daughter Morgan took one group; next-door neighbors Suzi and Lucas took another one; Glen and Barbie from two doors down took the third one; and, Melissa, from the court's end house, with Karen took the last one. Each group stapled posters on phone poles over a five mile radius and handed out flyers to anyone passing by while they worked. Local businesses were given stacks of flyers to hand out to customers and posters hung on their front doors. Greg and Brenda manned the supplies and designated areas for each group.

Greg left Brenda to pass out supplies when Phil Peters came to the door and asked Greg to join him for a moment over at the Andrews' house. Brenda and the neighbors, still in her house getting their posters and flyers, watched Greg's face as Phil placed his request. They were relieved that Greg's face reflected only worry and sorrow.

Greg waved to Brenda as he went out the door. "I'll be back in a moment, Brenda."

Catching up to Phil, Greg matched his steps and quietly waited for Phil to let him know what was on his mind.

"Greg, I know this is extremely difficult for you. How are you holding up?"

"Phil, I feel like the world tilted and I was standing on a cliff. Now I'm hanging on by my fingertips. Have your guys found anything yet?"

"I'm sorry, Greg, but no. Your wife kept a clean home, but not antiseptically clean. It's obvious that she vacuumed recently, but not the day she went missing. As you know, her purse with her wallet and passport were left here. Nothing has shown up on any of the searches for hits on your bank, her credit cards or at the airports and bus stations. There is nothing to suggest foul play inside. They have finished going over Laurel's car and haven't found anything but fingerprints. As you can see, they are starting on your truck now, but you and I both know they won't find anything there either will they?"

"No, Phil, they won't. I don't know what I can do to convince you that I didn't have anything to do with Laurel's disappearance. I love my wife, I can't imagine my life without her. Tell me, what do you want from me?" his voice was starting to rise with his frustration and he was running his fingers through his hair.

"Easy, Greg, easy." Phil looked over at a car pulling into the subdivision. Pointing it out to Greg he asked "Is that another neighbor arriving late?"

Greg rubbed his eyes to clear the tears, "No. I don't know who that is."

The sedan stopped in front of the Andrews house and Phil lowered his head and swore. "Christ! It's a reporter. Don't say anything, Greg, let me handle this."

"Okay."

The gangly reporter got out, stretched, and walked over to Phil and Greg. Fixing his eyes on the detective he calmly started in. "Good morning Phil, nice to see you again, although I hope I'm seeing you under better circumstances than last time."

"Morning, Gavin. As you very well know, any detailed news that I have cannot be released yet—this is an ongoing investigation. What I can tell you is that we have a missing person, Laurel Andrews. This is Greg Andrews, her husband. Mrs. Andrews went missing day before yesterday in the early morning, probably during her morning run. The search you have come upon is routine. At this time, we have found no evidence of foul play and we have found no medical incapacity in Mrs. Andrews history to suggest she may have wandered off. I can't tell you anything else at this time without compromising our investigation. If you would like to be of help, Greg can give you a flyer with Mrs. Andrews picture you can print with your story. Anyone who may have seen something can contact either me or Matt Johnson at this number." Phil took a card out of his pocket and handed it over to Gavin.

Gavin had already pulled out a notebook. "Greg, were you and your wife having any problems....?"

Phil cut him off and held onto Greg's arm to stop him from saying anything. "Gavin, stop it! I told you we have nothing to suggest foul play. Either take a flyer and ask some description and detail questions for your story or get out of here."

Gavin put up his hands in surrender, "Okay, okay. Greg, tell me your wife's height and weight. Also, what time was she running and do you know what she was wearing? Does she have a route she follows?"

Greg got a nod from Phil before answering. "Laurel is five feet eight and weighs one hundred and twenty pounds. She runs at 5:00 am—before going to work. I'm sorry, but I didn't take the time to check for what's missing from her clothing, only if there was any jewelry missing. Most of her running clothes this time of year are black running pants and long sleeve shirts. As far as her route, Laurel changes it every day just to make sure she isn't a target for a nut."

"I see. Phil, I'm assuming there was nothing missing to suggest a robbery?"

"No. The only jewelry missing is her wedding ring. We're checking pawn shops for that now. Greg, can you describe the ring for Gavin? Gavin, it's an unusual ring. If you can include the description for that in your article it could be something someone may have noticed."

"Good idea. Greg, what can you tell me?"

Greg was starting to look like someone suffering from the flu. Fear, worry and the lack of sleep were catching up fast. "We had the ring made. It's a fairly wide dual gold band. The band itself is open except for flowers out of diamonds between the bands. The flowers are divided by a single bar with a diamond in the center. There is a one carat marquis diamond on the top."

Gavin could tell there wasn't going to be anything "juicy" in this story. It was obvious that this guy was a wreck over his wife. No, this was something that was going to turn out to be a routine family tiff, his gut just knew it. Looking Greg over, he wondered if the guy got caught with his pants down and the wife took off to teach him a lesson. "You're right, Phil, The ring sounds very unique." Flipping his notebook shut, he looked at Greg and made it obvious he was ready to get going. "Greg, if you'll give me a picture of your wife, I'll take off now so I can get something in tomorrow's edition."

Greg pointed to Brenda's house across the street. "Just go knock on that door and ask for Brenda. She'll be happy to give you a flyer."

Looking at both men and not missing Phil's eyes warning him about asking any questions while he was at Brenda's, he nodded towards Greg as he put his hand out to shake his. "Mr. Andrews, I'm sorry for your trouble. I'll get right on this and I just want you to know that I hope everything turns out well and your wife returns home safely. Here's my card. If there's anything you find missing in my story that you, and of course you too, Phil, think might help bring Mrs. Andrews home, call me. I would like to keep in touch with you, if that's all right."

Taking the card, Greg looked the slight man in the eye. "Gavin, all I ask is that you don't sensationalize this. We're regular people with normal lives. I don't have a clue what's happened to Laurel, but I don't want to take any chances on pissing anybody off."

Gavin tried, and failed, to look innocent as he replied. "I understand. Good day, gentlemen."

Phil and Greg watched him leave, both feeling slightly uneasy. Phil could see Greg was fading fast. "Greg, I'm going to finish asking you a couple of questions and then I think you better lie down. Did you call your doctor?"

"No, the only people I called were those that might have heard from Laurel."

"You should. He can give you something to help you sleep."

"Later. What do you need to know?"

"As I said, we didn't find anything suspicious in our search so far, but some questions came up when I was doing the routine check on the information you gave me."

Greg eyes opened wide with shock. "Like what?"

"You said you were at work yesterday, but when we checked that out we were informed that while you were at work all day, you arrived an hour late. Why were you late?"

Fatigue was affecting Greg's reflexes and memory. "I was late? Let me think. Oh, yeah, I remember, I had to stop at the Home Depot to pick up some electrical switches missing from my order for the job. The electrical subcontractor called me on my cell when he was on the way letting me know that they didn't have those particular switches in stock. It would have cost me a day on the project so I stopped at the store on my way in."

"Isn't that unusual?"

"Not on this job. A lot of subcontractors have already gone under in the housing slump. Most of my subs on this job are from out of the area. My phone starts ringing just about every morning at 4:30 or so with one thing or another that I need to take care of first thing."

"I see. Greg, I hate to ask you this next question, but I have to, you understand?"

"I got it, Phil, shoot. I don't care what you ask me, I told you that. Let's just find Laurel."

"I know. Okay. You discussed you and your wife's fertility issues and told us that Joy Stewart had volunteered to be a surrogate for you and your wife. You also stated that she was like "one of the guys," and, that there was nothing romantically occurring between the two of you."

"Yeah, so what?"

"Ms. Stewart confirmed that she had volunteered for the surrogacy, but she also stated that she regretted that as she has romantic feelings for you."

Greg, mouth agape, stared openly at Phil trying to digest what he had just heard. "She said she had romantic feelings for me? Phil, I swear, she never said anything about that to me, I had no idea …"

Phil could see that Greg was plainly shocked. "Calm down. I understand. I told you I had to ask."

"I know, but, Joy, and me?"

"Let's move on. Greg, what was going on between you and Laurel that you took out a million dollar life insurance policy on her six months ago?"

Greg's head was spinning and his heartbeat was accelerating with each question Phil asked. It didn't take a genius to figure out he was with the "friendly" cop who also believed him to be a prime suspect. "I told you. Housing was taking a downturn and we were taking a big hit financially. When we were afraid I was going to lose our health insurance benefits along with my job, we sunk some of our savings into policies *for both of us.* If anything monumental came up, like cancer, we wouldn't be able to cover the costs for treatment. Did you even bother to look for a policy on me with Laurel as the beneficiary?"

Phil hung his head with shame. They hadn't, they had only asked questions about Laurel. "No Greg we didn't and I apologize. I'll have that confirmed immediately. Last question, then I want you to go in and lie down or you won't be doing anyone any good. You and your wife recently sold your home. Did your realtor report anyone showing an unusual interest in your wife—asking questions that weren't part of a normal home viewing?"

"No. Our house sold in the first week to the first prospective buyer that saw it. The new owner is a widow, hardly someone that would kidnap Laurel."

"Well, there's nothing there to check then." Phil could see the crew had completed the search on Greg's truck. The lead crewman shook his head at Phil indicating they hadn't found anything. "That's it, Greg. I'm sorry to tell you that the only lead we have left to follow is the delivery notice Ms. Vincent found on your door. Unless the delivery man saw something, we're out of leads. I'll let you know how that pans out, of course, but you should prepare yourself. I think our best bet at this time is that Gavin's story produces somebody who saw something."

Fresh tears sprang into Greg's eyes as he watched the teams returning to Brenda's, their duties completed. "Thanks for everything you've done Phil. I know you pulled strings to get on this before the twenty four hour period and I want you to know how much I appreciate it. I'm also aware that we're getting closer to that seventy-two hour window and what that means. Get back to me with anything you find out from the delivery guy. In the meantime, I'm going to pray that the news story helps us out."

The next morning Greg rose early to read the newspaper article on Laurel. Angry and disbelieving, Greg picked up the paper again to reread the story Gavin had put in today's issue. Slapping it down on the table as he left the kitchen nook table to get more coffee, Karen forced her attention back into their discussion on what steps to take now. "Greg, I don't know what to say, this is horrible."

"That goddamned reporter; my wife and I aren't famous, she's not pretty enough, what is it? We're just nobodies so my missing wife gets two inches on the back of the local section?"

"Greg, I'm just as upset about this as you are, but this isn't going to get us anywhere. I'm going to ask you one more time, what do we do now? It's almost a week and we don't have anything else we can do."

Exasperated, Greg put his mug in the sink and turned, lost in thought as he leaned against the kitchen counter. "I've got it! Karen, I'm going to call Tyler again and give him the lowdown on the story that came out. So far, all he and the rest of the family know is that Laurel is missing and we don't have any clues. Karen, Tyler's a broadcast journalist. I'm going to tell him that nothings being done here and see if he can pull some strings. He got his start here; he just may be able to get something out there that will get some action."

Karen was ready to try anything; she was drained from worry. "Don't just stand there Greg, start dialing."

CHAPTER 13

Tyler, with Jillian by his side listening, hung up from his call with Greg and instantly made three calls of his own: first to his boss to explain the situation and see if he could do a "mystery" piece; second to his old boss at the Keddie paper to see why Gavin dropped the ball; and last, to Detective Peters to see if he could meet with him early the next day. Jillian had used her cell to book the "red eye" flight while Tyler was making his arrangements and immediately went to start packing a bag for him.

Tyler was rattling off details a mile a minute when he entered their bedroom. "Okay, honey, my boss cleared me to do whatever I can to find Laurel up to and including a live broadcast. I'm meeting with my old boss at 7:00 a.m. before meeting with the detective at 8:00 a.m. I put in a quick call back to Greg so he knows what's in play. I assume since you're packing for me I'm on the red eye?"

Jillian lovingly looked at her husband while answering. "Yes, love, you are. I'm so glad you're doing this and so worried about Laurel. Promise me you'll call a zillion times a day to let me know what's going on."

"You know I will. Is it okay to tell everyone about the baby or do you want to wait a couple more weeks until after the first trimester?"

Eyes down, Jillian hesitantly asked "Would you mind if we wait? You know how nervous I am and I want to follow everything my doctor says. Besides, don't you think it would be more complete if we <u>both</u> got to spread the news? I also don't want anything taking the focus off of finding Laurel."

"You're right. We'll wait." Grabbing the packed suitcase in one hand, he grabbed his petite wife up with the other and kissed her hard. "Now, you promise me something. You will be very good while I'm gone and not lift, climb or in any way do anything I would not allow you to do if I was here. I don't want to have to worry about you or our child having a dented head."

Smiling, Jillian leaned into his warm embrace. "I promise" she whispered into his neck as he released her. Beaming into his face with a smile as they walked toward the door she turned to grab up the car keys and with lowered voice teased, "You know, if it would help relieve your mind, we could hire a housekeeper and I wouldn't even vacuum ..."

"Oh no, you minx, you know we can't afford it and it would be a waste anyway. You're one of those women who would clean before the cleaner!"

"Ah, you know me so well."

Happy and in love, they left for the drive to the airport. Tyler arrived just in time to get his boarding pass and make his flight. Jillian watched his plane as long as she could after takeoff.

The flight was smooth and Tyler was one of those travelers that could actually sleep on a plane. Immediately after retrieving his baggage, he rented a car and headed for his appointment at the paper.

His old boss, "Ace," nicknamed for a wicked poker hobby, was waiting in his office along with Gavin. After the warm handshake for Ace and a nod to Gavin they settled in.

Tyler started quickly so he would be on time with Detective Peters. "Gavin, tell me, what led you to downplay the story on Laurel Andrews and why no follow up?"

"Tyler, I'm telling you, there is no story. You came a long way for nothing. The "story" is that she and her hubby had a fight the night before and she took off, probably to shake him up and bring him to his knees. The cops have found no signs of any foul play anywhere—inside or outside of their home. The neighbors never heard or saw anything and no one else has called with any leads either. I did get a yarn on another woman issue down south at the husband's job and my guess is the wife found out and that's what the fight was about. I think she's going to waltz back in their front door anytime now and I'm not going to waste paper space on a story with no crime—especially with the two high profile cases that Keddie has recently been through."

Ace had been trying frantically to signal Gavin about his innuendoes about Laurel and Greg; he had forgotten to tell him about Tyler's relationship with them. As usual, Gavin was completely unaware of his surroundings, which is why he would never go far in the business. Putting a hand up to stop Tyler from leaving his seat, he glared at Gavin. "Gavin, I want you to know that the reason Tyler came all the way from Philadelphia on this story is because Laurel and Greg Andrews are his aunt and uncle. I'm going to ask you to leave the room now and stay off of the story, Tyler will be doing a special series until his aunt is found."

Shocked, Gavin's eyes had grown wider the more Ace talked. Still seated, Tyler tried and failed to keep the disdain out of his voice. "My aunt and uncle are a solid, loving and normal couple. If you had asked anyone at all, you would have known there isn't a vindictive bone in her body. If she gets mad, she yells and makes a less than wonderful dinner for her husband like many wives do. My uncle could be a poster child for a "good catch" of a husband. He would never cheat and he would bring flowers home to apologize to his wife even if he never quite knows what he did to make her mad. What I'm telling you, Gavin, is that something is very wrong. I've talked with the lead detective on the case and I'm meeting him at 8:00. You're right, they have found no evidence of foul play and they are leaning towards a kidnapping. The only problem is, they don't know why. There's been no ransom note or phone calls. So, Gavin, because you jumped to conclusions without doing even basic research, you've single handedly given whoever took my aunt more time to get away and conceal a crime!" Spent from his tirade, Tyler looked away as Gavin, thoroughly embarrassed, left the office.

Ace cleared his throat to bring Tyler's focus back. "Tyler, tell me how you want to handle this. Do you want to feed your story directly to me and trust me to the details for the layout?"

"That would be great, if you don't mind. Since so much time has passed, I want to start by putting this on the front page with Laurel's picture so we get all of our reader's attention. Hopefully, someone will have seen something. Let me call you after I meet with the police and I can give you more details on what my initial story will contain. If there is anything at all that they have found and don't want out to the public, I want to make sure we don't compromise the success of my aunt's return."

"I agree. For right now, I'll save you a quarter page on the front page. I think it would be best if we just put the face photo and her description in the first story. If we bring in a picture of their home you're going to have every Looky Lou out there on the Andrews' doorstep by tomorrow night."

"Good point. I'm going to stay with my uncle while I'm here. Their best friend, Karen Vincent, has been with him while they did the poster and flyer distribution and she needs to get back to her own home. I'll be able to keep involved in all sides of everything that's going on that way too." Glancing at his watch, he stood and reached out a hand to Ace. "I better head over to the police station. I'll bring my initial piece back here at 4:00 and fill you in on what the cops tell me, if that will work for you."

Shaking his hand firmly, Ace looked at Tyler's worried face. "I'll make it work. I've already told my assistant to find me wherever I am, whenever you call. Don't hesitate to let me know anything you need or anything this paper can do to help."

Tyler kept his tears in check as he headed out the door. Waving over his shoulder at his boss and friend, he huskily thanked him. "You're the best Ace."

CHAPTER 14

Shelby Abbott was just sitting down with a hot mug of herbal tea when her cell phone rang. Groaning, she perked up when she saw it was David on the line. "Hello, stranger, long time no hear."

Laughing, David was glad to hear some humor in his sister's voice—she was healing after all. "I see pregnancy has made you cocky Shelby! How is everything going on your end with the move?"

"Well, I've just returned from a meeting with my partner and my lawyer. I sold out my share of the boutique and agreed to work the holiday season beginning November first through the end of the year on a part-time basis. You should feel honored I answered your call, you know. I've given myself a break from phones, television and people for a few weeks that I'm sure Sam would whole heartedly have approved of. I appreciate everything our friends are doing, but with the home sale so soon, I really just want to give myself space and a little peace from the world while I pack up and prepare for the move."

"I'm so proud of you, Shelby, and so in awe. I knew you were bright, but I would have never dreamed you could be this strong in such awful circumstances. Is everything going smoothly for your move? What have you decided about your house? Are you going to keep it and rent it, or sell it?"

"Take a breath David! So many questions and thankfully, I have the answers. You know, I feel Sam all around me; not in a bazaar way, but in a warm and loving way. Don't worry, it doesn't make me sad, it gives me strength. Every time I've come to a decision, I can actually feel his approval or disapproval. It's like a warm touch on my cheek when I'm right or a complete absence of touch when I'm wrong. So, he's here with me and in some ways, I'm strong and strangely enough, happy. I know Sam is with me and will always be with us; I can feel it. It's because of that feeling I've been able to decide to let this house go. Some friends of ours, Mark and Jami, have always loved this house and had once asked us to let them know if we ever wanted to sell. I gave them a call and they still felt the same way. We used a realtor they know for the sale; Jeannie took a vacation right after we completed my paperwork. Since I have the boutique done and the decision on this house made, all I really need to do now is decide what personal items I want to take in my move. Anything that doesn't go with me or that I store for the baby when he's older is going to the women's shelter. Mark and Jami want to bring their own furnishings so it doesn't feel like "Sam and Shelby's" house."

"What about the move itself? Do you need me to make some arrangements for you? I'd come myself, but with Cat's arm still in the cast I'm uncomfortable leaving her right now."

"No worries, David. I contacted the local college. They have some kids that earn money by working as movers. All I have to do is supply them with a rented truck and some boxes. I explained my pregnancy to the woman I spoke with at the college and she's going to have one of the boys go with me for the rental and boxes. I won't be lifting a thing, just pointing. How are my wonderful niece and nephew by the way?"

"They're growing fast. They want to know when you'll be here for a visit. I hope you don't mind, but I told them about the baby and they are so excited."

"I don't mind at all. I know everything is fine and that this baby is healthy and meant to be. Did I tell you that I'm naming the baby Morgan? It works you know, whether it's a boy or a girl. I knew the minute that I saw the brass plate on the bedroom door next to my new bedroom that I didn't want to change a thing. That room will still be "Morgan's Room"—as a nursery at first. Will you tell the kids that because of the pregnancy I can't come until after the baby is born? Tell them I'll stay at least a month and give them a kiss for me."

"Henry is here to call me to dinner now. I'll give the children your message and try to give you a call next week. It's been wonderful to hear your voice and your news."

"Goodnight, David. I love you all."

Relieved and satisfied that their conversation revealed no alarming news about anything amiss in Keddie, David answered Henry's knock. "Yes, Henry."

"Dinner is about to be served sir."

"I'll be right there. I just need to change out of these work clothes."

Henry was very amused to hear Lord David singing on the other side of his door. The castle was in a complete uproar and his employer had never seemed happier. Considering that the source of his newfound happiness was a very married, kidnapped woman, Henry was more than a little worried.

Henry knew Lord David had fallen head over heels in love with Laurel; they all had. The only person who didn't seem to know was Laurel. By the third day of her arrival, there wasn't a one of them that could think about the day they would have to see her leave.

The first day of the "renovation" had started an unstoppable snowball that had captured everyone from the staff to the workmen hired for the duration. Laurel and David presented a united front in presenting Laurel's vision of the plan and David's working timetable to accomplish the plan. No one was prepared for Laurel's method of working. Part of Laurel's plan included putting an intercom system up in the fourth floor across from the ballroom so that concerts or music could be piped throughout the castle on special occasions. They quickly learned she preferred loud music, preferably songs of the seventies, while she worked and that she sang along with her favorites. Within two hours of starting on the main keep, Emily, Thomas, Roger, Henry and the children were laughing at the sight of workmen singing "YMCA" and a paintbrush waving, Lord David dancing "the bump" with Laurel! For days now, the Beatles, Journey, the Eurythmics, Laura Branigan and Celine Dion had filled the halls. Emily couldn't wait to tell them all about hearing Lord David beg Laurel to give in to her singing when they were working alone in Tim's bedroom.

Laurel knew all about Cat and Tim's fear of the dark. To solve the problem, she had worked with David to create a wooden wall in each child's room that was about three feet out from the longest stone wall. The wooden wall in Tim's room was painted in a mural that depicted an airport control room panel. Little colored lights were wired in from the back that the electrician connected to a light switch. One of the control boxes was actually a door so that workmen could get behind the mural for repairs if necessary. Tim's love of airplanes and rockets were the theme of his room. A special rocket shaped "Murphy Bed" was created and while David painted the mural, Laurel did a mosaic of an airplane on a step stool so Tim could pull down his own bed at night.

For Cat, ballet and dreams of being a prima ballerina filled her little heart. Her lighted mural was a scene from Swan Lake painted to appear as if in the evening. A knighted prince seated on his steed waited under a moon along the banks of the river. The little lights were reflected in the lake appearing to be moonlight. Cat's bed was a hollowed swan whose wings concealed her mattress above stair steps. Laurel's mosaic made especially for Cat was pink ballet slippers on top of a children's table that she also painted four chairs in pink to match.

What Emily happened to overhear was the end of David's attempt to help Laurel relax. "Laurel, I can't paint this mural correctly if you don't give in and be yourself. Start singing for God's sake. Do I really bother you that much?"

Letting out the breath she didn't realize she'd been holding, Laurel looked up from her work on the airplane. "I'm sorry, David, it's just that I'm not used to having anyone around while I do my projects. It was different when everyone was singing and dancing, but when it's just the two of us, you'll hear my voice and that makes me very nervous."

"Whatever for; you do know you have a very good voice don't you?"

"Thank you."

"If anyone should be nervous about being heard singing it should be me. I have no tone as I'm sure you must have noticed. How about this; I'll sing along with you and your only problem will be not laughing at how awful I sound, or getting the glue in your ears when you try to cover them. By the way, that is glue, correct? And, what are you using for your mosaics? I don't see tiles over there."

Smiling, Laurel reached over and grabbed a blown, dried goose egg. "I use these, not tiles. You paint them first and then break the eggshells up and use them just like tiles."

"Clever. I wondered why the orders you gave me to place included ten dozen goose eggs. How did you ever think of that?"

"I didn't. I read about it in a book. You know, you can learn just about anything you want to at the library."

"You still have to possess talent to use the knowledge. So, how about it? Personally, I happen to like Frank Sinatra a lot, but I'm willing to give in and start singing John Travolta's part in the theme from *Grease* if you'll be Olivia Newton John."

"You're on."

And so it went. Every day the music played, the workmen prepared rooms, and Laurel and David worked side by side accomplishing her plan.

CHAPTER 15

Tyler walked into the police station in Keddie at a few minutes past eight in the morning. Both Detectives Peters and Johnson came out to meet him when the Desk Sergeant announced his arrival. Phil was in the lead.

"Mr. Grant? I'm Phil Peters and this is Matt Johnson. Thank you for agreeing to come down here so early."

Shaking hands all around, Tyler anxiously greeted the two men. "Gentlemen, please call me Tyler. I appreciate your willingness to meet with me on such short notice, especially since I'm here not only as a family member, but as a member of the press."

Phil and Matt ushered him back into an interview room while Phil answered. "I agree, it is unusual, but we're hoping we can help each other out on this case; would you like a cup of coffee?"

"Yes thanks, black."

Matt pulled out a chair indicating for him to be seated. "You see, Tyler, we know your aunt is a crime victim, either as a kidnapped person or as a homicide, and I suspect your uncle." Tyler, instantly furious, stood and put his arms on his hips, ready to fire with a rebuttal. Matt reached out in a calming gesture, "Please, sit down and hear us both out. As I said, I suspect your uncle of wrongdoing, but my partner does not. Every bit of forensic testing we have completed has come back negative for blood. We also have no fingerprints other than your aunt and uncle's. So, while I should bow to my partner and agree that your uncle is not involved in a crime of passion, I still have some nagging details that I'm determined to clear. That said, we would like to fill you in on the investigation up to this point and have you answer some questions that may help me with those details."

Phil spoke up and brought Tyler's glaring eyes back on him. "Before we go any further Tyler, I need your agreement on how this joint venture of ours needs to proceed. As you indicated, you are here representing not only your family's interests, but as a member of the press. Because I am as certain your uncle is an innocent victim and that your aunt is a victim of a kidnapping as my partner is of your uncle's wrongdoing, there is a need to control what facts appear in any of your news reports. Therefore, I am going to require you to allow us editing privileges prior to any written or spoken reports before we can continue with this interview."

Tyler's demeanor visibly relaxed with Phil's words. "I understand and you have my word that I will run every article by you first and I will pre-record any telecasts to allow you to view them prior to their delivery to the television station."

Phil and Matt had agreed earlier that Phil, as lead detective, would have final judgment as to whether or not to move forward with Tyler. Phil had watched Tyler very closely as he answered affirmatively to the editing demand. Satisfied that Tyler was being honest and could be trusted, he nodded to Matt to go ahead.

Pulling a piece of paper from his file and a pen from his pocket, Matt slid both articles across the table to Tyler. "We had an agreement drafted stating the editing requirements that I need you to sign."

Tyler quickly read through the single page and signed where indicated. Unbelievably, he had just agreed to incarceration if he broke his word. Impressed, Matt took the signed paperwork back and looked at Phil while asking if he wanted to be the one to give Tyler the details of the investigation to date. Phil again nodded yes and leaned towards Tyler, folding his hands together and resting his arms on the table.

"Tyler, here's what we have so far. Your aunt went on her usual morning run five days ago at approximately five o'clock in the morning. The evening before, your uncle told us they had a disagreement over his desire to have your aunt resume fertility treatments. We also found out from your uncle, that a work associate, Joy Stewart, had agreed to be a surrogate if they decided to opt for that route. Your uncle left for work while your aunt was on her run and he was unaware she was missing until he heard a phone message from her work with concern over her not being there that day. Your uncle called around to several friends, including your aunt's best friend Karen Vincent, and then checked with hospitals before contacting the police. We know your aunt wasn't home in the late morning because a delivery receipt was left on the front door. Your aunt's purse with her passport, credit cards, license and money were all in the master bedroom closet. Your uncle cannot think of any missing clothing other than your aunt's running articles. As Matt mentioned, our forensic team found no blood in the house or any of the family vehicles. They also found no evidence of forced entry or missing jewelry or household items that would suggest a burglary that went wrong. We interviewed all of the neighbors and none of them saw anything unusual, either that morning or in the days prior that would suggest your aunt was being stalked. We have just one interview left to conclude and that is scheduled for late this afternoon with the deliveryman that left the notice on your aunt and uncle's door. It's a long shot, but if he's in the neighborhood regularly, there is a possibility that he might have noticed something out of place." Taking a deep breath, Phil leaned back in his chair and let Matt take over.

"Tyler, there are four nagging details that are staying with me. First, your uncle was an hour late to work the morning your aunt went missing. Then, we find out that the surrogate volunteer, Joy Stewart, has romantic feelings for your uncle. Third, your aunt and uncle signed paperwork for a sale of their home just two days before. This means your uncle would be sole beneficiary to not only the equity on that sale, but on a large life insurance policy he took out on your aunt recently. Finally, if this is a kidnapping, why hasn't your uncle had any word from the kidnappers?"

There was something about Matt's tone that just rubbed Tyler the wrong way. He had the same feeling about Matt as he did about Gavin—they just didn't delve deeply enough when they had already made up their minds about a story. As Matt bluntly stated his "nagging details", Tyler literally stiffened from head to toe trying to check his anger.

Oblivious, Matt badgered on. "So, Tyler, we know you lived with your aunt and uncle for several years. Is there anything you witnessed that caused you concern? Anything you can remember that would make your aunt so angry she would leave your uncle?"

Phil cut in front of Tyler with an outstretched arm before he could answer. "I should tell you, Tyler that my end of the investigation found that there was a dual life insurance policy on both your aunt and uncle which they took out in case of catastrophic illness when there was a gap in medical coverage due to your uncle's work situation. Your uncle also stated that your aunt had met Joy Stewart, knew they were just friends, and he had no idea that Joy was anything other than that—a friend."

Both men could see Tyler trying to digest everything he had heard. "Detective Peters, my gut tells me that you are the one that has come to a correct conclusion is this case." Looking directly into Matt's eyes, Tyler was prepared to convince him of his uncle's innocence. "Detective Johnson, I did live with my aunt and uncle while I was in college and briefly after graduation. I was also a regular visitor to their home while I worked for the paper before moving to my current position back east. I can honestly tell you that I have never witnessed anything but a loving relationship between them—a relationship that my wife and I hope to emulate. Detective, my uncle's honesty could be ranked with my wife's score in a recent *Cosmo* quiz she took on the subject—'honest to the point of non-tact'. He doesn't lie because he has no reason to; his life is literally an open book. In several conversations I've had with him over the last few months, I know that he's had to do a lot of the "grunt work" he would normally depend on a subordinate to do with the construction slow down. If he was late, I would guess that he was doing an errand. Since my uncle has never had eyes for anyone but my aunt, I'm pretty sure he wouldn't recognize another woman's invitation for playtime if she asked him outright. As far as my aunt just leaving in anger, my first thought is no way—she's a talker. However, I remember how awful my aunt felt when they tried fertility treatments the last time and I didn't know my uncle had brought it up again. Still, if she was going to leave him, I think she would do it sensibly. By that I mean she would pack a bag, take her purse and money, and leave him a letter telling him off royally. No, I don't think she left him and I know my uncle wouldn't touch a hair on her head. As far as why there hasn't been any contact from a kidnapper, the only thing I can think of is how pretty my aunt is. Do you think someone may have wanted to take her and keep her for himself?"

The detectives looked at each other and leaned back in their chairs. Taking a sip from his coffee, Phil answered Tyler's question. "That's where I'm at on this. I wasn't surprised no one in the neighborhood saw anything given the early morning hour. I'm sure your aunt disappeared during her run. What leads me to believe the kidnapper wants Laurel for himself and that he's from out of town is that no one has come forward from the newspaper article or from the posters and flyers around town. The tie I can't find is where someone from out of town would have seen your aunt recently to want to grab her. She's either been at work, at home, at the market or the mall. The only visitors to their home that weren't friends are those that bought their house. Now you know why I'm at that brick wall."

Tyler sunk back into his chair, his exasperation mirroring that of the two detectives. "Yeah, I can see your problem. I'm not surprised about a lack of response from that news story. Most people don't look at the back page of the local section. As I see it, the kidnapper either is someone she knows who's lying, or if she was at the mall, someone from out of the area that followed her home. Either way, this confirms my initial story line for the paper."

Matt looked up suspiciously at Tyler "Which is?"

"I have a quarter page space reserved on the front page. I'm going to run my aunt's picture and just the facts you approve of. My editor has assured me that this will run in all of the newspapers owned by this affiliate. That pretty much hits all the valley area and down through Los Angeles. If we still don't get any response, I have arranged for a live news broadcast that will hit every station throughout California."

Phil looked impressed. "That's good, real good. We're going to get a call from the delivery guy's boss when he returns to the shipping center this afternoon. Do you want to tag along with us when we meet with him?"

"Yes, if you don't mind. I want to participate in everything I'm allowed to while I'm here and get my aunt home."

"Great. It's only nine forty-five now. Why don't you write up your story to include just the day and time your aunt went missing and that there is no evidence indicating a medical problem or foul play? I don't think there's any need to have either your aunt and uncle's fertility issue or the infatuated Joy Stewart given their fifteen minutes of fame. We can meet back here at say, two o'clock, and we can review the story before you turn it over to the press before we go to the shippers."

"Sure, that works. I can also take some time with my uncle and get settled. How much can I tell him about what's going on?"

Matt quickly answered him. "Tell him as little as possible for right now. I'm going to go along with the kidnapping theory because there is no evidence to the contrary and at least we're agreed on one plan to follow. That doesn't mean I am going to ignore anything that comes up that could disclaim that theory. Assure your uncle that you are doing the news piece with police cooperation and mention nothing of his being cleared."

All three men stood up as the meeting concluded. Tyler threw the empty coffee cup in the trash as he was leaving. "Okay, I don't like it, but I'll follow your rules. My uncle is exhausted and out of his mind with worry."

Phil put a hand on his shoulder with comfort. "I know. I tried to have him call his doctor for something to help him sleep, but he refused. This is hard, but you have to trust us that it is for the best. We want to bring your aunt home safely and that means not tipping our hand to anyone."

Back at the reception area, Tyler shook both men's hands. "I understand. See you back here at two o'clock."

CHAPTER 16

Tyler pulled up to his aunt and uncle's house and pulled his bag from the rental car. His uncle spotted him through the window and had the door opened before Tyler could knock. "Uncle Greg, are you alright?"

Greg hugged Tyler tightly, "I'm just worried and tired, Tyler. I feel a lot better now that you're here. Come on in and let's get you settled in your old room. I'll put some coffee on and you can fill me in on what we're doing to get some attention on your aunt and bring her home. Have you had any breakfast?"

"Not really, I had a granola bar on my way to the paper from the airport and some coffee at the police station. You know me, Uncle Greg, I'm not fussy. If you have some toast, or a bagel, that would be great. I don't want you to go to any trouble on my account."

"You were never any trouble, Tyler. I haven't swallowed anything I can remember in the past five days. Why don't I make us some pancakes? They're easy and I think they may just sit in my stomach for awhile."

"That sounds really good. Let me check in with Jillian and get my stuff set up in the room. I'll be out in the kitchen in a minute." Poking his head back out the bedroom door he asked Greg's retreating back about his previous guest. "Did Karen get back home okay?"

"Yes she did. She didn't want to leave, but she had some loose ends at her house she had to take care of since she was supposed to be in India right now. She will be calling us tonight for you to fill her in on what's happening and let her know if you need her help with anything."

"Great. Be out in a minute."

Tyler took a moment to gather his composure before going out to the kitchen. His uncle was no fool and would know some parts would be missing when Tyler told him his news. He didn't want to hurt him, or worry him further, so this had to be balanced just right.

The smoky aroma of bacon cooking filled the kitchen as Tyler walked in. Greg looked up from stirring the pancake batter and gave Tyler another look at fresh worry lines etched on his face. "Uncle Greg, both of my meetings this morning went really well. My old boss, Ace, is going all out to start a series on Aunt Laurel to reach as wide an area as possible. All of the sister newspapers in the affiliate will have my first story and Aunt Laurel's picture on their front pages tomorrow morning."

"God, that's great news. What about the police; did they have any more leads?"

"No more leads than I think you already know about, but, they are allowing me to be in an interview this afternoon with their last lead—the delivery guy that left the slip on your door last Thursday."

Greg looked both excited and alarmed "Last lead they have?"

"You heard me correctly. Uncle Greg, there's only so much that I can tell you if you want to be able to utilize the news media, both in print and video. I agreed to allow the two detectives on the case editing privileges so that information to trigger people's attention get's out, but any details that could help, or alarm, whoever is involved in Aunt Laurel's disappearance get away or want to hurt her stays inside. I believe Detective Peters already informed you that the forensic tests were all negative and that the neighbors indicated nothing out of the ordinary."

"Yes, he did. The other detective doesn't believe me at all though, does he?"

"Uncle Greg, please, let me just tell you what my story is for the paper tomorrow and after we eat, I want to go talk to any of your neighbors that are home. I also have to write my story for tomorrow's edition before I meet the two detectives back at the police station this afternoon."

"Christ! I'm sorry, Tyler. I don't like this, I'm going freaking nuts, but if it gets Laurel home safely then I'll do whatever they want. Foods ready; let's eat."

Tyler volunteered to clean up and convinced his uncle to go lie down and try to rest. After writing his copy, he still had an hour and a half to talk with the neighbors.

Brenda, Glen and Melissa were all home. After talking to the three of them, he was actually anxious to go out to the shipping warehouse—one common point arose from all three of the neighbors. They all started to say nothing had been out of the ordinary and Glen happened to mention "except for my package delivery. I kept missing packages from anyone but Scott, so now I switch all my deliveries to him." Brenda's eyes lit up "Me too! I called and called the other company and they kept telling me they left a delivery notice, but they lied. That nice young Scott is the only one that ever followed up on a package for me. Use him any time I order now. He helped me with my water spicket too." Melissa was the clincher. "You're right! I almost didn't get a wedding gift in time for my best friend's wedding until I switched delivery to Scott. I never got a notice about a failed attempt on delivery either." Tyler thanked them as he left to head back to the police station. On the drive over he couldn't help but find three neighbors with missed packages and "attempt to deliver" notices too odd to be coincidental.

Tyler was directed back to Detective Peters' office when he arrived at the station. "Come on in Tyler and sit down. Our guy's boss called to say it'll probably be about a half hour or so before he's back into the warehouse. Did you finish your copy that you want me to take a look at it?"

Detective Johnson ambled in just as his partner finished talking. Tyler looked up at him and acknowledged his presence as he handed the pages to Phil. "Yes, I did. This is a primary story with just the facts to go with her picture. Let me know if there's anything you need deleted. I have until four o'clock to get it in."

Phil took the pages and started glancing over the story. "I have no doubt this will be fine."

As Phil started reading, Matt inquired about Greg. "How's he holding up?"

"It's just as I told you earlier. He's exhausted and worried out of his mind. He's not happy I couldn't tell him very much, but he's not going to fight about it if it means getting my aunt home safely."

"That's good."

Phil finished reading the copy and looked up at the two men. "This is perfect, Tyler. Do you want us to go by the paper so you can drop it off on our way to the warehouse?"

"That would make it a lot easier on the paper. My old boss has his ass hanging out a mile for me on this series to help out."

"Why don't we go ahead and go then; we can talk to the boss for some background if we have to wait."

As the three men drove to the paper, Tyler related the neighbors "coincidence" about missed deliveries to the two men.

"That's in the notes from the first day," Matt replied.

"Don't you think that's odd? I can't believe more than one delivery company would have a high number of missed packages on the same route. There's what, three overnight delivery companies altogether?"

"Four if you count the U.S. Express Mail service," Phil said.

Tyler found the odds completely against three other companies' route drivers making the same mistake. "There's something wrong here."

Matt was intrigued. "Yeah, we're here. Let's see what we can find out."

The men were directed to the back of the warehouse where Supervisor Graham Carver was sitting behind a desk that was up to his bushy eyebrows in stacks of paper.

Phil knocked on the door jamb before entering and holding up his badge. "Mr. Carver? I'm Detective Peters and this is Detective Johnson. We also have the missing woman's nephew, Tyler Grant, sitting in with us if you'll allow that."

Graham Carver slowly stood up, his paunchy sixty-three year old body unwinding stiffly. "Tyler Grant, huh, you the young fella that used to write with the paper?"

Tyler smiled, "Yes, sir, that's me. I'm in Philadelphia now."

"Not surprised a bit. You were always good. Come in, come in." As Graham started to move chairs around his desk, he glanced at the mess and had a better idea. "Oh, Jesus, what a goddamned mess. Let's move down to the conference room where we can spread out without needing a ladder to see over all this paper."

Graham grabbed a file off one of the piles and led them down the hall. Seated around the long table, he opened the file and started rattling off Scott Gregory's basic information. "Scott Gregory started working here just under two years ago. I'm going to be honest with you; I didn't think we should have hired him."

Phil was paying close attention to what Graham was telling them. "Why not?"

"Took one look at him and had his number. He's a punk, or at least I decided he was a punk. His high school record showed he squeaked by to graduate and he's got a juvenile record that's sealed. I wasn't his supervisor then so I was out voted. Turns out the first supervisor was right though."

"How so?"

"He's turned out to be a real go-getter. We're getting our asses kicked by our main competitors and Scott's taken the bull by the horns. He's been the only driver to kick back. He's had numerous compliments by the people on that route. He comes in early to get their packages out to them earlier than the other guys and really goes out of his way to deliver excellent service."

"Have any of your customers called to complain about missed packages or notices?"

Graham was curious why they asked him that question, but they were the cops, he was going to answer whatever question they asked. "No, just the opposite. Scott's made sure to take special care of the packages on that route. Seems the other guy's driver is not too good at his job."

"Appears so."

Graham looked out the window just as Scott was pulling in his truck. "Scott!" He waved his arms to indicate Scott should come to the conference room. "Come in here for a minute. There are some guys here that need to talk to you."

Scott looked past Graham and felt sweat starting under his arms. He knew cops when he saw them and these guys were cops. He wondered how much they knew and what it was going to cost him. Exhibiting a calm facade, he picked up his paperwork and sprinted over to the room.

"What's up boss?"

"These gentlemen are here from the police and have a few questions to ask you."

Scott held his paperwork so that he wouldn't have to shake their hands and reveal his sweaty palms. "Sure, what can I help you with?"

"Scott, I'm Detective Peters. We're here investigating the disappearance of one of the customers on your route, Laurel Andrews."

Scott's eyes just about bugged out of his head. "Mrs. Andrews? Disappeared? When?"

"Last Thursday and much earlier in the day than you would have been in her neighborhood. We know you had a delivery for her that day; you left an "attempt to deliver" slip. What we were wondering is if you happened to notice anything out of the ordinary or see anyone new hanging around?"

Scott felt sweat trickling down his back now. Big innocent eyes gave the illusion of trying to think of anything "out of the ordinary." "No, detective, I can't say there's anything that comes to my mind. I remember the package. It needed a signature so I couldn't just leave it. I just can't believe anything could have happened to Mrs. Andrews. That's a real safe area and she's so nice."

"Yes, well that's what we were afraid of. I'll leave you my card so if you do remember anything at all that seems strange, I'd appreciate you calling me immediately." Standing and motioning the other two men to join him he moved closer to Scott and slapped him on the back. "Your boss tells me you're a real go-getter Scott!" Scott almost dropped his paperwork he was so nervous.

"I'm just trying to make something of myself sir. I've got a girl that means a lot to me and I want to marry her."

Graham was trailing behind Phil and Scott. "That Angie you want to marry Scott?"

Scott was surprised the old guy remembered her name but he didn't mention that. He just wanted to get out of there—fast. "Yes sir, that's the one. I'll go turn in my dailies to your office." Turning towards Phil he flashed his most sincere smile. "I sure hope you find Mrs. Andrews soon. She's one of my favorite customers. When Angie and I get a house, I was hoping she would help us with the decorating."

Phil, Matt and Tyler exchanged a look. "You know about her decorating Scott?" Matt inquired.

"Only what I could see from the front porch when I delivered there. Never saw anything like it."

"What are your dailies Scott?"

"Oh, it's a list of all my deliveries and what action I took. Those that weren't able to be delivered get a notice, if they need a signature I turn in the proof slip, you know, that kind of thing. It coordinates with our handheld computers as backup."

Turning to Graham, Matt tried to keep his voice level. "Graham do you get these from all your drivers every day?"

"What do you think all that paper is on my desk? I sure do. I've got a quick system for sorting the papers; it's the new computer that takes me so much time."

Smiling, Phil took Scott's papers. "Scott, I'll take these off your hands for you. Graham, can I walk you back to your office?"

Scott's smile left his face as the detective took his paperwork. "Sure, thanks. I'm going to clean out the truck and get going. Goodnight boss."

Graham waved Scott off and turned to Phil. "What's up?"

"Can you pull Scott's dailies from last Thursday and see what he noted?"

"Sure thing. Follow me."

Matt and Tyler stood by the detective's car watching Scott while Phil went with Graham. Matt was the first to speak. "Well, it appears that Mr. Gregory is extremely nervous for some reason. All that delivering and he comes back dry as a saltine cracker. Takes one look at us and his khaki's look one shade darker. It also appears he's trying to hide that from us."

"Yeah, he's going to be bathing in his own sweat pretty soon. What do you think?"

"I think Graham's first impressions about Scott may have some validity and I want to hear what my partner is getting from those dailies."

Phil came out from Graham's office and strode purposefully towards the car. "Get in."

Matt was surprised at Phil's urgency. "What did you just find out."

"That every company gets "dailies" from its drivers. That guy is hiding something and I have an idea what it might be. Tyler you all done for today with the paper that you can spare me an hour?"

"Sure. What do you want me to do?"

"What I want is for you and Matt to contact Overnight Now and First Light Delivery. Talk to them about their driver's on the route that covers the Andrews' house. Find out how many, if any, packages were undelivered with notices left that customers called in on as missing. I specifically want you to find out if the driver's had a delivery close to last Thursday for the Andrews that were never claimed and the boundaries of their route. I'm going to go to the Post Office for that area and see what their records show."

Matt was catching on. "Okay. Drop us off. It's almost four o'clock and they probably close by six."

Tyler spoke up from the back seat. "It's a good thing I finished my copy, Matt."

"Yeah. Follow me. Phil, we'll use my office. As soon as you've finished at the Post Office meet us back there."

"Okay. See you in an hour or so. If I find out what I think I'm going to find out, I have a plan I'll need your help on."

Phil drove off and Matt and Tyler headed into the station to get started. Tyler was going to call one of the companies on his cell phone while Matt called the other from his office phone.

Forty-five minutes later, both men were sitting in an office crackling with energy. Matt was shaking his head and rubbing his eyes. "Who would have believed it huh? Two drivers. Not a blemish on either one's record except for a few blocks in Green Glenn. You did find out that a high number of the packages were returned unclaimed, not that they were stolen right?"

"That's right. My driver swears he left the first, second and final notices every time."

"My guy too. Did the dailies back that up?"

"Yes they did."

"Mine too."

"Do you have a city map? I think we should highlight the boundaries of their routes."

"Sure, there's one here in my desk. Let's see, I'll mark my guy's route boundaries in yellow; you hang on to the pink marker for yours." Matt looked at his notes and marked off his driver's route and then handed the map to Tyler. After Tyler marked his, he placed the map between them. "Do you see what I see?"

"I sure do. There's only three blocks in common on both drivers routes. Let's get a soda while we wait for Phil."

The two men were heading back from the break room with their drinks just as Phil entered the station. He had a huge smile on his face.

"What did you two find out?"

"Probably the same thing you found out. Perfect drivers, no missed deliveries except for three blocks the two drivers' routes have in common. I have the map we marked up on my desk if you want to add your postman's route. Packages were returned for lack of response to three notices for delivery. Same with you?"

"Yup. Postman was getting really angry about it too. He was actually making his co-workers nervous. Give me that map." Phil glanced at the two routes already highlighted and where they intersected. Grabbing a blue marker from the pencil cup, he marked the boundaries of the postman's route. He pushed the finished map into the desk center and looked up. "Check it out; two of the same three blocks as the other two routes. Let's sit down so I can tell you my plan. Tyler would you shut the door behind you?"

Tyler did as asked and joined the two men seated around Matt's desk. He had a perplexed look on his face directed at Phil. "I see the problem, but I don't see the answer. You think Scott has my aunt?"

"I don't know Tyler, but I think he has something to do with whatever happened to your aunt. He saw inside your aunt and uncle's home. He wanted your aunt to do him a favor and she's one of his favorite customer's. We don't have enough to be able to get a search warrant, but I have an idea about how we can find out about the missing delivery notices that resulted in missed packages. Right now, we know Scott's involved in a scam; now we have to prove it and find out what else he might be involved in."

Matt looked up earnestly at the other two. "Guys, I just want you to know that I'm feeling a lot better about those nagging details."

"It's okay Matt," Phil said reassuringly. "We aren't home free yet. You just made sure we didn't miss anything by raising those red flags. Now let's cut the bull, we're wasting time. This is what I think will trap our guy."

Matt and Tyler watched as Phil drew a US Post Office "Attempted Delivery" notice from his coat pocket. They hadn't noticed the package he was carrying when he came in. "Tyler, do you know anyone at the paper you can call to take this package to the shipping station by 5:30 tonight?"

"Yes. My boss' assistant. Why?"

"Because we're going to send this package to your uncle's neighbor, Brenda, via overnight delivery and I don't want one of us to take it down. Someone working there might recognize one of us from this afternoon and get suspicious. We're going to put this slip the postmaster gave me on Brenda's door tomorrow and ask her to leave for awhile. Then, we wait and watch in your uncle's gym which is directly across the street from Brenda's front door. I believe by tomorrow afternoon we will have one very nervous guy sitting in our interrogation room."

Tyler grabbed his cell phone out of his pocket. "I know I don't need to ask my uncle about a stakeout in his home. I'll call the paper."

Matt stood up and grabbed the case file off of his desk. "I have Brenda's number in here. I'll give her a call and see if she's home that we might stop by for a minute."

Phil stood up and walked over to grab the molding over Matt's office door. He did his first satisfying stretch in five days. Sighing he turned back to the men busily talking on their phones. When they both hung up simultaneously and looked at him with smiles he knew they were set. "Let's go get some answers."

CHAPTER 17

David found Laurel dressed for bed and searching the library's shelves for something to read. "Ah, there you are. Couldn't sleep?"

Laurel nearly jumped out of her skin; she had thought everyone had retired and that she would have some time alone. She tried to hide her head so David wouldn't see she had been crying when she answered. "No."

David had become so attuned to Laurel's sunny disposition he was completely undone to see her tears and immediately rushed over and turned her around to look at him. He didn't release her arms so she was forced to look him in the eye. "You've been crying. What's the matter? Has someone done something to upset you?"

"No, no. I've just had the most incredible day and I was feeling, oh God David, like I was soaring higher than the sun."

David had slid his hands down to hold hers and pulled her over to the settee. "I would never have thought I would see tears when you felt joy, Laurel." Laurel looked down at her slippers and didn't answer his questioning eyes. "I know it's late, but I was looking for you because I forgot to tell you that Anita and I have to fly to oversee changes to one of my projects tomorrow morning. You mentioned that you wanted to discuss the structural changes for the second floor."

Laurel's head popped up at the mention of another woman's name. "Who is Anita?"

David was surprised and pleased to see that Laurel appeared to be jealous. "Why, she's my pilot, don't you remember?"

"How would I remember your pilot David? Perhaps you introduced us when you were hauling my trunk aboard the plane? That would explain why I don't remember shaking hands...."

"Okay, okay, sorry. For some reason I thought Henry might have introduced you after I left the plane first to greet the children."

"No, he stood behind me in case I started to fall down. I was still a little woozy. I don't remember the doorway into the cockpit even being opened."

"Well, it's neither here nor there. I'll be sure to introduce you to her tomorrow if you're up. Now, which do you want to talk about first, your "joy" that's causing you to cry, or, the second floor of the castle?"

Laurel, composed now, smiled. "I think I'd better tell you about my emotional breakdown first since that has sealed the second floor's fate."

Curiosity peaked, David couldn't wait for her to begin. Just as he was about to ask her to explain, she zapped him with "Remember, I have complete control over the inside of this castle." Swallowing loudly, David groaned and begged her to get this over with.

Laurel sat back in the settee, looking as comfortable as a kitten sleeping on its pillow. David knew she wasn't really aware of him, she was actually categorizing and qualifying her thoughts and emotions.

"Today was the first day I have had confirmation of my God given gift to decorate when we showed the children their rooms. They were so thrilled and excited. It's a good thing we waited until after their lessons! All my life I have never had anyone that wasn't a family member or close friend confirm my unique talent. I never knew until today that what I do is artistically gifted and not just a "hobby" my family and friends tolerate out of love for me."

David cut in, "Surely you have to know that what you do is revolutionary, if not before Whitethorn, definitely after I went to such great lengths to utilize your services?"

"When I first saw Whitethorn, I was scared to death. Then I felt like I had an electrical current running up and down my body as one idea after another started charging through my mind while I looked at all of the stone and turrets. Even though I was so scared, there was nothing I could do to stop the overwhelming desire in me to work on a castle." She grabbed up David's hand and forced his attention to her face. David could see all the emotion she was trying so hard to convey. "It wasn't the money, David, or even fame that sealed the decision for me to move forward with this. It's something inside of me, my soul, that I just couldn't stop myself this time."

"What do you mean 'this time'?"

"Perhaps you've noticed that I'm above-average in intelligence?" David nodded affirmatively. "Well, I have craved art as long as I can remember, but my parents felt that my brain should be fed complete academics which the testing I was given at age six so clearly indicated would be appropriate. It was as if that was all they could see about who I was; my very being was merely a brain. When I would sneak a drawing or two into my binder, my mother would throw it out whenever she found them." David squeezed her hand with sympathy. "That hurt so much. By the time I was an adult, I was so used to hiding my interest in art that I felt incomplete so much of the time and never understood why. By the time Greg and I married, I knew I loved everything involved in making a house a home, but we needed the income from a job that my accounting skills could provide. Greg always assumed what I did at our home and in our friend's homes was nothing more than a hobby. I never pressed for anything more, even when I didn't need to work as Greg's income increased. I thought it was enough that those I loved enjoyed my talents."

"I cannot imagine how much you suffered and I find it hard to believe that someone before me hasn't badgered you about making a business of your gift."

"Thank you, but I really don't socialize much outside of my family and a small group of close friends. Growing up with so much structure, I was never comfortable in large groups."

"I see. So today, all of this joy, your tears are a release?"

"Yes and no. To be able to have the word "artist" ascribed to me is the most wonderful gift I've ever been given. But today, I also realized two dilemmas. I'm not sure how to resolve the one and I need your trust to resolve the other. That's what brings about tears of sadness."

"Well, spill it, at least the one that you need my trust on." Holding both hands against his heart he captured her eyes with his. "You have to know I trust you, don't you?"

"This is a conversation of yes's and no's isn't it? I believe you trust me as far as your home and with your children; but, with your secrets and communication outside the castle? No. How could I? You place all the orders for supplies and I'm not allowed near the computer. You've demanded my understanding about the reasons for a secluded life for you and your children, but you don't trust me enough to talk about your wife, or, is it your ex-wife?"

Exasperated, David dropped her hands. "Ex-wife and my reason for not discussing her had nothing to do with trust; it has everything to do with protecting Cat and Tim. That includes any outside communications." Realizing he had started to raise his voice and needing some time to calm down, he quickly changed the course of Laurel's discussion. "Why don't you tell me about your other dilemma and we'll come back to this one?"

Wanting to secure his cooperation tonight, Laurel gave in to his request. "The other dilemma involves my husband. Do you remember I told you our relationship was strained when you brought me to Whitethorn?"

"Yes—over having a child, correct?"

"Correct. Today when we went with the children and Thomas to the stables I watched you take such care in seating Cat and Tim on their horses. You hovered near to them while they trotted around and around that ring to protect them in case one of them fell off of their mounts."

"How did you see me? You and Thomas left us."

"Thomas told me there were some furnishings in the loft of the barn stored through time covering the history of the castle. He thought I might want to see if there was anything I wanted to use in the renovation. He's too old to climb up the ladder to the loft and stayed on the main floor. I watched you out of the hayloft."

"I see and this caused you a dilemma with your husband? I don't understand."

"It did because I am guilty of exactly what I'm accusing my husband of—not recognizing a need in his soul. Greg needs to be a father to a child of his the same way I need to have art and design in my life. And that's not the worst of it. I realized at dinner that I haven't actually thought of Greg or missed him because I've been so wrapped up in the castle and my design. I don't know how we are going to work this all out. I'm torn and I'm scared."

"I see. Give it some time Laurel. I know you both have a deep faith in God and in commitment. Let time be on your side. Let's get back to what you need from me."

Laurel moved slightly away from David before she began again. "David, I know you love Cat and Tim fiercely, but you can't meet all of their needs. In your parental desire to protect them from hurt, you have basically cocooned them from growth much the same way my growth was stunted by my parents."

"What? How can you say that?"

"Because David, children grow not only in their parents love, but also in their interactions with the outside world. That means they need other children; their peers. I can tell you that by not socializing with my peers growing up I had trouble when I went off to college. At the age of sixteen I was completely out on my own. I was not prepared socially, only academically. I trusted everyone and everything. Injustices and devious people were a huge surprise. I fell on my butt more than once. I know there's a way to broaden Cat and Tim's worlds in a way that they will be able to grow strong and someday, handle whatever it is they encounter—even the truth about their mother. You do know you'll have to tell them about her sometime don't you?"

David had crossed his arms across his chest closing into himself as Laurel talked. "Of course, although I had thought I would talk to them when they were older. I admit I hadn't thought of anything wrong in my keeping Cat and Tim away from the rest of the world. I thought they had everything they needed here, and they would never be hurt. But, you're right. Time goes by so fast and they will want to leave Whitethorn and see what else there is out there." He expanded his arms towards the ceiling as he spoke. "So, quickly since it's getting very late, tell me your plan."

Laurel didn't know why she was surprised at how quickly their minds connected—it had been happening ever since they met. "Right now the second floor of the castle has eight guest rooms, each with individual bathrooms. The third floor is identical to the second except that you have utilized four of the rooms and their attached bathrooms for your staff. It is impossible for me to think of Henry, Gwen, Roger, Thomas and Emily as "staff"; you have made them a part of your family. I believe that Thomas and Emily have been with you as long as you can remember. Gwen, Thomas and Emily have grandchildren about the same ages as Cat and Tim. What I propose is that the second floor be turned into four living quarters, each encompassing a bedroom, bathroom, sitting room and guest room. The third floor would be reverted into eight guest rooms, each with attached bathrooms. Then, I would like to have Gwen, Thomas and Emily to invite their children and grandchildren to visit from time to time. Cat and Tim would be able to play and have some interaction with others their own age. I think there's a possibility that you may be able to have Roger stay on at Whitethorn longer too if he could bring a bride here someday. If you agree to this, David, there is some risk involved in having "the talk" with your children sooner than you planned. Children notice everything. Cat and Tim are bound to notice families that have a daddy and a mommy and wonder why theirs doesn't. I believe with all my heart that this would be a good thing for them. It's better that they grow with this as just a fact of life; that people can be different in the world and that's okay." Laurel leaned in closer to David. "David, don't you see? You would still be controlling the speed at which the outside world would enter Whitethorn and Cat and Tim would have normal social interactions. They will be able to accept and embrace who they are and how they came to be rather than feel ashamed or embarrassed about something that doesn't even involve them."

David sat absolutely still and silent. Laurel watched his face in concentration and held her breath—she still had a little more to tell him. "Your right, of course, I was trying to stop the clock to forestall the day I would have to tell the children about their mother. I'm really not certain how I'm going to tell them; I can't stand knowing they are going to be hurt. I like your ideas for the second and third floor and giving my staff the respect of a home they are so much a part of. I'm going to trust you and your experiences as a child that this is the best way to move forward for Cat and Tim. It's late, but there really isn't much to do as far as structural changes. I think all we really need to do is remove some doorways to create walls. We'll add some doors so that each of the four quarters has two bathrooms—one private and one for their guests. I better leave you now so I can get started...."

"There's more."

"What? You have more? I can't believe there could possibly be more. Very well, go on."

"I've never had workmen to help me with my projects before. Even though Whitethorn Castle is larger than anything I've ever done, with so much help I believe I will be done in four more weeks. I've gotten close to Emily this past week and I've discovered that she and Thomas' fortieth wedding anniversary is November 1st. What I would love to do is have the new staff units kept secret for another week when Gwen will return. I want to have you gift Thomas and Emily with a three week vacation to Paris and Rome in honor of their anniversary. After they've left, I'll take Gwen into my confidence to contact all the families for a surprise party upon their return. From what I've learned about traditional festivities in town, I believe we can make this a daylong event. Plessey Woods Country Park has a Halloween "Gruesome Walk in the Woods" we can send all the children with their parents and grandparents to. Henry and Roger will stay behind and help you and I set up for the party. In keeping with the costumes the children will be wearing, I thought we might have a costumed evening where Thomas and Emily are dressed as "King and Queen" and honored for the evening. This would break the ice all the way around for future visits and celebrate a milestone for Thomas and Emily. It would also be a lovely way to celebrate the castle's new look and help take the attention off of my leaving to go home. We've all grown so close in such a short time. I can't imagine how hard it's going to be for me to leave knowing I'll probably never see any of you again."

"Wow! Thorough and melodramatic! Laurel, this is a lot for me to absorb. Why don't you start with the second and third floor designs for right now and you and I will discuss what to do for Thomas and Emily when I return?" David had felt slightly ill when Laurel mentioned "not ever seeing her again." "I wouldn't be so sure that you won't be seeing any of us again, either. I have some thoughts on your professional future I want to discuss with you. Preferably on another day and when it's not such a late hour."

Laurel found her first real smile of the evening. She felt so much better—except for her quandary about Greg. "You're right. I'm really tired and Roger's going to beat me on our run in the morning. When will you be back?"

"In two days. Laurel, tonight we talked a lot about trust. Tomorrow, I will trust you not to pester my staff into using the cell phone while I'm gone. I'll call Emily each evening for anything you need me to order by way of supplies. Go on to bed now. We'll talk in a couple of days."

Laurel had no problem agreeing to go to bed; she was exhausted. "Goodnight David. You don't have to worry about the phone. I have a lot to talk with my husband about and over the phone would be wrong. I'll use the next four weeks wisely. I hope you and Anita have a safe trip."

Laurel missed David's amusement over her mentioning Anita. He couldn't help wondering how long before she realized she had more to discuss with her husband than she thought.

CHAPTER 18

Greg and Tyler were in the kitchen at breakfast re-reading the front page of the morning newspaper. "Tyler, this is perfect. You said this is in all the papers in the affiliate? What area does that cover again?"

"Starting just north of Sacramento and going south, almost to Mexico's border. San Diego isn't part of the area. I'm glad you like the story, I'm happy with it too. If this doesn't get a response from someone that has seen Aunt Laurel, or at least something unusual in the last few days, I'll be shocked."

Greg heard a car pull up in front of the house. He glanced around the hall to see out the front door. "Looks like the detectives are here. I didn't expect them so early."

"Yeah, me either. I'll go let them in."

Tyler arrived at the front door just as Phil was about to ring the bell. "Good morning, Phil; Matt. Come on in. Uncle Greg has some coffee in the kitchen."

Matt hung back from entering the house. "Phil you go ahead. Tyler, we just wanted to make sure you were home to let us in before I move our car. We don't want anything to tip our guy off. Can you leave the door unlocked and I'll let myself in when I get back?"

"Sure thing. Do you need any help carrying anything in?"

"No thanks. All we really need for today is our camera. I'm going to stop by Brenda's and make sure she has plans for the day too."

"Okay, see you in a few minutes."

Tyler found Phil and Greg with their backs to him while looking at the paper when he returned to the kitchen. "Greg you must be much happier with this piece your nephew did for the paper."

"There are no words Phil. I feel like there's finally a chance that we'll find my wife."

Tyler was relieved to hear some hope in Greg's voice again. "Matt went to move the car and check in with Brenda, Phil. What do you need us to do for setup in the gym?"

"There's not much Tyler." Phil was glad he had a few minutes before Matt returned. He knew Greg didn't like him and he needed Greg's cooperation. "Greg, I know you aren't going to like this, but I need to ask you to take your truck and leave for at least six hours too."

Greg was shocked and let it show. "What? How can you say that? We know this guy knows something and you're going to make me leave? Why?"

"Because I need our guy to feel that there isn't anyone around so we can catch him. If he thinks you're home, he's probably not going to do his usual scam—especially now that he knows there's an investigation. We need this house to look empty. Tyler, you're going to have to move your rental car too."

Greg started to calm down when Phil explained about the house being empty, but then when he realized Tyler was going to be able to stay he tensed up again. "Why does Tyler get to stay? I have more reason to want to find out what this guy knows that he does."

"Because Tyler is a seasoned reporter and can remain detached. All we have on this guy right now is a scam involving his company's competition. If he's somehow more involved in the crime of your wife's disappearance too, we want Tyler to be able to get the facts into a story, if we need it, for the newspaper. You've already concluded that this guy is not only involved, but that he acted alone. We don't know that. If he is involved in your wife's disappearance and didn't act alone, Tyler can put what we do have in a story for tomorrow and help lead us to anyone else he's working with. This is important to have ready if we don't get some names out of him during our interrogation. We also need to trust that when this goes down today, no one is going to come charging out of this house and interfere with the arrest."

Matt had come back into the house as Phil was trying to get Greg's cooperation to leave. "The car's moved, Phil, and Brenda just left with one of her friends to go shopping for the day."

"Thanks, Matt. Tyler, why don't you move your car while I finish talking with your uncle?"

Tyler was only too glad to comply; it was killing him to watch his uncle continue to go through pain. "Sure. I'm going to go a few blocks over so there's less chance of Scott noticing the rental car tag."

"The slip you stole off the door today was a US Express Mail notice—federal. When we add that do the charges you face for the standard delivery companies you've been bilking, well, let's just say you're in deep shit here."

Scott jumped up, sending his chair sliding forcefully backwards into the wall. "You're the one that's full of shit here!" Scott yelled. "So I took some paper off a door, you can't prove anything other than that. I didn't steal anything!"

Phil was up the minute Scott burst out of his chair. "Sit down, Scott."

Scott, furious, remained still and glared hatred at Phil.

Pointing to the chair, Phil raised his voice to a yell. "I said sit down, now!"

Scott kicked his chair with his feet back to the table and sat down, resigned to his fate.

Phil regained his seat and started in on Scott again. "That "paper" you took is federal property and I don't need anything more than that to prove a crime was committed. What I want to know is what's in it for you and who's in it with you? Is somebody working with you to make your competition look bad? Guarantee you some payback money? What?"

"No! You're way off base here man. I just wanted to get a promotion and make some money to get Angie back, that's it. I figured if customers started missing packages from everybody else but us, I'd look good and be first in line. And it was working, damn it! People were noticing me, asking my name and calling the company talking good about me. I just wanted to get Angie back, that's all."

"That's very touching, Scott, but I'm not buying it. I've got a forensic team going over your apartment right now. I'll tell you what, you tell me the truth about this scam and I'll put in a good word for you; see if I can reduce your prison time."

Scott started shrieking the minute the "p" word left Phil's mouth. "Prison! I'm not going to prison, you're nuts!"

"Nuts, huh? Well, number one, the feds don't ignore crimes against the government and number two, who do you think your company's going to go after when your competition you've been setting up wants restitution for slander and lost income? You don't think you have some charges coming your way from your company? I think you're nuts."

Scott's head was pounding and he started to beg. "You've got to help me, man, I'm nothing, really. All I wanted was to get my girl back. I didn't mean to cause any harm to anybody."

"But you did, Scott. And, of course, we have the problem of the disappearance of Laurel Andrews …"

"I'm telling you, I don't know anything about that!" Scott yelled at the top of his lungs.

Phil kept his tone neutral and kept right on talking. "Well, as I said, we have forensics covering your apartment as we speak and I should have their report within the hour. I want to help you, Scott, I really do; but, you've got to give me something."

Rolling his eyes toward the ceiling and affecting a snide tone, Scott mimicked back "I don't know anything. How the hell can I give you anything if I don't know anything?"

"Scott, we know there weren't deliveries made to the Andrews home from the day before Laurel Andrews went missing to the day after she went missing. The only missing notice on the door was the one you put there that you told us about."

Scott missed what Phil was trying to telling him. "That's right. She had a package I needed to get a signature for and no one was home, so I put the notice on their door and left."

"Yes, we know that Scott, but by any chance did you find a notice on the door that you swiped?"

Phil could tell by the guilty look on Scott's face that he had. "Okay, there was a notice, you got me. I took it and left mine in its place."

"What do you do with the notices after you take them Scott?"

"I tear them up and put them in the garbage bag in my truck."

Phil was having a hard time remaining still in his seat. Matt and Tyler were standing with jaws dropped to the floor in the next room. "Scott, if I go out to your truck right now and grab your garbage, am I going to find the notice you took off of the Andrews' door?"

"It's possible. The bag was getting full so I dumped some of it in the company trash this morning."

Phil shot out of his seat like a bolt of lightning and pointed at Scott "Stay there!" and sped to the room's door.

Matt was already in the hallway dialing his cell phone when Phil came out. "Are you calling Graham?"

"Yes. Hold on, he's answering."

"Graham, this is Detective Johnson calling. What? Oh, yes, we do have Scott in custody. Graham, Scott emptied his truck's garbage into the company trash this morning. I need you to hold that trash for me. What? When? Oh my God, just keep everyone away from the trash until I get an officer over to pick it up. There may still be something. A police officer will be down there within a half hour."

Phil didn't like Matt's face or what he heard. "Well?"

Matt clicked his cell phone shut, "The city garbage collector picked up the trash this morning."

Phil turned and pounded his fists on the wall. "Shit. Okay, get someone to bring me the trash from Scott's truck. You never know, we may get lucky."

"I'll go get it myself."

Phil waited with Tyler while Matt went to get the trash bag. He couldn't take Scott's strong urine smell any longer. Ten minutes later, Matt walked in carrying a bag with gloved hands.

The three men looked into the bag and found several small pieces of torn paper stuck in dried soda at the bottom. Phil motioned for Matt to turn the bag over onto the table and then used a ballpoint pen to search through the debris so as not to disturb any fingerprints. Flipping over a piece of a white notice, he found it. A torn yellow piece of post it paper had the beginning of a note written in scratchy black ink: "*Mr. Andrews: Your wife is unharmed . . .*"

CHAPTER 19

David's inflated ego from the previous evening died a quick and painful death early the next morning. In spite of claiming Roger would be up first this morning because she retired at such a late hour, Laurel was actually a full ten minutes earlier to arrive outside for the morning run—just in time to make sure she met Anita. David had a horrible time reigning in his grin while pretending not to notice Laurel's curiosity about "the other woman" in his life. The grin departed rapidly as fate turned against him. He received nothing but a bruised ego at the seemingly delighted Laurel quickly making a new best friend. What David didn't see as he set his tea cup down and left the table in search of his briefcase was where Laurel's eyes looked with her cheery "Good Morning! Oh! You must be Anita," on her way to shake the gorgeous woman's hand. She purposely held her running hat in her right hand thereby forcing Anita to produce her left hand for the introduction.

Anita was a tall, curvaceous redhead with startling blue eyes and a perfect "peaches 'n cream" complexion. She also had a left hand bearing a full two carat diamond wedding ring. "Yes I am and good morning to you too. You're dressed for running; not joining my flight this time?"

Laughing, Laurel shook her head. "No, I'm afraid not. One of us has to stay here and keep up the work on this place."

Anita had a quick wit and a huge sense of humor. "That's a shame, I would have enjoyed some conversation with you this time. I took a quick tour of the main keep before our breakfast and I have to tell you, it's simply magnificent. I am completely in love with it. Any possibility you could visit my home in town before you leave and give me a pointer or two?"

Beaming, Laurel and Anita walked with their heads together as they chatted, non-stop, on their way to the hangar with a deflated David trailing behind. He noticed the two women made perfectly matched friends immediately; something Gwen and Emily grew into only after a few years together. David used the guise of last minute details to pull Laurel back to him as Anita boarded the plane to begin pre-flight preparations.

It took every bit of restraint David could muster not to kiss the glowing upturned face presented to him in answer to hearing her name. "Laurel, is there anything more we need to cover before I take off?"

Pure delight etched her face as she thought before answering. "Hmmm, no, I don't think so. I'm glad you're leaving Henry here with us."

"Why?"

"I thought I might go ahead and take advantage of your absence to complete the master bedroom suite, including the nursery. That way, the entire private family wing of the castle will also be complete."

Startled at the thought of Laurel in his room, David thought he could divert her plan. "When will you have time to start on the second floor staff quarters if you do that now?"

"Actually, I think I can do them simultaneously. The workmen are going to be a little while adding and removing doorways and making walls. With Henry's help, we can get your artwork moved up to your new studio area on the fourth floor. I would also be able to utilize Henry in placing the pieces in the room to suit your preferences." Laurel had years of practice at hiding her feelings. David never guessed that she was trying to make her time as filled as possible. She wanted to make time pass more quickly in his absence. She thoroughly enjoyed her work days with David sharing her vision right beside her.

The fact that Laurel would be completing the rooms so close to his heart without him was exactly why David was trying to divert her into the upper floors instead. "I see. Are you sure you don't want to wait until I return to tackle that area? I mean, I am the current occupant and might want some input in that regard."

"Ah, but even if you were here, I wouldn't allow that, David and you know it. You gave me complete design control, remember? Everyone else has had to place complete trust in me while I create their rooms. So far, I believe I have a one hundred percent satisfaction score. Besides, you know that I like to create one unique "surprise" in each room. I want you to have the same pleasure I have planned for everyone else."

Sighing, David could do nothing but concede the point. He knew he was going to be exhausted when he got back. Between client meetings and anticipation over how Laurel had read his personality for his private quarters, there wouldn't be any sleep in his foreseeable future. "Very well, proceed. Did you meet the workmen's wives that want to help you with the sewing yet?"

"Yes, I did and we are making some gorgeous drapes and pillows. I can't wait for you to see the results." The engines started on the plane and David and Laurel looked up to see Anita signaling for David to board. Laurel was surprised to find herself tearing up the same way she did every time she said goodbye to Tyler at the end of one of his visits. "You better get going, David. Have a good trip." She squeezed his hand goodbye as she headed back towards Whitethorn where Roger was probably waiting for their run.

David's hand felt her warmth and he watched her until she entered the gardens and the bushes hindered his sight of her before boarding the plane. Laurel stopped still as she heard the plane gaining speed, peeked above the tall bushes behind her and watched until the plane was a speck on the horizon. Anxious to clear her thoughts, she ran her way through the now familiar gardens to meet Roger and get started on their run.

Roger was glad to have Laurel to himself for a couple of days. David had been monopolizing her during their running time and had even started joining her on the off days for lap swims. He found her both invigorating and interesting. He also found an increase in his energy level since starting his days with a run and wanted to talk to her about marathon running.

Roger ran to her when she came into view at the garden entrance. "I'm already warmed up; let's just keep going."

"Great, you lead and I'll pace myself next to you."

"Would you mind sharing some information about marathon running with me as we go? I think I may be interested in upping my training and giving one a try."

Laurel was pleased and excited at the prospect of adding another partner to a marathon run. "Are you serious? That's wonderful! David was considering the same thing. Wouldn't it be fun if the three of us could run a marathon together in six months or so? You two would be able to train together while I'm gone and we could meet up for the run."

Roger hated to think about her leaving. The castle had such warmth and life with her here. "Do you really think Lord David and I could run a marathon?"

"Absolutely; you two haven't even noticed that you are running a little under nine minute miles and I haven't heard you straining to breathe for awhile now." Laurel had the nerve to smile as she revealed her knowledge about their deceiving her and the price the two men had paid.

Roger was courteous enough to laugh at being caught. "Okay, I give; we shouldn't have tried to best you. Honestly, what kind of training am I looking at here?"

"It's not as bad as you think. I follow a twenty-two week training schedule that our coach for The Leukemia Society's *Team in Training* gave each of the team members at our first marathon. You will be shocked at how quickly you will be racking up the miles—especially since men are naturally better at running over women."

"Why is that?"

"Men have greater muscle mass than women and therefore, more glycogen. That's why women's marathon finish times are always longer than the men's."

"I see. Will you have time to share the schedule with me with all the work you're doing?"

"Sure, I know it by heart by now. Why don't you and I meet over lunch and I can pencil it out for you then?" Laurel paused for a minute and then added, "You know, I'm getting back home after the marathon I was planning on running. Since you and David are already running six miles easily, I could cut back into the training schedule to work it with the two of you."

"That would be fantastic, although I'm sorry, I didn't realize you were going to miss your marathon. Can't you talk to Lord David about taking the time off to do your marathon and then returning to complete the castle?"

Laurel had to think fast in her answer so Roger wouldn't know about her working "arrangement." "That would be impractical, Roger. It's not like this is my first marathon, you know. I wasn't even doing this one as part of the team. I'm at the point where I enter them when I feel like running one just for the fun of it. Surely you've noticed I'm much more excited about getting the castle project over the finish line?"

"I think we've all noticed your excitement about that! If you're serious about sharing the schedule and starting the training while you're here, I think I'll take you up on your offer."

"This is going to be fun!" The overcast morning sky that had deepened during the past half hour finally gave way to a gentle rain. "Oops, guess we didn't beat the rain. Are you okay to keep on going?"

"I don't believe either one of us will melt. I can take another half hour if you can."

"I can't believe you have any doubt! Do you think you can handle Cat and Tim joining us for lunch?"

"Sure, why?"

"I told them the next time we had a rainy day I'd talk to Emily about having a pizza lunch."

"This is my lucky day! I haven't had pizza in years."

"Bring the children down to the kitchen at about eleven thirty and you can jot down some notes on the new running schedule while the children and I pretend we're at a pizzeria."

"I'll try to turn the morning into a lesson about pizza not being Italian."

The two laughed together and ran along in the rain before parting ways for the morning when they were back at the castle.

Laurel bathed and returned downstairs in search of Henry. Not seeing him inside, she had just started to go back out into the mud room on her way outside when Thomas and Henry came in. "Oh, Henry, there you are."

Henry was surprised that Laurel was looking for him and stopped removing his rain gear to question her motive. Thomas was relieved Laurel hadn't been looking for him; he had some tea and biscuits with his wife that had been calling his name.

"You were looking for me, ma'am?"

"It's Laurel, Henry, and yes, I was looking for you. With David off for a couple of days, do you think I could enlist your aide in the private master quarters? I think your knowledge of where David needs his daily living pieces placed would be invaluable."

Henry was initially thrilled at being needed. He had been feeling somewhat melancholy over seeing everyone else taking part in the castle that had become his home being renovated without him. Just as he was about to answer in the affirmative, Henry remembered something about the way Laurel and the other's worked that, while he enjoyed watching and listening to them immensely, he was not gifted with either voice or rhythm. "Well, Laurel, I would be more than happy to lend you assistance, however, not foreseeing your desire to work on Lord David's private rooms, I'm afraid I did not think to secure his permission prior to his leaving this morning."

"No problem, Henry, I met with him before he left and he is expecting us to go ahead."

Henry's complexion paled, but he had no exit open to him. "Very well, Laurel. When did you want to begin?"

"Why now; of course! Oh! Have you eaten? I can check in with the work-men first if you need some time."

The last thing Henry wanted in his stomach, which was rapidly becoming queasy, was food. "No need. I'll follow your lead."

Smiling broadly, Laurel asked Henry to start gathering David's artwork and supplies together. Laurel was going to send a couple of the workmen's wives to help transfer the items to the new studio on the fourth floor and take the opportunity to discuss the work schedule for the staff quarters out of Henry's presence. She also had to get any carpenters that could be spared from the staff quarters started on the special projects for the nursery and master bedroom.

Laurel couldn't help but notice that Henry looked as if he had a broom stuck in the back of his pants when they were about to start clearing David's items out of the room and begin. She thought she knew why. Laurel had never seen Henry so much as tap his foot while everyone else was boogying their way through the days. She had even caught Emily shaking a plump hip once or twice. "Henry, you appear uncomfortable. What can I do to help you so we can enjoy creating your employer's new quarters together?"

Henry pulled at the neck of his shirt before confessing. "Uh, well, um, you see, I don't know how to dance and I've been told I can't sing either."

"I see; and, exactly what makes you think you can't learn to dance and carry a tune? Or that you have to?"

"I'm sure I'd be awful and I really don't want to make a fool of myself."

"Oh, Henry, I'm so sorry you believe that I would ever think you foolish. Do you enjoy music Henry?"

"Yes, very much."

"Let's do this then. I won't turn the music on until after lunch. Roger, the children and I are going to be having a pizza party by the way, and you're welcome to join us. I think I'll take advantage of this morning to get to know you better and make some decisions for when I work on your room."

Laurel could hear excitement in Henry's voice. "My room? I had no idea you would be doing the staff's quarters."

"Why not? You must have noticed that we did Gwen's quarters while she's away on vacation."

"I knew you changed her room in the family quarters to that of an older child. I didn't know you were creating new rooms for the staff. I thought you simply moved Gwen's old quarters to a room upstairs with the rest of us."

Laurel was relieved to see Henry's color had improved and that he was smiling again. "Well, now you know."

For the next few hours, Henry and Laurel worked side by side removing all the articles from the master bedroom. By the time they broke for the pizza party, Laurel had discovered Henry's love of anything connected to the movie character, James Bond, and had mentally plotted out his room.

Cat and Tim were bursting with excitement when Henry and Laurel joined them in the kitchen to start the pizza. Roger, Emily and Thomas were all standing by.

Laurel took count of all the extra people and quickly asked Emily for more pans. "Emily, it appears we will be making more pizza than I thought so we won't be freezing any of the dough you've already prepared. Do you mind making a green salad for us?" Emily had placed all the ingredients that Laurel requested on the counter top when she was making Laurel's dough recipe earlier. She nodded affirmatively as she went to retrieve the raised dough on top of the stove and the salad ingredients. "Thomas, how much sausage do we have?"

Thomas had a twinkle in his eye and was patting his portly belly. "When Emily told me about the pizza, I knew you would need more than enough for four people. We've never had anything like it and I knew you would rope Henry in on trying some too. You might have noticed that I like to eat and I want to see what you do with my sausage. There's more than enough sausage for however much pizza you want to make."

Laurel couldn't remember the last time she had such impromptu fun. "Cat, Tim, come over here and put an apron on. Men, stand back!"

For the next few minutes, the men watched as the two women helped the children knead the dough and pat it into pans. The children had flour in their hair and on their noses and were giggling the entire time. Next, Emily brought the sauce she had made at Laurel's direction over and they spread it over the dough. Laurel thought the men should get in on the activities too. "Okay, you guys, up out of your seats and get ready to work for your lunch! Thomas, would you please stir the sausage until it browns? Henry, I need you to grab up the cheddar and grate it into a bowl. Roger, would you grate the mozzarella into another bowl please?"

As soon as the pizzas were in the oven, six anxious faces looked at Laurel for what to do next. "We have twenty-five minutes before those pizzas are done. Why don't we go ahead and set the table and have our salad while we wait?"

Everyone, aprons still on, headed into the main dining room to do just that. Cat and Tim were thrilled to be at a "grownups" party and to have helped make the food. While rain continued outside, they all enjoyed a wonderful pizza party inside. Laughter abounded and conversation flowed. Thomas and

Emily, consistently English style food consumers, were very surprised to find they loved pizza. The children didn't want the party to end, especially since that meant they had to return to their lessons. Laurel had enjoyed the lunch and her time with the children tremendously, but she was anxious to get back to work with Henry. "Emily, why don't Henry and I help you with cleaning up?"

"I wouldn't think of it, Laurel. You and Henry go along back to your project and my Thomas and I will take care of things here."

"Thank you very much, I appreciate that." With that, Laurel and Henry removed their aprons to head back to their project. She was relieved to see that Henry was looking very mellow with his tummy filled.

Back in Lord David's sleeping quarters, Henry was surprised to find a couple of carpenters busily working—to music. Laurel could sense Henry's panic and she rushed to assure him. "Henry, it's going to be alright. The men are going to be creating some built in cabinetry while you and I stain this wall," she explained pointing to the opposite wall from the workmen. "I want you to know, that even if we sing or dance a little, in no way do you have to participate. If you do want to join in, let me know and I'll work on a song with you."

Henry completely trusted Laurel and relaxed. A few hours later, Laurel noticed just the slightest of movement from one of Henry's feet and she inched closer to barely hear him singing to their song. She was surprised to find that Henry was correct about one thing—he couldn't sing worth a damn. She smiled as the solution came to her in a flash. "Henry, I mean, Sonny, do you mind if we try "I Got You Babe"?

Shocked, Henry caught onto her very quickly and chanced a smile. Wanting to be a part of all the fun, he shyly nodded.

Emily had more she couldn't wait to share with Gwen upon her return when she walked by with linens to be put away just in time to hear "Sonny" croak after Cher's intro "Well I don't know if all that's true, but you got me and baby I got you...." and shamelessly stood outside in the hallway, once again biting the insides of her cheeks to keep quiet during the remainder of *Sonny and Cher's* performance.

CHAPTER 20

Jeannie Lawson, refreshed from three weeks in Vermont, grabbed the stacked mail left by the house sitter and entered her cozy kitchen. Dropping the mail on the kitchen nook table, she brewed a pot of coffee and grabbed a croissant. Before sitting down, she checked the time and was happy to find out she had five minutes before Veronica Garcia and "Eye on Keddie" started. Tuning the small television to the proper channel, she sat down with her morning break-fast and decided to sort through the mail while she waited for her program. She had time to weed out all the advertisements and occupant mail before the introduction music started.

The vivacious brunette's smiling visage filled the screen. "Good morning Keddie and welcome to "Eye on Keddie"! I'm your host, Veronica Garcia, and we are going directly to our weather report so we can move without interrup-tion through an in depth report on the mysterious disappearance of one of Keddie's citizens. Our first story this morning is dedicated to helping find Lau-rel Andrews."

The croissant paused in mid air on its way to Jeannie's mouth as Veronica finished her opening line. Closing her open mouth, Jeannie dropped the crois-sant back on to the plate, positive that she must have misunderstood what she just heard. The weatherman finished up and, after the longest commercial break in history, the program picked back up with Veronica.

"Today, we have Tyler Grant, Detective Phil Peters and Detective Matt Johnson with us. Good morning gentlemen."

The three men answered in unison "Good morning."

"For all of you tuning in, I'm sure you have been following the mysterious disappearance of Laurel Andrews for the past three weeks. Today, we are jointly broadcasting with *US News Report* hoping that one of our viewers may have information that will lead to finding Mrs. Andrews."

Veronica swiveled her chair to face Tyler directly. "First of all, Tyler, I understand that you have both a personal and professional interest in this case."

"That's correct, Veronica. Laurel Andrews is my aunt and I got my start at the newspaper here in Keddie. I'm a broadcast journalist in Philadelphia now. I contacted my old boss at the newspaper the minute my uncle contacted me with the news about my Aunt Laurel. With full cooperation from the newspaper, I'm here combining the role of mediator between my uncle and the police, and the police with the newspaper. I'm hoping that the joint efforts of the police, coupled with responsible reporting, will help find my aunt."

Veronica swiveled her chair again, towards Phil Peters. "I see. Detective Peters, as lead detective on the case, why don't you give our viewers an accurate history to date and perhaps Detective Johnson can follow that with the case's current direction."

Phil Peters was very happy that Veronica was complying with a request to keep the broadcast on a tasteful level. "Laurel Andrews disappeared three weeks ago at about five o'clock in the morning during her daily run. Greg Andrews, her husband, arrived home from work that evening and discovered that his wife was missing and called the police. When we arrived, we found no signs of burglary, forced entry or foul play. Forensic testing confirmed our initial findings. We zeroed in on a kidnapping based on the negative forensic testing and the fact that Mrs. Andrews' purse with all of her money, credit cards and identification was still in the home. The last lead we had to follow up on came about due to the neighbors comments about missing package deliveries and an attempted delivery notice left on the Andrews door the day of the kidnapping. An interview with the delivery driver that left the notice raised our suspicions that he might have been involved in the kidnapping, or actually be the kidnapper. Instead, surveillance of the driver, Scott Gregory, unveiled a scam to discredit the competition. Part of that scam, removing competition's attempted delivery notices and discarding them, led to the discovery of a piece of a note the kidnapper or kidnappers had left on the Andrews' front door which Mr. Gregory removed." The camera panned away and did a close up of a photograph of the torn and stained note on the coffee table in front of the three men. "Matt, why don't you take it from here."

"Sure, Phil. As you can see, the note is part of a yellow post-it note and stained from soda. Forensics was unable to identify any singular fingerprint for identification from the note due to the soda stains and an overlapping of several different prints. Some prints were actually smudged together. What we can tell you is that the pen used to write the note was a fountain pen with a script head."

Veronica raised her hand to interrupt and picked up a pen from the side table next to her chair. Holding the pen up for the viewers, the camera moved in on her hand. "You mean a pen like this one used for calligraphy?"

"That's correct. The only thing we know from the part of the note we have, is that Mrs. Andrews was unharmed. What we would like your viewers to do is take a close look at the note and contact the Keddie Police Department at the telephone number on your screen if the handwriting looks at all familiar to you."

As the telephone number flashed at the bottom of the screen, the camera did another long close up on the note while Matt commentated on unusual characteristics in the handwriting. "As you can see, one thing that stands out is the writer's "m's." Grabbing a pen from his pocket to use as a pointer, Matt leaned over the note; careful not to obstruct the camera. "See how there's this peculiar loop on every "m"?" It doesn't matter whether it's a capital or not. Look at the capital M in Mr." Matt looked up at Veronica. "See the loop?" Veronica nodded in the affirmative "Yes."

"Now look at the small m in "unharmed." See the loop again?"

Again, Veronica nodded agreement. "Uncanny isn't it?"

"We think so."

Veronica looked back towards the three men and singled out Tyler. "Tyler, please take this opportunity to tell our viewers any requests on the family's behalf."

"Thank you, Veronica. Folks, please, only contact the police if you feel you definitely recognize this handwriting. As Ms. Garcia mentioned, we are broad-casting live across the nation. The family is doing this because publishing the story throughout California's newspapers has produced no credible results. Anyone contacting these two detectives simply out of curiosity will use precious time we may not have." Scott's voice started to break as he reflected on the circus of events since Scott's arrest was made public. "On behalf of my uncle and our family, we would respectfully request that all reporters and their crews camped outside the Andrews' home leave immediately. This request also goes for the reporters stationed at my uncle's place of business and at the home of his co-worker, Joy Stewart. Any further updates in this case will be handled through press releases by the police. I believe that everyone watching can understand that this is tremendously frustrating and worrisome to all of our family, my uncle in particular. While we appreciate the kind intents of those who have called, we would prefer not to accept the psychic services offered or those wishing to express thoughtful sentiments at this time. Since the note was torn, we don't know what else the kidnapper was requesting. We would like to keep any means of communication open, not only for a possible contact from the kidnapper, but also in case my aunt is able to break away and contact us herself."

Veronica could tell Tyler was near his breaking point and signaled the cameraman back to her. "Thank you Tyler. On behalf of everyone here at the station, please express our support to your uncle in helping in any way we can to bring your aunt home. For all of our viewers, please look one more time at the note and see if you recognize the handwriting. If you do, please call the telephone number on your screen immediately. Detectives Peters and Thompson, thank you for being here with us today." The two men nodded and waved. "Tyler, I appreciate you taking the time to be here this morning, especially since you are heading home today?"

"That's correct. There isn't anything more I can do here and I will be returning to my wife tonight. We are expecting our first child in six months and I need to get home to care for her. My superiors at the television station in Philadelphia have pledged their support with national broadcasts as news breaks until my aunt is found."

Veronica's large, dark eyes looked at Tyler, clearly expressing her compassion and understanding. "That's wonderful." She placed a hand on Tyler's, "Have a safe trip home." Patting his hand goodbye, she stood and moved across the room to her mark near the "Eye on Keddie" logo. "We'll be right back after these words from our sponsor with some fall design tips for your home."

Jeannie's coffee had gone cold and she hadn't taken a bite of her croissant. Breathing heavily, she shot out of her chair, flipped off the television and ran for the collected newspapers in her study. Taking a seat behind the beautiful mahogany desk, she turned the stack over to start at the beginning and scanned the front pages. An hour later, she noticed a headache that was growing with each headline. The first story was alarming enough that her client's future home was involved in a kidnapping. Succeeding stories of possible infidelity, a scam artist for a deliveryman, and an interview with an Angie Desmond revealing that she had been stalked by the deliveryman, all added up to the probability that spending her commission before closing was a huge mistake.

"God, Oh God, Why?" she caterwauled to herself. She started to pace up and down in the study. "How am I going to convince Shelby Abbott this neighborhood is safe and get the sale to go through? What to do, what to do?" She continued to pace and picked up a pen and tablet to make a list of what she would do in order to salvage the situation. "Okay, first, oh! First check my messages!" Freshly alarmed, she scurried back to the kitchen again and saw the flashing red "four" on the message machine. Pressing the button, the messages began to play.

"Good morning, Jeannie. This is George Yager, Greg and Laurel Andrews' realtor, calling. In light of the news, I thought we should discuss setting up a meeting with your client and Greg Andrews about how the home sale should or should not progress. Give me a call as soon as you can. My number is 516-8371."

"Hello again, Jeannie. I called your office when I didn't hear back from you and got the phone message regarding your vacation. I cannot contact your client directly so I am going to wait for your call before contacting Greg Andrews about any meeting. Give me a call when you get this."

"Good morning Ms. Lawson. This is Betty, your house sitter, calling. I forgot to leave you a note letting you know when I last watered your houseplants. It was just yesterday so you have a good week before they need more. Hope you had a great vacation and that you'll call me if you ever need my services again."

The last message just about clinched Jeannie's entrance into a mental facility. "Hello, Jeannie, it's Shelby Abbott. I hope you had a wonderful vacation. I've spent the last three weeks cut off from the world while I packed up my belongings and readied for the move. I think we should get together so you can let me know exactly when the escrow is set to close. I've hired some movers from the college and I need to give them details as soon as possible. Also, Jami and Mark are setting their move into this house based on my date. I'm so anxious to get on with my life! I'm sure you have tons to catch up on, but, please call me as soon as you can."

Jeannie listened as the machine clicked off, dropped the pen and pad on the counter and plopped in the first chair she could find. Rubbing her hands over her drumming brow, she tried to focus on what to do as her four limbs quaked with fear. As soon as she was able to control her tremors, she reasoned that she wasn't going to solve her current crisis without several aspirin and a shower to clear her thoughts.

Jeannie took her time under the steaming water after downing the aspirin and searched the recesses of her mind for divine insight on how she should proceed. The water massaged her head and neck succeeding in somewhat relaxing her taught muscles. Resigned to the distressing facts at hand, she decided that calls needed to be returned and was determined to take care of the easiest one first—George Yager.

Stepping from her shower, she toweled off and donned her robe to get the call over with. The call to George actually took some of the weight off of her shoulders. Not only was George in a similar situation as her with the current real estate climate, but he had been forced to contact Greg Andrews last week when bankruptcy loomed over his head in the form of a lost commission if the sale didn't go through. Mr. Andrews was understandably distraught, but assured George that he was sure Laurel would want the home sale to go through and welcomed any meeting to resolve the situation! Now all Jeannie had to do was talk with Shelby Abbott, convince her that the neighborhood was indeed "safe" and find out her thoughts about closing the sale.

Jeannie's headache was much better as she ran off to finish dressing and then returned to her study to make the call to Shelby Abbott.

Across town, Shelby Abbott answered the phone on the second ring. She wasn't surprised that it was her realtor returning her call. "Jeannie! Hello! How was Vermont?"

"Very restful and absolutely beautiful in all its fall glory thank you."

"I appreciate you getting back to me so quickly. I know you just got back last night. Do you think we can get together over coffee and go over the escrow details?"

Jeannie had scraped the lipstick off her bottom lip. "Absolutely, that's why I'm calling. You see, there's been a development that might cause a delay I would like to discuss with you."

"Development? What development?"

Jeannie could hear the alarm in Shelby's voice and rushed to calm her. "No worries, dear, no worries! I assure you the sale is going through, however I don't want to go over this in a lengthy telephone call. Are you available for lunch today?"

"Yes."

"Why don't I pick you up at noon and I'll take you to a new little deli I've found and we can discuss your move?"

Shelby didn't like the idea of waiting until noon to find out about the "development" and her voice didn't sound any happier as she accepted Jeannie's luncheon invitation. "That would be fine. Are you sure you wouldn't rather I meet you at the deli?"

"No, I think it would be best if I picked you up. I'll see you at noon."

Rubbing the first crease of worry she'd felt in three weeks streaking across her forehead, Shelby politely replied, "See you at noon" and hung up the phone.

CHAPTER 21

Laurel was very surprised to find Henry walking in on her and two of the workmen's wives sewing, cell phone in hand. "Laurel, Lord David is on the phone and needs to speak with you."

Smiling broadly, she extended her hand from the sewing machine in front of her to retrieve the phone. "Hello, David?"

"Yes, Laurel. I'm sorry to bother you in the middle of the day, but I'm afraid I am going to be detained here for awhile longer and I wanted to check in with you."

Laurel's smile immediately vanished with his news. "It's no problem; the girls and I are working on drapes for the second floor rooms with the fabric that arrived yesterday."

"Perfect. That leads me into my next question Do you know what other fabrics you may need soon? The fabric outlet I've been utilizing is here in town and I can place your order directly. I can bring it all back with me."

The women couldn't get over the rapidly changing expressions on Laurel's face. First her smile was like sunlight entering the room, and before they knew it, night had descended. Seconds later, whatever Lord David said, had her face looking as excited as one of their men with a fish on his line.

"Oh, David, that would be wonderful! Do you have a pen and paper handy? What am I saying, of course you do."

The whirring of sewing machines had paused with Henry's entrance into the work area. The women tried not to listen to Laurel's conversation, however that was impossible as their chairs were positioned closely to take advantage of an electrical outlet in the make-shift work area. The two women's machines ceased entirely as they were shocked at noticing Laurel, her eyes closed, recite a list from her mind's vision. Her list was specific, including even minute details, to include the exact color, type and yardage of fabric she needed for the remaining rooms of the second and third floors. Henry seemed to be the only one completely at ease with Laurel's gift; he busied himself looking at the morning's work as if nothing at all unusual was occurring in his day.

Finished with her list, Laurel opened her eyes as she spoke to David. "Did you get all of that David?"

On his end of the phone, David, so in tune with Laurel's vision for Whitethorn and thrilled to have advance knowledge of the remaining rooms décor, hadn't missed a single word of her entire recital. "Do you have any doubt?"

Laurel could hear the sewing machines humming once again and smiled her gratitude to the ladies for what she thought was their courtesy of silence while she was on the phone. "None whatsoever! Have you talked with Cat and Tim yet?"

"You must know I have. I have a bone to pick with you upon my return."

"Whatever for?"

"My children are not missing me! I don't have to ask what you've been up to, they couldn't wait to tell me about pizza, Cat's ballet DVD, Tim's rocket that really blasts off, and that you read to them before bed from the "Boxcar Children" books you had me order right after Gwen left. Seriously, I appreciate your taking so much time with them when I know how busy you are."

"David, you don't have to thank me, I'm having a blast. I can't tell you how much I'm enjoying my days. I love this project and with all of the help, the incredible speed with which it moves is like icing on the cake. You see, for me, the hardest part of designing is the time I have to wait between starting to work and the ending where I find if reality lives up to the pictures in my mind. As far as Cat and Tim are concerned, the organization and work schedule we set up leave me pockets of time I'm enjoying with them as a treat to myself. Much like I do whenever I get a visit from my nephew and his wife, or Morgan comes to stay. I'm not going to want to have the children go back to sleeping in those rooms we so carefully created when you return."

David, tired from lack of sleep, found himself wanting to get off the phone, find his client and shake some sense into the man so he could finish his drawings and hurry home—to her. "Too bad; I plan to take them for the day immediately upon my return and spoil them until they are completely enamored with me again."

Laurel, never one to pass on a dare, teased "Good luck with that, David."

David erupted in laughter on his end of the phone. "Touché; I better ring off. I'll see you as soon as I can finish here. Would you connect me back with Henry please?"

Standing up from her sewing, Laurel tapped Henry, who was stooped closely over a drapery panel, on the shoulder. "Henry, David wants to speak with you again."

Henry, slightly embarrassed at being caught snooping in her sewing, politely took the phone and left the room while talking with his employer.

Laurel returned to her sewing as if nothing out of the ordinary had just happened. Taking her cue, the work began again. Secretly, she was glad to have a little more time before David returned. Truth be told, her nervousness about his reaction to the master quarters, the nursery in particular, had grown from softball to beach ball in its proportion. She planned to use the extra time to bolster her confidence and calm her nerves.

David's excitement to see the room matched Laurel's in apprehension resulting in a late flight home two days later. Anita was surprised they were flying home so late. Lord David usually chose an early morning departure. She was further surprised upon landing at Lord David's hasty "thank you and goodnight" as he bolted out the hatch the minute the plane came to a stop at the rear entrance to Whitethorn's gardens.

The night was clear, but cool. David used the chilled air as his excuse to run through the gardens and into the castle. With no one about, he didn't worry about excuses as to why he continued to run directly through the mud room, kitchen, formal dining room and main room straight to the hall in the family wing. He couldn't wait a moment longer to find out if she really saw him, as a man, and not as the figurehead at Whitethorn Castle. David took a deep breath at the door to his private quarters and then quickly opened it.

The only words that could describe him when he turned on the lights and took in the room were "astonished glee". He dropped his briefcase where he stood and forgot the laptop tucked under his arm as he moved further into his room. She had captured everything unique about him, just as every other room she had designed at this point had suited each individual or purpose. How could he have doubted what he thought he saw in her eyes? His room reflected all of his tastes and interests while somehow managing to make room for the addition of a future Lady Whitethorn. The room was predominately created using the male colors of slate blue and grey. She softened the room by adding the feminine mauve in tapestry panels gathered under round fabric cornices. The built in oak cabinetry along the wall opened the room. Instead of a large desk and credenza he used for his home office, the floor was cleared and part of the built in wall contained a desk area with overhead open bookshelves above a three-drawer filing cabinet below. Along with the work area, his armoire had literally been fused into the wall on the opposite side of more open shelving and a chest of drawers, just as if it had always been the initial design. An intimate seating area graced the resulting open floor space. A plump blue and grey tweed loveseat topped with mauve pillows, its back placed four feet from the built in wall and facing his massive bed, was flanked by oak end tables topped with hurricane lamps. A matching oak coffee table was centered in front of the sofa. He sat down and looked at the room's central point—his bed. He was sure he was looking at Laurel's surprise for him—Whitethorn's coat of arms hung above the headboard of the beautiful four poster bed. He couldn't wait to find out where she had discovered it. She had softened the immense bed by using more of the mauve pillows on the patterned bedspread. She had also added rails connecting the four posts and hung drapes in more of the bedspread's patterned material tied at each corner post with mauve braided rope. Rising to look more closely at the window cornices, he discovered Laurel had stamped a fabric paint border of three inch gnarly limbed, whitethorn trees against the grey background. On his way to see the bathroom and nursery, David took in the architect's instruments used ornamentally on the shelves and the careful placement of "feminine" Neptune shells on the room's tables. The gleaming oak hardwood floor was slightly interrupted with tapestry area rugs under the coffee table and on either side of the bed.

Laurel had continued with nature's colors and David's love of the sea in the bathroom. Neutral grey, mauve and tan towel sets hung on racks next to a four head, walk in, slate stoned shower stall. Clear apothecary jars of varying heights held soaps, shells, cotton balls and natural ocean sponges. Just as she had in the bedroom, large candlesticks were placed on a small oak table next to a chair and on a vanity. Thick tan area carpets dotted the stone floor.

The Whitethorn nursery was the most amazing room he had ever seen. He wished he could have seen the workmen's faces when she described what she had in mind. She had completely done the room in a theme to the lullaby "Rock-a-bye Baby". A realistic looking, artificial oak tree appeared to have a cradle in a low lying bough winding along the floor. The lightest tones of slate blue and grey had been stained onto the walls to appear as if the sky surrounded the tree. Again, oak cabinetry had been built into one wall encompassing dresser drawers, a changing table and open shelving. Laurel had managed to keep the room childlike with the addition of Disney's *Bambi* in a plush toy on the floor and patterned fabric in the cradle and draperies. Instead of a cozy seating area, she had placed a dove grey cushioned rocker and floor lamp in one corner. The entire floor was covered with a dark grey, sculptured carpet. David had to search for Laurel's surprise. He was immensely pleased when he did—she had sewn a monogrammed "W" on a pocket of a baby pillow top. As a backdrop, she had used an outline trailing stitch scattering the words "pacifier", "bottle", and "tooth fairy" with outlined caricatures of the baby items.

David couldn't help himself as he disregarded the late hour and took the elevator up to Laurel's room. Quietly opening her door, he tiptoed over to the bed and stared at the slumbering threesome before reaching over Cat to gently shake Laurel's shoulder. He was relieved that her enormous eyes opened without fear.

Laurel was surprised to find a large hand waking her when she expected a much smaller one. Half awake, she followed the hand and arm up to meet David's anxious glance. Sitting up, Laurel had to check herself to keep from hugging him in welcome. Startled as she realized what she had been about to do, she focused her attention on pulling up the bed covers and glancing to the window trying to gauge the time. "You're home," she whispered. She kept her eyes downcast, embarrassed to look him in the eye as she quietly inquired if he had seen his room.

"Oh, yes," he whispered and grabbed her hand. Scared and confused at her emotions, she forced herself not to react to his touch. "Come and talk with me for a little while will you?"

She could tell he was pleased. "Hand me my robe from the chair."

David released her hand and fetched the robe as Laurel, careful so as not to disturb the children, climbed out of the bed. She tied the belt of the robe as she stepped into her slippers. Turning, she had thought to follow David out of the room but he retrieved her hand and led her over to the seating area across from the bed and continued his whispering. "I want to talk here in case the children wake up. I don't want them to be scared thinking they're alone."

Laurel nodded her understanding as David seated her in one of the chairs. She watched as he retrieved a footstool, placed it close to her chair and then sat down on top of it and grabbed her hand once again in a single motion. Laurel quickly became accustomed to his touch. It seemed the most natural thing in the world for him to hold her hand. Even though they were whispering, David's emotion was loud and clear. "I love my room. You never cease to amaze me."

Golden curls tumbled around Laurel's shoulders and a smile appeared on her sleepy face. "I'm so glad. What about the nursery? I know we fought about it, but can you live with it there for awhile waiting for a baby Whitethorn?"

"It's the most fantastic room I've ever seen! You were right, by the way. I do hope my children will make Whitethorn their home. Someday, that room is going to delight a Whitethorn heir."

"That's a ways off, I'm sure. I'm thrilled you like your rooms, but, you felt this couldn't wait until morning to tell me?"

"How is it you can know me so well as to design the perfect rooms for me, but not understand there is more than that I cannot wait to discuss with you?"

"More? What is it?"

He put a single finger against her lips as a signal for her to listen. "I did a lot of thinking while I was away regarding the children and what you said about letting people into their world. I already knew I trusted you, but seeing the rooms made me realize how much a part of this family you have become. I believe you are right about my children needing other children and I want to go ahead with your idea for the surprise party for Emily and Thomas and the living quarters for the staff."

All remnants of sleep left Laurel's eyes as excitement and pleasure fill her face. David pushed firmly with his fingers on her lips for her to remain quiet before he trailed his hand across her face and cupped her cheek. He pulled the footstool as close as possible to her chair and held both her hands in his own. "I want you to understand the enormity of my decision and why it was so difficult for me." Locking his eyes with hers, "I believe it's time I told you about the children's mother."

CHAPTER 22

Laurel didn't move a muscle or break eye contact with David. She didn't want to do anything to give him cause to change his mind. She needn't have worried. David was relieved to finally talk about it with someone after all these years of keeping his silence.

"My parents married late in life. My father, more than my mother, was very concerned with tradition and doing the "proper thing." When I was thirty-four, I received a call from him requesting that I meet with him here at Whitethorn as soon as I could possibly arrange it. In a private meeting, he informed me that he had terminal cancer and was unsure how much longer he would live. My sister had already married, but any children of her marriage would not be a direct Whitethorn heir. My father wanted to make sure the Whitethorn lineage would continue and had me promise I would not only marry, but that I would have children. I loved my parents very much and never hesitated before pledging the promise. He died three months later from an inoperable brain tumor. My mother passed, away, from grief I believe, two months after that. I had dated a lot before my parents' deaths, but I had never had a serious relationship. In my youth, I hadn't realized how unique my sister's marriage was. It wasn't until I was older that I grew up enough to realize how very lucky she and Sam were. Elizabeth and I had grown up together. Our parents were close friends and part of the same social circle. By the time we were teenagers, I had noticed something different about her. Elizabeth never once mooned over me or any other boy. Whenever I tried asking her out, she was always busy with a girlfriend. I eventually gave up and at the wise age of twenty decided she just wasn't interested in me and that we would always be the best of friends. Shortly after my mother's death, Elizabeth arrived unexpectedly at Whitethorn, obviously extremely upset."

David couldn't look Laurel in the eye as he told her the next part of the story. "Elizabeth's father was every bit as concerned with tradition as my father. One day, he walked in on Elizabeth and one of her "girlfriends" in the middle of a kiss." David heard Laurel's sudden intake of breath and he looked her in the eye again, tightening their joined hands. "You can imagine how upsetting this was to him. As a result of her careless behavior, Elizabeth was issued an ultimatum from both her parents. She was never to be the cause of any gossip of a perverted nature and she was given one year to marry someone of a suitable station. Failure to fulfill these terms would result in the family fortune bypassing her for the first male cousin in the family lineage."

Laurel's heart broke when she knew what he had done.

"All Elizabeth ever wanted from anyone was to be accepted for who she was. She had no alternative but to comply with her parents' ultimatum. What could I do? I was her best friend and I hadn't met anyone to marry and fulfill my promise to my father. So, we agreed to a partnership, of sorts. Elizabeth and I would marry, and remain married, until she bore a son. We would then divorce without divulging our reason, and she would move to America and live as she pleased. Our son would remain at Whitethorn and she would maintain a regular visiting schedule. I'm sure you've already found the flaw in our plan. Elizabeth's parents were very pleased with our marriage and how quickly their daughter became pregnant. Elizabeth was surprised when she bore a daughter, but she didn't appear overly upset at the prospect of staying married longer than we anticipated. Elizabeth was just like any mother with her firstborn. She nursed Cat and worried if she was getting enough milk. She walked with her when her tummy was upset and cried with the pain of a first tooth. We were getting along well and I was convinced that Elizabeth and I were happy and that we wouldn't be divorcing after all. I so wanted a relationship like Shelby and Sam's that I exaggerated every little event in my mind as proof that Elizabeth and I were soul mates." David stopped his whispering when he heard one of the children stirring. When they looked over at the cause, Laurel thought she would die if Tim didn't stay asleep so she could hear the rest of the story.

Tim must have heard Laurel's silent prayer as he pulled the blankets tight about his neck and fell back asleep. David leaned his head closer into Laurel's and whispered even lower.

"It took Elizabeth two years to get pregnant with Tim. When he was born I was on top of the world and felt like the luckiest man alive. I was in love with my beautiful wife and we had two gorgeous children. Four months later, Elizabeth's parents were killed in a traffic accident while on a vacation in Germany. Shortly after receiving her inheritance, Elizabeth began taking what she called "shopping trips." When she came home from one of her trips, she cornered me in my study after the children were asleep and reminded me of our agreement. She had met a woman she was in love with and wanted to divorce me and live openly with her."

Laurel could still feel pain emanating from David as the story poured out of him. "She had completely fooled you?"

"Yes—but not intentionally, I'm sure. I think she loved the children and honestly tried to stay in the marriage. It just wasn't meant to be. Anyway, there was no arguing with her, she had made up her mind. She and her lover were going to move in together and live in New York. Elizabeth promised to return to her family's estate for a week every two months to visit with the children. She was packed and gone within a week. Cat was almost three at the time and cried for her mother continually. I was too wrapped up in my own anger and pain to comfort her. Gwen joined my staff and worked wonders with the children. She never said a word about their mother. She just loved them with all of her heart."

"The visiting arrangement went well for the next six months. On Elizabeth's last visit, she informed me she would no longer be returning to England. She and her lover had decided they wanted to be recognized as a family and live exactly as any other family would. Her lover had already been artificially inseminated and was expecting their first child. Elizabeth decided it would be better for both her and the children if she no longer participated in their lives. She was tired of living a lie and wanted to be free to live with her life partner and their children. I had no choice but to accept her decision and do whatever I could to protect Cat and Tim. I trusted my staff not to speak of Elizabeth and secured Whitethorn from the outside world. I was sure old gossip would rear its ugly head if I allowed anyone in and my children would be hurt. I never want them to feel unwanted." Tears had started in the corner of David's eyes as he finished his story. He dropped Laurel's hands and made a show of standing to stretch his back while he blinked them away. Exhaustion was clearly winning as he regained his seat on the footstool.

"Now you know why I've lived as I have and how much trust I have in you and your instincts. So tell me this; are you still sure in your view that I should let the world in, and if so, what do I tell my children about their mother when they ask?"

Laurel leaned forward in her chair and, this time, she took hold of David's hands. "Yes, David, I'm more inclined than ever to feel you must have children here for Cat and Tim to grow up with. They must not go out in the world as adults completely unprepared. As to what you should tell them about their mother, I suggest the truth." David tried to break his hands free when she said that, but Laurel held fast. "David, the "truth" of the matter is that you and Elizabeth had a good marriage and she loved her babies very much. After Tim was born, Elizabeth realized she had changed and wasn't happy being married to you anymore. That doesn't mean she could ever stop loving Cat and Tim. Because she did love her children so much, she felt it was best that they grow up here with you at Whitethorn and she would visit. When she could tell it was hurting the children every time she had to leave, she made the biggest sacrifice a mother can make. She decided it would be best if she remained out of their lives. That's all you need to tell them for now. David, as they grow, you will be able to explain the different kinds of love people can experience without judgment about Elizabeth's sexual preference. This will be no different than explaining a stepmother to them if you decide to remarry." David raised his eyebrows when she said that. Smiling for the first time in an hour, she pushed on his hands. "In their minds, you were sure you and their mother were in love: how could you possibly be in love with someone else? You said you trust my instincts. I trust your children and their ability to learn from you that a heart has room for all kinds of love."

David stood and raised his arms overhead again to stretch the tension out of his body. Shaking his head as if to clear his mind, he looked relieved as the weight of the world he'd been carrying for three years died. "Isn't it funny how simple a disastrous situation can actually be when viewed from the outside? I appreciate your wisdom more than you'll ever know. As much as I'd love to stay up all night and talk with you about the party, I'm too anxious to miss sleeping in my new room. Have I disrupted your sleep so that you'll be too tired in the morning to spare me some time?"

The devil was back in Laurel's enormous green eyes. "Tired? No, but I will be taking advantage of your children not knowing you're home and your threat to spoil them rotten. Looking at you, there is no way you'll be up before nine o'clock. I'm planning to enjoy an early swim with them before a breakfast of my famous chocolate chip pancakes and bacon." Eyebrows shot up to his hairline as his mouth dropped open, disbelieving she was taunting him at this hour of the night. Laurel stood and walked over to him so that they were standing toe to toe. Her head tilted so she looked up at him in profile with mischievous eyes. "I never promised to make it easy for you to win your dare."

CHAPTER 23

Jeannie pulled her Lexus in front of Shelby's Piedmont Estates home promptly at noon. Glancing at her watch, she couldn't believe she had made it on time. After hanging up with Shelby, she had gone through all of the saved newspapers, pulled the ones with the kidnapping story, and put their front pages in date order. She then called the deli to reserve a table and was delighted to find out some old friends from college were the new owners. Steve and Julie not only reserved a table, they gave her a private room upstairs when she asked if they had somewhere quiet to conduct a private business affair. She placed a quick call to George Yager to see if he could join them and, with a clear calendar in the current market, he said he would. Just as Jeannie was gathering up her purse and the papers to leave, George phoned back to tell her Greg Andrews would join them. He might be a little late since not all of the journalists in front of his home had left, but he assured George he would be there. Jeannie left for Shelby's with her heart a little lighter at the newly acquired reinforcements. She'd picked up the current *US News Report* with this morning's story on her way to pickup Shelby.

Jeannie placed the *US News Report* on the bottom of her stack in a bag on the back seat before getting out of her car. She was a little breathless from all the running around when she rang Shelby's doorbell. She was just about to ring the doorbell a second time when Shelby pulled the door open. "Jeannie, come in! Sorry I was so long answering the door, I was on the phone with my brother. He's been checking in on me at least once a week and I wanted to make sure I told him to wait for me to check in with him next week. I wasn't sure when I would be moving and I didn't know when I would be having my phone transferred."

Jeannie followed Shelby into the hallway and waited while she put on her coat and some gloves. "Shelby, you are looking so much better. You must have done something right—aside from looking like you could still use some sleep, no one would ever guess you so recently suffered a loss."

Shelby tensed up at the word "loss" and missed putting the button through its hole. It had been so nice not to hear words like that or see sympathetic faces for three weeks. "Thank you Jeannie, I'm trying to move ahead. I did tell you I had cut myself off from the world since you were away didn't I?" Finished with her buttons, she grabbed up her purse and keys indicating she was ready to go.

"Yes, you did. Let's go, shall we? I'm parked just out front."

"Great. I'm starting to get my appetite back. Where is this new deli you're taking me to?"

Jeannie opened the car doors and both women climbed in and fastened their seatbelts. Jeannie was relieved that if Shelby noticed the bag of papers in the rear seat, she didn't mention it. "It's in Hughson of all places and I had the nicest surprise when I phoned for reservations. A couple of friends I knew in college are the new owners."

Shelby had always been very good at "reading" people and she could tell that Jeannie was very nervous. This made Shelby nervous. "Oh, then why don't we discuss the development on my new house on the way so we can just enjoy lunch when we get there?"

Jeannie swallowed loudly; the moment had come. "Yes, that's what I had in mind. Can you reach the bag of newspapers on the back seat?"

Shelby hadn't noticed the bag when she got in the car and had to turn her head to see where it was. "Yes, I can."

"Excellent. While you took your escape from the world, there was a mystery that involves Laurel Andrews."

"Isn't she one of the current owners of my new house?"

"That's correct. Because it's a long story, I took the liberty of putting newspapers together in date order before I picked you up. I would appreciate your getting the bag and reading the papers while I drive." As Shelby started to do as requested, Jeannie stopped her hand. "Promise you won't say anything until you've finished with the entire stack."

Puzzled and a little alarmed, Shelby promised and then retrieved the bag. She slowly pulled the stack of a dozen or so papers out onto her lap and began to read as Jeannie drove.

Jeannie was gripping the steering wheel so hard her rings were cutting into her hand. As she navigated her way to the deli, the only sound in the car was

Shelby's gasp followed by "Oh My Lord!" and "That poor man." Shelby took a long time staring at the note pictured in the *US News Report*. Thirty minutes later, Jeannie was just parking the car in the lot as Shelby looked up at her. "I can see why you made me promise not to say anything."

"Yes and why I wanted to meet with you in person. As I told you on the phone, the sale of the home will go through, but it is up to you as to when, and if, you want to continue with the escrow. While Laurel Andrews was kidnapped outside the home and there is no sign of any foul play within the home, this still qualifies as a disclosure issue on the sale. We're here, let's go in. I hope you don't mind, but George Yager, the Andrews' realtor, and Greg Andrews will be joining us later."

Shelby did a slight pause in her walk and turned to Jeannie with that bit of news. "Do you think that's a good idea?"

Linking arms with Shelby, Jeannie continued to the deli's front door. "Absolutely or I wouldn't have gone to so much trouble for privacy." Jeannie held the door open for Shelby and was somewhat relieved to see no signs of anger in Shelby's face.

Jeannie followed Shelby through the door and a moment later was warmly greeting Steve and Julie. Shelby noticed they were a particularly attractive couple. Steve was the definition of tall, dark and handsome. Julie was the most feminine creature Shelby had ever seen. Hugs were passed all around and a smiling Julie planted a kiss on Jeannie's cheek. "Jeannie it is so nice to see you!"

Giggling and holding both Steve and Julie's hands, Jeannie nodded towards Shelby. The pleasure at seeing her old friends made her forget her worries for a moment "It's wonderful to see you too. May I introduce you to one of my lunch guests?" The stunning couple looked at Shelby. "This is my client, Shelby Abbot. Shelby, this is Steve and Julie Evans."

Shelby extended her hand towards Julie first. "It is very nice to meet you both. This is an absolutely charming little deli and the smells are wonderful."

Steve, his chest puffed with pride, put his arm around his wife. "It's all of my wife's idea. I think the aroma you're smelling is her mile high lasagna. Why don't I take you upstairs to your table with a couple of menus?"

Jeannie's mouth was beginning to water. "That would be great, Steve, but I don't need a menu. I think I'm going to have some of that lasagna. Will it be too much trouble to send the other two men in our party up when they arrive?"

Julie headed back behind the counter and Steve grabbed three menus while leading the way towards the stairs. "For you, Jeannie, anything. Will the men ask for you?"

"I told them to say my name."

"Then you don't need to worry; I'll bring them right up when they get here."

Steve ushered them into a single, warm nook created at the top of the stairs holding a table for four. He pulled out two of the chairs to seat the ladies and gave Shelby one of the menus. "Do you want to wait for the men to order or would you like to start with your salads now?"

Shelby looked up from perusing the menu and exchanged a look with Jeannie. "Shelby, do you know what you would like to order?"

"It all looks wonderful, but I agree with you, the lasagna smells fantastic."

"Steve, why don't we go ahead with the salads and bread. I'm not sure exactly how late the men will be."

"I'll be back in a minute with your salads. Raspberry vinaigrette sound good to you two?"

Both women nodded their agreement and Steve left them alone.

Jeannie placed her napkin on her lap, folded her hands under her chin and placed her elbows on the table so as to appear relaxed. "Shelby you now have all the facts in the case. Tell me, what are your initial thoughts about continuing with the escrow?"

Shelby couldn't share her first reaction with Jeannie. How to explain that she was extremely relieved that she had told her brother to wait for her to call him? If he knew what was going on with the house, he would have insisted she catch the next plane to Whitethorn where she would be "safe". "Jeannie, my first thoughts were for Greg Andrews. This must have been horrible to have to stand by, knowing he was innocent of any wrongdoing and wait for the process to get underway to find his wife. I cannot imagine the worry and stress he is going through. I know the neighborhood is safe, Jeannie, I searched the police records myself. I definitely want to buy the house, but I don't want to be involved in a circus of reporters flashing my business to the world."

Jeannie had just released her hands and sat back in relief when Steve, salads in hand, brought George Yager upstairs. "Ladies, the first gentleman has arrived."

George thanked Steve and leaned over to give Jeannie a kiss on the cheek. "Jeannie, it's nice to see you again. I wish the circumstances could have been better." Taking a seat, George reached his hand across the table to Shelby. "I'm George Yager, the Andrews' realtor and you must be Shelby Abbott?"

"Yes, I am. Thank you for taking the time to meet with us."

"No need to thank me, this is my job." Just as George was going to open a menu, Steve reappeared with Greg Andrews. "I believe everyone's here now, Jeannie."

"Thank you Steve. Can you wait a moment to see what the gentlemen might want to order?"

Before Steve could answer, George piped up with "I'll have whatever the ladies are having."

Greg had just taken the last seat at the table. "Make it two."

"Lasagna for four; Jeannie, would you like a house wine for everyone or some iced tea?"

Jeannie looked around the table for some votes one way or the other.

Shelby couldn't have alcoholic beverages while pregnant. "Steve, if you don't mind, could I have a glass of low fat milk?" Shelby blushed slightly as she realized she had certainly taken everyone by surprise.

Jeannie, ever the perfect hostess, continued without a hitch, "Gentlemen, what are your preferences?"

Both Greg and George wanted the iced tea. "Steve, could you bring a pitcher of iced tea and a glass of the wine for me?"

"The lasagna is ready, so I'll bring all four orders, the two salads and your drinks back up with me. I promise I'll leave you alone for the rest of your meal unless you ring that bell," he said while pointing. No one had noticed the little bell sitting next to a fern on a plant stand.

"Thanks so much Steve."

Jeannie put her hand out to Greg. "Hello, you must be Greg Andrews. I'm Jeannie Lawson and this is my client, Shelby Abbott."

Greg shook both ladies hands. "It's nice to meet you both and I want to thank you in advance for agreeing to this meeting given the circumstances."

George wondered aloud if Greg had been followed. "No, Karen Vincent, my wife's best friend, is back at the house to help out. Her car was parked in the garage. We used the automatic opener after I hid down on the passenger side so she could drive me here. I will call her cell phone when we're done to pick me up."

Shelby couldn't get over the haunted look of the man seated next to her. He looked like he had aged ten years from the picture she had seen on the home tour. "Mr. Andrews, may I say how very sorry I am about your wife?"

"Call, me Greg, and thank you."

Steve brought up the orders and George barely waited for him to leave to get down to business. "Jeannie, I presume you and Mrs. Abbott have discussed the situation?"

Shelby interrupted Jeannie's response. "Please call me Shelby."

"Yes, George we have. Shelby would like to move ahead with the escrow, but we need your input as to how to handle this. Greg, have you given any thought to the sale?"

"I admit that it was the furthest thing from my mind until I got the call from George. I know my wife would want the sale to go through. Just tell me what you need me to do."

Shelby had been listening intently as everyone else buzzed around her. "Please, may I say something?" All eyes turned to her. "I need to explain my situation so that you will understand exactly what my needs are. You all know I was recently widowed?"

Three voices answered to the affirmative. "What you don't know, what no one else knows, is that I'm three months pregnant." She paused a moment to let that sink in. "That's why I personally checked the neighborhood's safety record with the police and your alarm company. I'm responsible for keeping Sam and I's baby safe. That's also why I really need to move on time, I'm determined to get on with the business of living. I know I'm buying the house and all the furnishings, but there was one change I wanted to make and it must be done soon. That said; I'm sure we can't finalize the escrow until Laurel is found. We'll need her signature on the final paperwork." Looking at the two realtors, she continued. "I have the ability to pay your commissions up front and they can be deducted at the closing. What I can't figure out is how the changes can be made on the house and how I can get moved in without the newsmen finding out."

She swore she felt sighs of relief emanating from the two realtors. Greg had been toying with his salad while Shelby talked. He thought she was an extremely attractive woman when they were introduced. After her speech, he thought she was beautiful. "What change did you want to make?"

"I want to remove the master bedroom walk in closet and turn it into a seating area that will be open into Morgan's room. I will need to utilize the space as a nursery with connecting doors on either side of the seating area."

"George, I think I know how we can work this out."

"Well don't just sit there, man, speak up!"

"Shelby, you may not know this, but I'm in construction. I can move into the front guest room and start the nursery renovation immediately. It will give me something to do before I go nuts. If you don't mind living with our things for awhile, we could have you and your luggage moved in using a van exactly the way Karen got me here today."

"I don't get it, how would a van go unnoticed?"

"We would have Karen drive her car out of the garage and go over to get you and your things. She would return with you ducked down in the back of the van and pull straight into the garage using the automatic door opener. You would enter the house from the garage and no one would know you were there. Karen could pack her stuff out using the van and return for her car. Unless you open up the front windows and look out, no one is going to know you are there. I just talked with my boss yesterday and he expects me back at work in two weeks. I think I can finish your renovation of the nursery in one. Would you mind if I stayed in the guest room for a bit if it isn't quite done?"

Everyone watched while Shelby gave Greg's suggestion some thought. Nodding her head back and forth in a sing song motion, she smiled and lifted her milk glass. "Shall we toast to the new homeowner?"

CHAPTER 24

Lord David, dressed in swimsuit, robe and slippers, strolled down the corridor to the swimming pool with a cocky smile perking up his early morning face. He couldn't wait to see Laurel's face when he won their dare. She had underestimated his sleep requirements. He had never needed more than four or six hours sleep at night. His attitude did an abrupt about-face however, as he was about to enter the double glass doors into the pool. What in God's name was Roger doing frolicking in the pool with Laurel and his children? Unobserved, he watched them for a moment to see what was going on.

Roger and Laurel stood two feet apart facing Tim and Cat seated on the edge at the shallow end of the pool. Laurel could see that the children, while excited, were a little scared. "Now Tim, Cat, we practiced this before while you sat on the edge. This is just a little different. I want you to both get up on your knees and put your arms and hands out to prepare for a dive into the water." Cat and Tim exchanged a look to see who would do it first. Tim stayed put and Cat knew she was going to have to prove to be better than her little brother. She did exactly as Laurel directed. Tim immediately followed.

"Oh! I am so proud of you two, that's perfect. I'm going to count to three and Tim, I want you to dive in and swim to Master Roger. Cat, you dive in and swim to me. Ready? Okay here we go; one, two, three!" A big splash followed by a series of little kick splashes followed.

Tim, whether out of fear of the water or being a better swimmer, reached Roger first. "That's it Tim, excellent!"

Cat came up sputtering in front of Laurel a moment later and quickly became an extra limb attached to Laurel's body. Laurel hugged her close and patted her back. "Cat, that was wonderful!" Looking from one beaming face to another she gave them their due. "I have never seen any children learn to swim so quickly. You two are naturals." Still holding Cat in her arms, Laurel walked closer to Roger. "Master Roger, what do you say to a children's choice of a pool game as a reward for their remarkable achievements?"

"I agree, they have certainly earned it." Cat fell into the water, forgetting where she was and moving to jump up and down in her excitement. Laurel was pleased that she didn't panic and came back up to the surface sputtering, but also giggling. "Tim, I pick keep away!"

"But I wanted to play tugboat."

Lord David came through the double doors clapping his hands. "I say you deserve both!"

All heads turned in surprise at Lord David's entrance. He was pleased to see a shocked face from one swimmer in particular.

Both children had started swimming for the edge in record time at the sight of their father. Cat, ever the daddy's girl, beat Tim to the edge. "Papa, you're home! Did you see me dive? We've been practicing for four days."

Lord David had discarded his robe and slippers and taken a seat on the edge of the pool while he waited for Cat to run out of her bulleted prattle. He lifted Tim out of the water and onto his lap. "I got home late last night and your racket in here woke me up!" He tickled both giggling children's tummies. "Master Roger and Laurel I can't thank you enough for teaching the children how to swim. I've always been so concerned about their getting into the pool area. Now I can rest much easier. Do you mind if I join in?"

The children were thrilled at the thought of their father playing in the water with them. "Yes, oh yes, please?" they cried in unison.

Roger wasn't as thrilled as the children at his employer's entrance. He had completely enjoyed his time alone with Laurel the past few days. Hoping Lord David didn't notice how he felt, he graciously replied, "Lord David we would appreciate you helping these two tired adults with the games." He swam to the side of the pool, easily pulled himself out, grabbed a beach ball and hopped back into the water. "Cat, you picked keep away first. You get to pick who goes in the middle."

"I pick Laurel!"

Laurel groaned, "No fair! Oh, alright, I'll get in the middle." Laurel moved to the center dividing line in the shallow end.

Roger felt her misery. With Lord David on one end to help catch the ball and he on the other, she might never get out of the water. "Lord David, why don't you and Cat take one side of the pool and Tim and I will take the other."

"Come on Cat, let's go."

And so it went for another hour. The beach ball was tossed back and forth until Laurel finally caught it and put Cat in the middle in retaliation. Cat proved to be a clever minx when she waited until Tim was tossing the ball and gained her freedom. She put her father in the middle next and Roger and Laurel had great fun keeping him there for awhile. He finally got the ball and put Roger in the middle and thoroughly enjoyed the art of retaliation. The children never noticed how little they had the ball; they were having too much fun. After everyone had a turn in the middle, Lord David called a halt to the game. "It's getting late and I heard a rumor that we're having some ghastly concoction called chocolate chip pancakes for breakfast. Children, Roger and I will play Tim's tugboat game with you twice around the pool so Laurel can get started in the kitchen."

As Roger watched Laurel exit from the pool and prepared to grab Cat's hands, he wondered how Lord David knew about their breakfast plans.

Laurel had showered quickly and hurried back down to the kitchen. Emily had already started browning bacon. "Good morning, Emily. Did you notice David returned last night?"

"I started the bacon for you when I heard Lord David's voice from the pool. Can you manage the rest of your breakfast if I go get the children bathed?"

"You are amazing! Thank you."

Laurel pushed up her sleeves and donned an apron as Emily left for the pool. Thirty minutes later, David, Roger, Emily and the children were taking their places around the formal dining area. Laurel was happy that Emily was going to give the pancakes a try and shocked when Thomas, with Henry in tow, showed up as well.

The usually reserved Thomas confidently sat down next to his wife. "Laurel, could you feed a couple sorry blokes some breakfast?"

"I've made more than enough. I'll get some more place settings. Henry, could I request you serve Thomas and yourself some tea?"

"Thomas, are you wanting tea this morning?"

"Henry, I think I should drink something English if I'm going to chance a fancy Cal-I-forn-eye-ay concoction!"

Laurel was coming back with the place settings just in time for Thomas' joke. "I heard that and you better pray you don't find these pancakes to be your new favorite because you won't get more than three out of me!"

The happy group was seated and everyone had just filled their plates. Lord David tapped the side of his water glass with his spoon. "Everyone, I believe

I'm going to take advantage of our all being together to make an announcement. "Thomas and Emily, it has come to my attention that you have a fortieth wedding anniversary soon."

The couple had suspended their forks mid-air and given all their attention to their employer when he spoke their names. Thomas cleared his throat, "Yes, sir, we do. On November first I am proud to say I have been blessed with my Emily for forty years."

Everyone clapped their hands and cheered congratulations. Lord David used the spoon on his water glass again to quiet them down. "Congratulations! I hope I have made it clear to you both, well to all of you actually, that you are more to me than employees. Thomas and Emily, after breakfast you are to pack your bags for a two week trip to Paris. I have made all the flight, hotel and meal arrangements. I want you to go and celebrate a rare accomplishment in style."

Emily had gasped and covered her face at Lord David's surprise. Thomas was awestruck. "I don't know what to say, sir. Thank you."

Emily had recovered and started to think. "But, Lord David, we can't possibly go. Who will keep the house, grounds, order supplies, and do the cooking for two weeks?"

Lord David smiled benevolently at the woman who had been a second mother to him. "Emily, we will be 'enjoying' California cuisine and the women who have been helping their husbands and Laurel in the renovation have volunteered to take on the housekeeping. I'll take care of the gardens myself. I've also contacted Gwen and she will be returning tomorrow. Now, I won't take no for an answer and I want you to quit worrying. Anita has an eleven o'clock flight planned and she gets upset if you're late."

Emily and Thomas were hugging and holding hands. Roger caught a smile and a look between Lord David and Laurel. Henry was oblivious; his sweet tooth was enjoying his pancakes very much. The children had stopped paying attention the moment they realized there wasn't a surprise in store for them and continued eating.

As pandemonium ebbed, Lord David motioned to everyone to eat their breakfast. "Laurel, after the breakfast is cleared, are you available to meet with me and go over the fabrics I brought back for you?"

Laurel was happy to see every single one of her pancakes disappear. "Yes, David, I need to confirm I have everything I need to finish all of the curtains, spreads and pillows I've planned."

Lord David looked at his watch. "It's ten o'clock now. Why don't I meet you back here in forty-five minutes and we can see Thomas and Emily off on their trip first?"

"That would be perfect. Emily, do you need any help with anything?"

"No, thank you Laurel, I did laundry just yesterday. I should be able to pack for Thomas and me with no trouble."

"I guess I'll see everyone back here in forty-five minutes then."

With that, everyone left the tables to do their individual tasks. Roger took the children for a quick lesson in their reading to calm them down after securing permission for them to join the send off. Henry and Lord David left to take care of the necessary correspondence and messages accumulated over the past four days. Emily and Thomas, holding hands and talking in hushed excitement with their heads bent together, hurried to get themselves packed. Laurel, heart bursting with happiness, tackled clearing the table and cleaning up the breakfast dishes.

Forty-five minutes later, everyone bundled in coats against the chilled air and then walked out to the airstrip to see Thomas and Emily off. Anita helped them board and then briefly stopped to talk with Lord David. "I think we're going to make it before the rain starts."

"That's good news. I'm not sure if Thomas and Emily are nervous fliers or not."

Anita smiled, "Judging by the smiles on their faces, I don't think they would even notice a lightning storm."

"Well, we'll pray your theory goes untested. Have a safe flight."

Anita, waving hello and goodbye to everyone, turned and headed for her plane, "Thank you, I'm sure we will."

The children stood at their father's feet as everyone watched the plane take-off. "Children, I want you to return to your studies with Master Roger. I'll see you again after your lessons."

"Yes, papa," they happily replied. The weather was simply too cold today for them to beg to ride the horses.

Henry watched the threesome depart and inquired about the morning plans. "Lord David do you need my assistance in opening the fabrics for Laurel's review?"

"Actually, Henry, I would appreciate it if you would start spreading them out on tables while I discuss some business with Laurel. We will be up to help with the task in, oh, I'd say about thirty minutes or so."

"I'll see to it immediately."

"Laurel, I had hoped to walk in the gardens while we talked, but it is too cold. Do you mind another cup of tea in the library instead? I don't want to be overheard."

"I think anything hot in any room <u>inside</u> sounds wonderful."

Taking her arm, Lord David quickly walked them back inside the castle. They hung their coats in the mudroom and made their way to the kitchen. David sat on a stool while Laurel prepared the tea. "How did someone living in California learn to prepare tea properly?"

"I didn't. Emily taught me shortly after I arrived as a caution against her "having a heart attack". She's actually explained "high tea" and all of that to me in case you need me to take care of that while she's away."

David had started laughing at the thought of Emily's disgusted face when she observed Laurel brewing tea improperly. "No, I think I'll be fine for a couple of weeks. You do know that Henry is completely capable of preparing tea, don't you?"

"David, I've only figured out everything Emily does to keep this castle running. I haven't had time to figure Henry out beyond what I am going to design in his quarters."

"Simple designing I would imagine."

Laurel looked up, clearly surprised. "You've never really talked with Henry, have you?"

"What do you mean? Of course I've talked with Henry."

"You lie! If you have ever really talked with him, other than as his employer, you would know that his quarters are the biggest surprise of all."

One of David's eyebrows rose up to his hairline in vexation. "What are you doing for Henry?"

Laurel smirked and shook her head as she put their tea on a tray. "There's no way I'm telling you that mister! You're going to have to wait and see just like everyone else."

David was trailing the laughing Laurel carrying the tray on their way to the library. Frustrated at not having his curiosity satisfied, he spouted "Is everyone else paying you to design his quarters?"

Setting the tray down on the table, Laurel turned and crossed her arms across her chest. "No, you are. And as I keep reminding you, I have complete design control over the interior of the castle. I don't recall our bargain containing any language about your having advance "peeks" because you were giving me a million dollars...."

Both David's eyes rolled to the ceiling as he seated her in a chair to quiet her and took a seat across from her for himself. He wondered how long it was going to take him to learn to watch for her traps and not accept the bait. "Fine, you win! I'll wait along with everyone else."

Laurel, satisfied that she had won, calmly poured him a cup of tea and passed it to him. "Do you want cream or sugar?"

"One sugar, please. Thank you."

David was appalled at Laurel's drinking her tea plain. "You're going to drink it like that?"

Glaring, "Yes, David, I am. Do you want to continue critiquing my likes and dislikes or get down to business?"

Put in his place, David rose to retrieve a pen and paper from the desk. Seating himself again, he wrote the word "Party" at the top of the page. "You are correct, I apologize if I hurt your feelings. I suggest we make three lists: one that is an itinerary of sorts for the party, one for guests, and the last one for supplies and/or vendors."

Laurel noticed his pen and beautiful handwriting. "That's a gorgeous pen. Where did you get it?"

"It was a gift from my father when I graduated from university; I take it with me everywhere I go."

"May I try it?"

David wasn't surprised at her desire to write with the pen. It was simply a design tool she couldn't resist using to make ordinary handwriting into beautiful script. He passed the pen and paper across the table to her. "Be my guest."

Laurel wrote her name at the top of the next page. "I love it!"

"You're going to have to settle for the money; I'm not giving you my father's pen."

"Okay, okay." She slid the paper and pen back across the table to him. "I like you're idea of the lists. Before we start, though, did you give any thought about how we are going to get in touch with the family members?"

"Yes, I did. You and I will meet with Gwen tomorrow night. She is due in at seven o'clock. By the way, are you going to put Gwen in her new quarters?"

"No. That wouldn't be fair to everyone else and we already have to trust her with our secret about the party. I was thinking of putting her in the "older girl's" bedroom in the family wing while we finish all of the staff's quarters."

"That is a very good idea. She will be close by the children if I should get called away on business again."

He was very pleased to watch Laurel's emotions in her huge green eyes. First, sadness; he supposed over not having the children in with her again, and then alarm. "You have to leave again? When and for how long?"

"Good God, woman, you're starting to sound like Cat. I don't get to answer the first question before you toss out another one!"

Laurel's huge eyes never wavered, "Well, are you leaving again?"

"Not that I'm aware of, but I wasn't given advance notice of my last meeting either."

She relaxed down in her seat. "I hope you don't have to go again, I mean, it will be hard to pull this party off in two weeks as it is, let alone by myself."

"Stop worrying. Now, tell me what you are planning for the day."

Laurel did better than that. Before David could stop her, she grabbed the paper and pen from him. She put the page with "party" at the top to his left. On a second page, she wrote "guests" at the top and put that directly in front of him. On a third page, she wrote "supplies" at the top and put that to his right. She then handed him back his pen. David could do nothing but fill the three pages with hastily scribbled notes as she closed her eyes and recited every detail of the day's requirements. Laurel finished her recital and opened her eyes to see David finishing his last note. He looked up at her expectant face, clearly impressed with her peculiar talent, as she asked, "What do you think?"

Smiling, he dropped the pen and put his hand on top of hers, "I think we're going to have one hell of a party!"

CHAPTER 25

A week after Shelby Abbott sealed the deal on her new home, Karen Vincent waved goodbye to Greg as she went out the back door of his house and into the garage. She took a look around after opening the garage door to see exactly how many reporters were in front of the house. Relieved at the sight of only one, she got in her car and headed out to pick up Shelby Abbott. Driving carefully, Karen glanced in the rearview mirror occasionally on her way to Piedmont Estates. When she was sure no one was following her, she turned at the next stoplight and circled around to park in the Abbott driveway.

Inside, Shelby had just finished a long letter to her brother. Talking to herself, and to Sam, she skimmed over the letter one more time. "This has to be perfect, Sam, so David won't give me a hard time. Let's see, I told him I checked the police reports and security company so I know the neighborhood is safe. I mentioned twice that Mrs. Andrews was not taken from her home—she was on the street and that her husband has been proved innocent of any involvement whatsoever. He'll see the kidnappers note for himself when he reads the papers." Satisfied, she was placing the letter in a box filled with the newspapers from her meeting with Jeannie when the doorbell rang.

Karen knew from Greg's description that the woman answering the door was Shelby Abbott. "Mrs. Abbott? Good morning, I'm Karen Vincent."

"Good morning Karen. Please come in and won't you call me Shelby?"

"Thank you, I will. Are you ready to play famous person hiding from paparazzi and check out the progress on your new home?"

"You have no idea. Would you mind if we stopped at the mail center a few blocks from here on our way?" Referring to Karen's celebrity from her link to the Andrews, she teased "I have a package I want to send to my brother and I don't think this famous person should go to the post office with another famous person."

Shelby had just made a friend for life. Laughing, Karen volleyed back "I have no problem making the stop, I just want to watch you try to casually duck down in my car, in that suit, when you try getting back in." Karen couldn't help but envy Shelby's simple long tan skirt over stylish brown boots. "Didn't Greg tell you I'm driving a Honda Civic?"

Without missing a beat, Shelby finished putting on her coat as she replied, "Yes he did and I want you to know that this famous person is extremely graceful." Both women doubled over in laughter at Shelby's quick retort. Remembering their mission, Shelby turned serious again, "He also suggested that I put some of my things in grocery bags so it will look like you've been to the market." Going to a coat closet in the hallway, Shelby pulled out three filled grocery bags, each filled halfway with shoes. "Do you think this will do?"

"I think they're perfect. You grab your package and I'll carry the bags."

Shelby locked the front door behind Karen and took a deep breath of the cool autumn air. "Were there many reporters in front of the house when you left?"

Setting the bags in the back seat, Karen opened the passenger side for Shelby, "Just one. I think Tyler's appeal on *Eye on Keddie* actually got through to them. They know the only news that will be released to the public will come through the police. I'm curious which rag this reporter is from. He has to be from something like *The National Enquirer* if he's staying in front of the house. If he wanted something credible and not juicy, he would be at the police department."

"I think you're right. Turn left at the next light. The mail center is in the little corner complex at the far end. Did you bring a blanket to throw over the top of me?"

"Yes, it's on the floor behind your seat. Ah, there's the mail center and an open parking space right in front of their door. I'll wait here while you go in."

"I'll just be a minute."

Out of habit, Karen perused the parking lot for reporters while Shelby was in the center. Ten minutes later, her business done, Shelby came around to the passenger side of the door. Karen burst into laughter as she flung open the door with an exaggerated motion and "floated" her way knees first into the car. Her stomach flat on the seat and head on hands, she tried to stifle her laughter as Karen checked out her position. "Am I down far enough below the windows?"

Karen did a combination hiccup-snicker as her laughter came to a stop, "Yes." Reaching behind the seat, she pulled out the blanket. "Let me put this over you and I'll buzz us over to the house."

The single reporter was still in front of the house when Karen returned. She hit the garage door opener from the street so she wouldn't have to wait in the driveway while it opened; she didn't want the reporter to have time to get close to her car.

Once inside the garage, Karen sat still as she punched the button to close the door. Shelby popped out of the blanket the minute she heard the heavy door close against the concrete. Karen could tell Shelby was having a hard time trying to get out of the car. Just as she was going around the car to help her, Greg came out of the house and pulled the passenger side door open. "What in the world? Shelby however did you get yourself in there like that?"

"Didn't you know I was a very graceful famous person?"

Karen laughed so hard at Shelby's comment and the expression on Greg's face she dropped her purse. Greg didn't know what the hell Shelby was talking about, but he'd learned a lot from twenty years of his wife's dry wit and knew when not to ask questions. "Well, thank you for sharing that information. Here, grab my hand."

Shelby tossed the blanket into the driver's seat and let Greg assist her from the car. "Thank you Greg. This really worked! I'm in here and the reporter didn't see me! Let's get the grocery bags and go in; I can't wait to see the nursery."

Greg handed each of the women a bag and then took the last one. Karen led the way as they followed each other like mules on a mountain trail through the back door.

Karen and Greg waited at the nursery door and let Shelby look over the room. "Oh, Greg, I love it! I can tell it's going to be perfect. Your suggestion to use French doors on either side of the seating area was a good one. I like that I can leave one or both doors open to hear the baby." She moved into the seating area where a new closet area and the walls weren't quite done. "How long do you think it's going to take you to finish?"

"I need a little more lumber to finish the closet space. I called one of the guys at the lumber yard that I know. He'll be delivering the wood tomorrow. I have to texture the walls that remain from the walk in closet to match the other two rooms before I can paint them. Given the rain we're expecting, I think it's going to be about a week if I allow for drying time."

"Hmmm. I scheduled the utility changes and my move for five days from now. Would it be possible for you to texture and paint first?"

"I guess so, why?"

"I think you and I are going to be roommates for a couple of days and I can't be in paint fumes; it might hurt the baby."

"Oh, God, you're right. Okay, I'll texture tomorrow and put a couple of fans in here. I should be able to paint the day after that. If I keep the fans running, I should be able to get all of the fumes out of here before you move in."

Retracing her steps to where Karen and Greg stood, she put her hands out to both of them. "Thank you, both. I appreciate more than words can say what you're doing to help me get settled in our new home, especially under the circumstances. Greg, what are your plans once you leave here while the search continues for Laurel?"

"I have to go back to work." Putting a hand on Karen's shoulder, "and Karen has to go to India and write the book that's been delayed. I'm going to house sit for her so I can still be in town in case there's a break in the case and they find my wife."

"My prayer is that they find her safe and sound. I hate to do this, but could I ask you two for one more favor?"

Karen and Greg were more than happy to help Shelby get started on her new life. "Sure" they replied in unison.

"Would you mind terribly taking down the bed in the nursery? I have a crib to put up in there and a basinet on wheels for somewhere in the seating area. I can't have anyone in here to help me and I can't take the bed down by myself."

Greg got a little misty eyed at the thought of the baby that would be living in his house. "I'll take care of that tonight. Do you need me to put the crib and basinet together?"

"How would you be able to do that? My movers will take them to storage until after the reporter's have seen you move out."

"Are they at your house now?"

"Yes they are."

"Karen, are you up for a little more cat and mouse play?"

Karen knew exactly what Greg had in mind. "Greg, you know me; I'm always up for a little adventure."

"Shelby, I'll ride back to your house when Karen takes you home. I can duck down in the back seat. Once we're there, I can assemble the crib and basinet for you."

Shelby's face brightened at Greg's offer. "You'd do that for me?

"You bet."

"You two are the sweetest people I've ever met. I'm glad my hormones have calmed down or I'd be blabbering all over your sleeves, Greg."

Greg took hold of her upper arm, "Shelby, we're glad we could help. You've been a real blessing for me. I can't tell you how much I appreciate your giving me something to keep my mind from going crazy." Squeezing her arm gently, he released her and turned to Karen.

"Karen, what's your reason for going out this time?"

"I'm so glad you asked, Greg. We have some clothes to be picked up at the cleaners I forgot earlier and some books to return to the library."

"That's urgent stuff, we better get moving. Shelby, why don't you lead the way so you can teach me how to get my posterior gracefully into the back seat of the car." The two women fell into each other's arms in hysterics. They grabbed Greg between them when they straightened up and pulled him along as they led the way out.

CHAPTER 26

Late in the afternoon, four and a half weeks after Laurel's arrival at Whitethorn, Lord David decided to take a grand tour of the completed project. He walked from one room to the next spectacular room, as a sense of peace, warmth and contentment grew brighter and brighter. He knew his heart was going to stop beating in a few days when he had to take Laurel home. Looking around him and feeling newly born, he didn't care what price he would be paying for his actions.

The end of his tour landed him at the top floor of the keep. He could hear everyone rehearsing their program for the party in the ballroom. He kept his pace slow as he first looked at the conservatory and art studio side of the floor. Walking across the hallway, he entered the wide double doors to the ballroom. Laurel was just finishing practice on a ballet routine with Cat. His staff, along with the workmen and their wives, was all up on stage gathered around the grand piano. "Am I late?"

As usual, Laurel gave him her complete attention when she heard his voice. She became a little flustered at his stare. She could feel heat from the caress of his eyes across the vast room, "Only a little bit." To break the spell, she put her hands on Cat's shoulders. "Roger played Cat's music a little slower and she is now able to match her dance to the tempo perfectly."

"That's wonderful, Cat. We better get started. We only have three days until the party."

David caught up with Laurel and Cat on his way to the stage. He couldn't believe he agreed to the program they were putting on, or that he was having so much fun doing it. Laurel was delighted to find out from her talk with Gwen when she returned that all four of the workmen and their wives were part of the same church choir as she. She was even happier when she sat down with Gary, Diane, Lewis, Teresa, John, Lucy, Leighton and Charity that they adored Thomas and Emily and wanted to be part of the program. The group had worked well together and David knew they would dazzle the guests of honor.

Cat hurried to sit next to her brother so they could watch everyone perform. Laurel took her place next to the ladies and had just turned to await Roger's opening chords. Lord David interrupted Roger's beginning, "May I have everyone's attention for a moment please." All eyes turned to Lord David. "Thank you. I want to take a moment before we begin our last practice session to tell you I took a complete tour just now of the new Whitethorn Castle. I can't tell you how pleased I am with the magnificent results and how exceptional your work has been. That you are now going above and beyond to join me in making fools of ourselves for the love we share for Thomas and Emily is to be commended." Everyone clapped and laughed with good humor at Lord David's speech. "I want to make sure everyone has their costumes and their invitation for dinner before the performance."

Various voices in the group erupted with "yes sir" and "yes, thank you."

"I would also like to request that my staff stay after the practice for a brief meeting." Roger, Gwen, and Henry all nodded their agreement. David, his arm extended, palm up toward Roger, continued "Maestro will you please begin our first number?"

One hour later, the workmen and their wives left and Lord David took center stage. Looking at the happy faces surrounding him, he pulled Laurel away from the group and next to his side. "Some of you may remember my friend, Donovan Metcalf, a photo-journalist I worked with when President Clinton was touring some of my buildings. He will be arriving here the morning of our celebration and spending the night. He is going to be creating a piece about the castle renovation for publication." Everyone was speechless. There had been so many changes—good changes—in such a short time. The staff had become familiar with Lord David's penchant for seclusion and had only adjusted to the opening of the castle doors within the community. To open the castle to the world in the form of a publication was quite a leap.

Roger, happy that Laurel's talent would be shared with more than just the castle and its inhabitants, stepped forward to shake Lord David's hand. "That's amazing and wonderful, sir. What can we do to help Mr. Metcalf?"

"First of all, just be yourselves. I will give him a tour upon his arrival. He will be taking photographs both in daylight and during the dinner party in the evening. Right now, I think we need to get you three settled into your new quarters, don't you agree Laurel?"

Laurel put her hands up in surrender, "You'll receive no argument from me David."

David looked at the others, "You all heard her say that didn't you?" Laughter abounded as David took Tim's hand and Laurel took Cat's to lead everyone on their way.

Exiting the elevator at the second floor, David turned to Laurel. "Laurel, where shall we begin?"

"I was taught "ladies first" in California."

"Yes, well the custom was started in England," he replied smugly. "Gwen, are you ready?"

Gwen was about to bust the seams out of her dress, she was so excited. "Yes sir!"

"Laurel, would you do the honors?"

Laurel was getting nervous as she took the lead to Gwen's suite. She always dreaded having to watch and wait for a reaction to find if a patron truly loved or merely tolerated her creation. Laurel opened the door to the main room of Gwen's quarters and stepped aside. She had planned to wait in the hall, but David pulled her along with him as he entered at the back of the pack.

None of the staff had been told they were going to be assigned suites to live in. Gwen was awed at the beauty of her bedroom. Laurel's talks with Gwen produced knowledge of a teenager's love of anything having to do with California. Laurel did the entire suite in royal blue and the exact gold of the California poppy. The bedspread and the pillows of the seating area chairs were made from chintz in blue with scattered poppies. All of the furniture was rattan to give the room the feel of the beach. Seashells decorated the tables and ocean themed pictures hung on the walls. Two coffee table books were on the table in the seating area. The book on top was a pictorial of California's favorite tourist attractions. Gwen's surprise was the book on the bottom. It was filled with surfers, all tan and gorgeous men, of course, and their boards. "Oh my God" Gwen twirled and danced through the room, obviously delighted. She turned and charged through the group to get to Laurel. Practically hugging the breath out of her, Laurel could barely hear her. "I love my room and I love you! Thank you, this is the most gorgeous room I've ever lived in!"

Lord David tried to pry the woman off of Laurel. "Gwen, don't you think you should see the rest?"

"Oh, yes, Lord David, I'm so sorry." Looking at Laurel, "Whose room are we seeing next?"

Lord David took hold of Gwen's elbow and turned her back into the room, "The rest of yours." Surprised, Gwen stared up at Lord David, not comprehending what he was talking about. Lord David looked from Gwen to include the two other men in his vision. "Laurel seems to not only have a talent for interior decorating, but also for living life. She brought to my attention that you have all become part of a family; my family. Roger and Henry, I'm surprised that neither of you said anything about being moved from one room to the next on the third floor as redecorating took place. Each of you now has a suite on this floor that will be considered yours." Laurel was both humbled at David's praise and happy to see the three faces light up with pleasure. Pointing to one of two doors, Lord David set out to explain, "You heard me correctly. Gwen, that door is not a closet, but a doorway into your personal water closet. The other door leads to a private sitting area, kitchen nook, and guest room with another water closet. I want each of you to accept your suites as your personal homes. That means that Gwen, you should invite your children and grandchildren to visit you and spend the night as guests. Roger and Henry, I have no idea if you have friends or family nearby that you would like to invite, but if so, please do. Also, if either of you decides to marry one day, I hope you will bring your brides to live with you at Whitethorn rather than leave."

Gwen, Roger and Henry were all feeling extremely blessed. The explicit invitation about bringing a bride to Whitethorn particularly touched Roger. "Sir, I don't know what to say. I must admit, I've been giving some thought to settling down and starting a family, but I am really happy here. I was sure I would have to leave Whitethorn, and all of you, if I was ever going to marry."

Lord David pulled Laurel next to his side again. "I'm very glad we were able to accomplish righting the situation. I'm just sorry I didn't realize the need sooner. Gwen, hurry and look at the rest of your suite so we can move on!"

Gwen was only too happy to comply with this particular order. Everyone but Lord David and Laurel quickly followed Gwen through the door to the sitting area. David put a finger under Laurel's chin to raise her face so that she was looking at him. "Do you think you can calm down now? I repeat, I did a complete tour of your work earlier and judged my home to be magnificent. I can feel your nervousness from ten feet away. I promise you, everyone is going to love what you've done." Lifting his hand and tapping her on her nose, he pulled her along to join the others, "I command you to relax and enjoy your moment in the sun immediately."

The moment David's fingers lifted her chin and her eyes stared directly into his, Laurel forgot her worries about design and started worrying about the feeling curling through her body. Lowering her gaze when he tapped her nose, she tried to hide the conflicting emotions even she didn't quite understand. She responded lightly with "I believe I have already agreed not to argue with you—at least for today."

The group moved on to tour Roger's suite. His was right next to Gwen's. It didn't take Laurel long to discover Roger's love of music. She had done his room as a masculine melody. Mocha stained walls were complimented by a bed covered with a creamy, off-white cotton spread dotted with musical note covered pillows. Plump, mocha, cotton covered chairs had black piping outlining their curves. The group was delighted to find a violin, viola and mandolin hung in ivory matted shadow boxes on the walls. Taking Roger's position into consideration, the sitting area included a set of mahogany bookshelves and a desk. Laurel was thrilled with Roger's joyous reaction to his surprise—she had done a mosaic in cream, black and tan in a paisley print on the face of a cello and placed it on a stand in the room. He had to stop Cat and Tim from trying to play with it.

Henry was having a very difficult time maintaining his usual reserved manner. He was so impressed with Gwen and Roger's suites that he was finding it impossible not to keep mentioning the closeness to the dinner hour so that they would hurry along to his. Unfortunately, Lord David didn't properly catch his hint. "Yes, Henry, I can tell by the delicious smells coming from the kitchen that dinner is close. Laurel, what are we having for dinner?"

Looking at Henry's face, Laurel came to his aid, "We're having Yankee Pot Roast, Red Potatoes, Carrots, Green Salad, Fresh Bread and I made an apple pie for dessert. I think we had better move on to Henry's suite so things don't get overdone."

Henry stopped himself from a loud cheer by clapping his hands together. Lord David didn't realize he had been manipulated. "Oh, well then, let's go across the hall to Henry's room, shall we?"

Henry almost caught Lord David's heel with his shoe, he was following so closely. Laurel moved next to him and took his hand before opening the door. Second only to the master suite, Henry's rooms were her most enjoyable part of the project. Lord David was jealous as he observed her watching Henry's face closely to catch his reaction. He didn't like her holding his hand either. Henry took a sweeping look at the room and had never been so touched. She had designed a room that was so tasteful and he instantly recognized elements reminiscent of his favorite James Bond movies. Unlike the natural wood and rattan of the other rooms, his had been done with modern chrome and glass furnishings. The headboard on his bed was a sleek, six inch wide polished matte chrome surface. Laurel had covered the bed in a deep navy satin quilted spread. Six pillows covered in quilted satin shams in the colors of ivory, navy and silver were layered against the headboard. On top of the headboard, a standing, glass covered, domed clock had been placed at the center. At just that moment, the glass split open down the center and the face broke into four even pieces revealing seven o'clock on a digital insert. The chairs next to the bed were more of the matte metal in an s-shape with striped navy, silver and white pillows. A chrome edged glass table was between the chairs and had a black and ivory striped, bowl shaped pipe and ashtray on top. Henry squeezed Laurel's hand. "Thank you. This is remarkable."

"I'm glad you're pleased, however, as we discussed many times, I would really like you to consider giving up smoking. You should never think I'm going to give up on you just because I gave you a pipe. It is perfectly acceptable as an accent piece," she admonished.

"For you, dear lady, I'll try."

"Let's look at your sitting room quickly before the meat burns."

Henry took one look in the sitting room and knew what she had wanted him to see—his surprise. On top of a mirrored bar in the corner, she had put a martini set. He moved closer to read a note folded next to the set and burst into laughter. *Remember, shaken, not stirred, Love, Laurel,* had been written in script. She had also framed two James Bond Movie posters in floating glass within a silver edged frame above a simple navy sofa.

Lord David couldn't take another moment of the obvious affection between Laurel and Henry. Jealousy erased his ability to see Henry as a father-figure and the folly of his emotion since she was, after all, a married woman. "I'm glad you are all so pleased with your new rooms but I think we had better get down to dinner before it's burned and you have no time remaining to move your things before retiring this evening."

Henry turned around as he was about to go through the door and faced Lord David. "Sir, I forgot to tell you a large package from Lady Shelby arrived today. I put it on the desk in your room for you."

CHAPTER 27

Early in the morning on her last day at Whitethorn, Laurel was busy packing for the trip home. She knew the light knocking at her door had to be David. "Come in."

David's heart clutched at the sight of Laurel packing to leave him. He had been up most of the night thinking about how he would get through the day. "I see you received the luggage I ordered." He looked over her shoulder at the pieces spread on the bed. "Do you need more?"

Laurel stopped her packing, turned and looked at him with a bemused expression. She noticed that he seemed different. She couldn't explain how, but she could feel it. "How ironic that you are wondering if you can purchase more of the luggage you purchased for me to take home a designer wardrobe you also purchased for me. No, David, there's plenty of room in these."

"Can you take a break and sit with me for a minute before things start getting crazy? I need to talk to you."

For a brief moment, she thought she saw concern in his eyes and worried that something had gone wrong for today's festivities, "Of course. Is everything alright?"

He took hold of her arm to escort her to the chairs and regretted it instantly. The silky satin robe was enticing to look at on her fabulous form and, at his touch, too tempting a combination for him to resist without a will of iron. "Yes, no need to worry. I wanted to talk to you about some business; specifically I want to talk to you about becoming a partner with me."

David would be forever grateful that he learned to read her emotions by watching her beautiful green eyes. He could tell she was pleased with his offer.

"You want me as a partner in your business? David, I'm flattered, but let's be realistic. Even if I wanted to accept, I couldn't possibly. I live in California and your business is in England. I can't just up and leave my home for six weeks at a time whenever a client wants to utilize my services."

"Laurel, I wouldn't make you an offer like this if I hadn't thought of a way for it to work successfully. We haven't talked about your husband since you told me of your difficulties. Have you made any decisions regarding your personal life?"

Laurel looked at her lap and played with the wedding ring on her finger. "Yes, David I have however, I don't want to talk about any decisions I've made with you before talking with my husband."

"I'm sorry, I didn't mean to interfere somewhere I don't belong. I had two different solutions in mind, one if you continued to live in California and one if you became free to move to England."

Her head popped up fast and eyes opened wide when he said that! "Move to England? David, whether I remain married or not, I'm not sure I could live in England. All of my family and friends are in the United States."

This time it was she that read emotional turmoil in David's eyes. He was surprised at how quickly the familiarity of pain and sadness could return at the thought of losing the woman he loved. "Very well, I'll tell you my plan that allows you the ability to remain in California. If a client having their castle renovated or built desires your interior design services, I could take a virtual tour video hosted by the clients of any existing structure and send it to you with a complete floor plan and copy of the work schedule. You would be able to get a feel for what the clients would like in their living spaces and work out the logistics from the floor plan while at home. You would only need to meet with the clients once early in the project to confirm the colors, fabrics and style you have planned. You would give me any details requiring skilled workmen to complete at this time. Then, during the manual construction phase, you would be able to order your supplies. I think you would only need to return for three to four weeks at the end of the renovation to complete the interiors."

Laurel listened carefully while he detailed his plan and, since their minds were completely in sync, easily followed his thinking. "You've just made my day much lighter David. I was trying to think how I would make it through the day without completely breaking into tears. I have enjoyed designing the interior renovation of Whitethorn more than you'll ever know. I was extremely depressed at the thought of never getting to do something like this ever again and at not seeing you, I mean all of you, on a regular basis. This would work,

David, no matter what happens with Greg and I. Is it alright if I accept your offer of partnership now?"

She would never know how much of his soul David had just sacrificed for her. If she stayed with her husband and he could only be near her a few weeks a year, and then never as he desired to be, a part of his heart would die. David leaned forward in his chair and took Laurel's hands between his own. "We're in agreement then. You do know that, as a partner, you will only get a percentage of the profits from any project you complete don't you?"

Warmed by his hands and his humor, she was able to tease, "Yes and I don't care about the size of the percentage. You do know I would have taken on Whitethorn for considerably less than a million dollars, don't you?"

"If I had I wouldn't have deposited the money into a Swiss bank account for you this morning." Releasing her hands to reach into his coat pocket, he removed an envelope. "In here you'll find all the information you need to personalize the bank account and move it however you like. I've also put five thousand dollars in cash in here for your immediate use."

"Oh, David, it's too much. I know I said you had to pay me a million dollars, but surely you know I really didn't expect that, let alone a bonus."

"Laurel I would have paid more than that for what you have brought into our lives. I insist you take the money. You are going to have to consult with an accountant about any taxes you will be responsible for paying. I thought by depositing the money in a Swiss account you may not have to declare it as income, but I didn't have time to verify that."

"I hadn't even thought of that. How do I ever thank you?"

"You already have, you brought me and my family back into the world." Looking out her window he could see the sun starting to rise. "I better let you finish your packing so you have time for breakfast before Donovan arrives."

An hour before Donovan Metcalf was due to arrive at the castle, Laurel and Gwen were showing Gwen's son, Richard, and daughter-in-law, Rosemary, their guest room. Their three children would be staying with Gwen in her suite. They had no sooner finished introducing Cat and Tim to their new friends when Thomas and Emily's daughter, Maryann, and son-in-law, Daniel, arrived with two more children. Laurel showed Maryann and Daniel to their guest room while Gwen made sure all of the children became acquainted with one another. Everyone gathered back at the great room to pick up their Halloween costumes. Tim started pealing his clothes off where he stood he was so excited to get the "rocket man" costume Laurel had made for him on. She had made a delicate looking, white feathered swan ballerina costume for Cat. The nine family members had just left to change into their costumes when Lord David came through the front door with Donovan Metcalf.

"Donovan, let me introduce you to the interior designer responsible for Whitethorn's renovation. Laurel, this is Donovan Metcalf and Donovan, it is my pleasure to introduce you to Laurel Andrews."

Donovan didn't move to shake hands right away as he was craning his neck left, right and then straight up in wonder at his surroundings. If he hadn't walked through a doorway into the main keep, he would have thought they were still out of doors. The room had a full size, live oak tree surrounded by an ornamental iron fence, centered in the room under a colorful canopy provided by the most gorgeous stained glass windows he had ever seen. The entire room had been altered so as to appear to be gardens, complete with stone walkways and a fountain spilling water into a pond in front of a mauve stained stone wall. Country styled sofas and chairs in shades of slate blue and mauve were at each of the four corners. Dried heather had been strategically placed in painted clay vases throughout. Realizing he was gawking, he brought himself into the present and put his hand out to the stunning woman standing before him. "I'm so sorry, but I could have sworn I was still outside. It's my pleasure to meet you Laurel. Lord David, how did you get a tree in here?"

David wasn't surprised at Donovan's reaction—it was exactly what he knew anyone's would be. "Donovan, you've only just begun to experience the fruits of this beautiful woman's mind. Why don't you just enjoy a tour for now and I can fill you in on the details of the renovation over our lunch?"

"That works for me. Let me just check my camera lighting and I'll follow your lead."

"Actually Donovan, you and I will both be following Laurel's lead." David silenced the stunned recipient of his intended command with a confident look. "Laurel, why don't we start with the family wing?"

Laurel was thinking of a certain duet they had during tonight's program that would give her the perfect opportunity to get even for David's latest surprise. Ever the gracious hostess, Laurel used her arm to indicate the direction to the family wing. "Certainly; Donovan, we'll be starting in this direction."

Donovan, reassured he would get the castle's plan details at lunch, never asked another question during his tour. He was in seventh heaven over the large quantity of photographs he could snap everywhere they went. He couldn't wait to take photographs of Cat and Tim's rooms in the evening light to capture the murals in their rooms. He also wanted to see the great room with all of the candles lit and the lighting placed on the underside of each of the four floor's edges shining up to the stained glass windows. Donovan took an adorable picture of all of the costumed children enjoying *Beauty and the Beast* in the former salon that was now a state-of-the art theater. He was also able to take a picture of Roger swimming laps in the pool and then working out in the gym. He was as delighted with the staff's suites as the occupants were. While he was shown the third floor guest rooms, David took the opportunity to show him where he would be staying. The eight guest rooms and their accompanying baths had been done completely in jewel tones: two red, two blue, two green and two purple. Every one of the rooms had ornate four poster beds and renaissance era wardrobes and chairs. In keeping with the renaissance look, ornate banners had been hung on the walls. Laurel had relaxed after Donovan's response to Cat and Tim's rooms. Workers, under Henry's supervision, were busy setting up tables in the ballroom on the fourth floor. David had planned carefully for them to be done before Emily and Thomas returned at three o'clock. Donovan did get one detail of the renovation before lunch. David couldn't resist showing him the sound system that had been installed. It was now possible for music to be heard throughout the castle.

Donovan simply gazed out the glass as the elevator returned them to the main floor. As they walked through the beautiful gardened main room towards the kitchen, dining area and rear gardens he couldn't help commenting on what a perfect room this would be for a wedding reception.

David grinned and took hold of Laurel's hand. "Funny you should mention that Donovan. Laurel found the remains of the chapel at the rear of the garden and mentioned just that thought should I ever choose to rebuild it."

"And; are you going to rebuild it?"

"The work has been scheduled to begin after the New Year." David's heart skipped a beat when Laurel squeezed his hand and smiled up at him. "Laurel, do you have time to show Donovan the kitchen while I check in with Henry and the progress in the ballroom?"

"Yes, I can check on our lunch while we're there."

Donovan showed no surprised at David's disclosure of Laurel acting as the cook. After touring the castle, nothing she did would ever surprise him again. "I can't wait to see what you've done with the kitchen and find out what that delicious smell is."

"Well, let's not wait a moment longer." Laurel led Donovan through topiary decorated doors into the kitchen. She had changed the smooth stone walls into something more rustic by having the workmen chip into the stone at varying levels. The addition of a copper hood over the six burner gas stove and copper pots suspended over a well-worn wooden work table all contributed to a feeling of having stepped back in time. Green granite stoned counters surrounded the room. Donovan was busily taking one photograph after another as Laurel checked on the Mediterranean chicken casserole bubbling in the oven.

David found Henry just as the workmen had finished their work on setting the tables and chairs. "Henry, would you join me in my room for a moment please? I think we need to discuss Lady Shelby's package I received yesterday."

CHAPTER 28

Everyone was gathered on the main floor in the great room of the keep at two o'clock in the afternoon. Lord David looked at the motley crew, all dressed in various Halloween costumes, and pulled Cat and Tim forward in front of him. He was sending everyone except for he and Laurel to the Plessey Woods Country Park *Gruesome Walk in the Woods* so Thomas and Emily wouldn't know about any of the evening's "special guests."

"Children, especially you two," he began while pointing at Cat and Tim, "it is extremely important that you stay with the adults at Plessey Woods. There are going to be a lot of families there for the walk and if you wander off on your own, it would be hard to find you in the mix of costumes, and you might become lost in the woods. I don't care what your costume is when you leave; when you return, you are all going to be quiet little mice so you can sneak up to the ballroom without being heard." He scrunched his face into a somewhat threatening pose, "None of you wants to spoil the surprise party and go to the dungeon do you?"

Tim's eyes were huge. "Papa, what's a dungin?"

Lord David broke up with laughter. "It's a secret place in the castle for children who spoil parties to spend a time out in."

Shaking his head and staring wide-eyed at his father, Tim quickly made his pledge. "I'm going to be the best mouse, papa, I don't want to see the dungin."

Lord David swung his little Rocket Man up on his hip and gave him a hug. "Tim, I don't think you'll ever get to see the dungeon. Now, Gwen, is there anything you want to add before you leave?"

"Yes, thank you. Children, do you all remember whose hands you're holding?" Seven costumed heads all nodded that they did. "Wonderful. Let's take each other's hands now and follow Henry and Roger to the cars." As children formed lines attaching themselves to their appointed guardians, Gwen was excited to leave for their adventure. "Quickly everyone, let's go for a walk."

Laurel, dressed in a full skirted, black satin gown and a tiara on her head, knew David was worried about his children's first venture outside the castle property. She moved closer to the "Prince" and took his hand. "They're going to be fine, David, and they are going to have the most wonderful adventure. Don't worry, Gwen, Henry and Roger will make sure they are safe."

"In my heart, I know they will, but in my mind I can imagine all sorts of real monsters they could encounter. I think this must be how all parents feel the first time their children go somewhere out of their parents sight."

"My sister-in-law told me the first time Tyler insisted he wanted to walk a block by himself to a friend's house to play, she hid behind bushes and trees to watch him until he was inside the house."

"So you're saying there is one thing normal about me?"

Glad to see his humor return, she smiled and verbally knocked him on his butt. "When did I ever say my sister-in-law was normal?"

Laughing, David accepted defeat. "One of these days, I am going to best you in one of our colloquial volleys."

Shaking her head left and right because she knew today obviously wasn't the day, "I suggest you up your vitamins then to make sure you live long enough to make good on your boast" and turned to lead the way into the elevator. They needed to finish the last touches to Thomas and Emily's suite before they went to meet the plane.

David held the door open for Laurel to enter into the suite and waited for her instructions on what was left she needed him to do. Laurel went straight into the sitting area and grabbed a silk miniature rose garland from the kitchen nook counter. "David, I left a ladder behind the counter. Would you please get it and take this garland? I need you to place it in and out of the chandelier's sconces for me."

He quickly found the ladder and positioned it under the chandelier. Taking the garland from Laurel, he started to mount the ladder, "I have absolutely no talent in this department so you are going to have to be my eyes while I'm up here and tell me exactly what you need me to do."

Fifteen minutes later, Laurel was satisfied with the final touch to the room. "Perfect. Okay, now I need to open the wardrobe in their bedroom so they see the King and Queen costumes hanging on the doors."

David moved the ladder out into the hall while Laurel adjusted the wardrobe and costumes to her liking. She stood back to see if she had her desired effect; realized she had, and then reached in the bottom to pull out the matching shoes and placed them on the floor. "There; I like that."

"Laurel, this is my favorite suite among the collection you did for my staff."

"I would have never guessed you would like this one the best. What is it that stands out more for you in this suite than the others?"

"It's English, and perfect for the very English Thomas and Emily; I feel extremely comfortable in here."

The minute he had remarked about the suite's native influence, Laurel had her hands on her hips and was facing him squarely. "Of course the suite is English; it's all done in English roses for God's sake," she dryly replied while rolling her eyes. Dropping her hands, she swatted David's arm lightly on her way back to the kitchen nook counter. Opening one of the drawers, she pulled out a framed invitation. Using David's script pen, she had created a beautiful invitation for Thomas and Emily.

Prince David and Princess Laurel
Respectfully request the honour of
King Thomas and Queen Emily
For a celebration of
Their fortieth wedding anniversary
On the evening of their return from Paris
In the ballroom of Whitethorn Castle

Paige Henry Will Arrive to Give
The royal couple
Escort to dinner promptly at
Six o'clock

David took the frame from Laurel and looked at the invitation. "This is beautiful, Laurel. When did you find the time?"

"I used your pen; the calligraphy seems to flow of its own accord. I don't think I spent more than ten minutes on it while you and Donovan were having your lunch."

"This will be a nice keepsake of the day for them." David looked at his watch, "It's quarter to three now. We better take the ladder down and head to the airstrip so we're on time for their flight. What story are we using for everyone being away from the castle?"

"I'll tell you on our way."

At just five minutes past three o'clock, Anita stopped the plane behind the castle gardens. Thomas and Emily looked wonderful as they dismounted through the hatch door. Thomas' barrel laugh at the sight of the two of them in their costumes was probably heard for miles. Emily couldn't wait to get to Laurel's open arms for her homecoming hug. "Laurel, we had such a marvelous time, but I must confess I truly missed you. I was so afraid you would have left for home before we returned."

Hugging Emily tight, Laurel wallowed in the warm emotion before she answered. "I promised you I would be here. I never break a promise."

Thomas left Lord David's handshake and lifted Laurel off her feet with his bear hug. "So now you're a Princess, are you? Emily, we've been gone for two weeks and come back to find ourselves serving royalty now!"

Oh how Laurel had missed Thomas' teasing. "Unfortunately, I'm sorry to say this is only borrowed rags from my Fairy Godmother for the day."

Emily had been looking around for the others. "Where is everyone?"

Lord David glanced at Laurel and quickly got on with the concocted story, "Henry took the car into town for service and Roger rode along to pick up some personal articles he wanted. Gwen just took the children for a short ride on the horses. She's hoping to get them to take a nap before a little Halloween fun Laurel planned for this evening."

The couple wasn't suspicious at all and started to pick up their luggage. "Thomas, let me give you a hand with those bags. We have a surprise for you two. Laurel finished all of the castle renovations and we'll be escorting you to your newly decorated quarters."

Emily beamed. "Laurel you said you were going to do our room, but I can't believe you had time. What did you do?"

"Why don't we let the men follow us with your bags and you can see for yourself?"

Thomas and Emily both spoke up to try and stop Laurel from exiting the elevator at the second floor. "You've made an error Laurel, our room is on the third floor," Emily said while trying to catch her arm.

Laurel kept right on moving out through the door and never turned around as she replied, "Not anymore."

Lord David was sucking in his cheeks at her cocky response. Thomas and Emily looked dumbfounded, but at their employer's urging, followed behind the Princess.

Emily burst into emotional tears the moment she was inside the suite. Thomas' deep voice went gruff with gratitude. "Laurel, this is the most remarkable thing anyone has ever done for us. In our hearts, we hope you know that you will always be considered a daughter to us."

"I'm honored. David, would you like to show my parents their rooms?"

Thomas and Emily were so caught up in the vision of the rose covered spread on the sumptuous bed and the shell pink throw over ivory cushioned chairs they failed to notice the plural. "Yes, I would thank you. Thomas, Emily I see you've noticed the costumes on the wardrobe. As I mentioned, Laurel has planned a little Halloween festivities for this evening and we will all be in costume. After we've left and you've gotten settled, I would appreciate it if you would consent to a change of clothing and wear the costumes for the rest of the day. Now then, you seem not to have noticed that there is more than just a bedroom for your private use."

The pair had been moving around the room, touching the bedspread, holding up the costumes in front of themselves and, just as David wound down his speech, they were testing the chairs. Thomas was first to return to earth and inquired what Lord David was talking about.

"If you two will follow us, you now have an entire suite that is yours. Laurel was quick to point out to me that each of my staff is really a part of my family. As part of my family, you now have a suite that includes your bedroom, your personal bath, a sitting room, kitchen nook, guest room and guest bath. I want you to feel free to have your family start visiting you here whenever you'd like."

The two had been following the royal pair in a daze as they walked through the rooms. Emily loved the chandelier, but Thomas was the one that found Laurel's real surprise. She had made a picture using dried roses, heather, and moonbell flowers placed between sheets of glass surrounded by a rich cherry wood frame. A beautiful tea set was on the coffee table in the sitting area. Emily was the one who found the framed invitation.

"Thomas, look at this."

Thomas took the frame from his wife and looked up, first at Laurel and then at Lord David. "You are honoring us with a dinner this evening?"

"Yes, _we_ are. I would like you to unpack and rest for a bit after your flight. Just as the invitation reads, Henry will be here for you at six o'clock."

Emily became all emotional again and hugged her new daughter. "This is too much Lord David; you've already sent us to Paris."

"Forty years of marriage demands recognition. I expect you both to prepare yourselves for a well-deserved evening in your honor."

Emily knew she needed to accept graciously. "God bless you, I love you both."

Thomas was holding his wife as Lord David and Laurel left them alone to explore their suite. Outside, David stopped Laurel as she headed to the elevator. "Laurel, I have something important to tell you and I was going to talk to you on the plane tomorrow, but it's bothering me, and even though the caterers are waiting, I think we should talk …"

Cutting him off as she pulled her arm away, "Whatever it is will have to wait until later. It's already four thirty and we have to get the props set up before the dinner begins. Let's go!"

David was sure he was going to regret not stressing his need to take the time to talk now, but since he dreaded what he had to tell her, he succumbed to procrastination. "Calm down, we have plenty of time."

Promptly at six o'clock, Henry, dressed as a Paige, knocked at Thomas and Emily's door. The King and Queen opened to hear him say "I am here to escort your majesties to an evening in their honor." Emily stepped out of character to quickly give Henry a peck on his rouged cheek. The King commanded him to move along.

Five feet before the ballroom's closed double doors, Henry stopped, turned and lifted his hands, palms at right angles to his arms, signaling the couple to wait for a moment. Advancing to open the doors, he stood at entry and bellowed "All stand and prepare for the King and Queen!" and stood aside for their entrance.

Thomas and Emily, heads held high, tried to walk regally through the door. They had a small slip of composure at finding four workmen dressed in jesters costumes lined two across from two and blowing horns.

The children had been fed every snack Gwen, Laurel and their parents could get their hands on in an effort to keep them quiet. With the sound of the horns, pandemonium reigned' "Surprise!"

King and Queen resorted to loving grandparents in the wink of an eye. As hugs and kisses were passed all around and introductions made, caterers were busily circulating with trays of champagne. Donovan, dressed as a servant, had already taken twenty pictures. Prince David with Princess Laurel at his side; took one glass off of a passing tray and handed another glass to her. Holding his glass up high, the Prince perfectly declared "I propose a toast to King Thomas and Queen Emily. Your majesties, congratulations on your fortieth wedding anniversary; we wish you many more. All hail the King and Queen!"

The group raised their glasses high and rang out with "God bless the King and Queen!"

While soft jazz played through the sound system, the honored guests circulated for a brief cocktail prelude. Henry, signaled Lewis to play his horn to get everyone's attention. "I'm sorry to interrupt the familiarities, but our feast is prepared. I beg the King and Queen to take their rightful seats and start this assembly in a most delicious dining experience."

Thomas and Emily burst into laughter when John and Leighton appeared with "thrones" and placed them at the center of a long dining table. The Prince was seated to Emily's left and the Princess to Thomas' right. Roger, Henry, Gwen, Donovan, Cat and Tim completed the table. Seated at round tables filling the room were the workmen and their wives, Gwen's family and Thomas and Emily's family.

Chattering conversation flowed over a dinner of butter lettuce salad, dutch crunch rolls, apricot glazed roast turkey, twice baked sweet potatoes, and baby green beans with bacon and caramelized onions. A beautiful three tiered wedding cake decorated with fresh pink rosebuds completed the meal.

The music stopped and Henry stepped up to a microphone on the stage. Lights were dimmed on the tables and a spotlight beamed over Henry's head. "Your majesties, in honor of this auspicious occasion, we, your humble servants, have prepared a program for your enjoyment. We pray you enjoy our efforts." The curtain rose as Henry left the stage to reveal Roger seated playing the grand piano and Laurel singing the beginning lyrics of *Beauty and the Beast*. The children were delighted when the beast, aka Prince David, joined her in song. The program progressed with the workmen doing their rendition of *YMCA*, a choir of workmen and their wives singing a rousing *Love Can Move Mountains*, Cat doing ballet to a small part of *Swan Lake*, Gwen singing and moving to *I Will Survive* and Henry and Laurel, wigged and dressed as hippies, singing Sonny and Cher's, *I Got You Babe*.

The curtain dropped and "Sonny" announced a ten minute intermission. Backstage, Laurel found David after changing her costume, just before the curtain was lifted for the next number. David's guard went up when he saw her obviously innocent façade. "David, have you ever known me not to retaliate when someone springs something on me, like, oh say leading a castle tour, unexpectedly?"

David's alarm bells were ringing loudly as she shoved him in the back to start the routine. The entire cast was on stage three fourths through the theme from *Grease*, the men in slicked back hair and the women in poodle skirts, when David's voice suddenly went high. The audience thought it was little Tim, his hair greased back, waving from the window of the wooden "Greased Lightning" car prop slipping out a shriek in his over-excitement. Only David and Laurel knew it was because just as they came together to start the finish to *Summer Loving*, she reached behind him, straight into the back of his jeans, and gave the Prince a royal wedgie. David didn't do anymore dancing through the rest of the number.

Henry remained on the stage as the rest of the cast went backstage to change. "We're going to interrupt our show to return to reality for just a moment. As we all know, tomorrow Laurel Andrews will be leaving to return to her home in California. She has asked to sing a special song to all of us."

The curtain lifted and Laurel entered from the rear of the stage looking absolutely beautiful in an emerald green silk gown. The form-fitting gown, from the front, appeared to be a simple chemise. She had left her golden curls down around her shoulders and the spotlight on her hair made her look somewhat angelic.

"Thank you Henry. I have Lord David's permission to announce that this morning, I accepted a partnership with his company. So, while I am going home tomorrow, you haven't seen the last of me. The song I selected to sing for you is one that I've used to remember family members I've lost whenever I hear it. Today, as I was faced with thoughts of not being at the breakfast table with all of you tomorrow morning, it occurred to me that it also perfectly fits my feelings for all of you. Each of you has become family to me. I will miss you all and I expect lots and lots of emails until my next visit." Leaning her head toward Roger at the piano, she quietly placed a request for the music. "Roger, if you please."

The music started and there wasn't a dry eye in the house a minute into *My Heart Will Go On*. Laurel's pure voice did the song justice and she blew a kiss to Thomas and Emily as the curtain came down.

Henry appeared on the stage again when the curtain rose. "We are back in time and it brings great pleasure to announce the Prince and Princess will be performing the next number for the King and Queen's personal pleasure.

Lord David, dressed in a black silk suit and a hat reminiscent of one Frank Sinatra would wear, took the microphone from Henry. "Your majesties, we were unable to find knowledge of your favorite song and the Princess and I

have chosen to sing *All The Way* in hopes that you will find it acceptable."
Roger started the music and David and Laurel performed the song as a duet
just as Celine Dion had done with a taped Frank Sinatra.

Henry announced the final performance of the evening. "Your majesties,
ladies and gentlemen; Gwen will be performing our last song. She requests that
any of you feeling the desire to dance during the song surrender to the urge
and enjoy yourselves. A moment later, Gwen's deep, throaty voice filled the
room with Donna Summer's, *Last Dance*.

The cast had gathered in front of the stage and David grabbed Laurel close
to him and started to dance. As one couple after another gyrated near the
Prince and Princess, they didn't find Laurel looking quite as angelic as she first
appeared when they saw her back. The dress was cut into a deep 'v' stopping
just above her tailbone. David and Laurel were oblivious to the gawking assembly as they danced. Donovan, still busily taking photographs, managed to capture the exact moment when Laurel lifted her head from David's shoulder,
stared unseeing at David's chest as if having an epiphany, and then looked into
his eyes revealing her deep love shining into his.

The evening ended with Henry escorting the King and Queen back to their
suite and parents gathering up sleepy children to tuck them into their beds.
Prince David wished everyone a good night as he picked up Tim and Laurel
picked up Cat.

Laurel and David changed the children into their pajamas and tucked them
in. Turning on their mural lights, each child was already asleep before their
goodnight kiss. The electricity between David and Laurel was palpable as they
traversed the quiet hallway, hand in hand.

David stopped in front of his room, "Join me for a brandy?"

Still holding his hand, Laurel moved in front of him and looked him
directly in the eye. Her eyes huge in a pale face, she huskily braved what she
had wanted to ask him during their last dance. "David, do you feel that we're
soul mates?"

He said nothing. He opened the door to his room and lifted her into his
arms, all the while holding her gaze. With her arms around his neck, he
answered "Yes" and bent his head in a deep kiss as he crossed the threshold
with her and kicked the door shut.

CHAPTER 29

Laurel watched the slumbering David as long as she dared. Just before twilight, she rose and went into the master bathroom. Behind the closed door, she used the facilities and ran water in the sink to cover her sound from opening the medicine cupboard. She found the sleeping capsules she remembered from her renovation of the suite and quickly opened the bottle, removed two capsules, and returned the bottle to the cupboard. She took a glass and filled it with water before turning off the tap. Shaking, she opened the capsules and poured their contents into the glass and threw the shells in the garbage.

David came awake with the noise that interrupted his deep sleep. He looked up at the door as it opened and enjoyed his sight of Laurel's nudity as she returned to his bed.

Laurel walked over to David's side of the bed and held the glass out while bending over his prone form to give him a kiss. "Good morning, love. I thought you might be as thirsty as I was."

He rose and braced himself sideways to take the welcome glass from her hand. "Good morning. Yes, I can't understand why I'm so thirsty; one would think I'd been making love to a gorgeous, energetic lover all night." She was amazed at how quickly he drank the glass dry. Setting the empty glass on the bedside table, David swung his arm back and brought his other arm up to circle Laurel's waist to pull her down on top of him. "That's better," he whispered into her neck. "Get your delicious body back in this bed and let's get thirsty again."

An hour later, Laurel's tears fell on David's sleeping face as she kissed him goodbye. Before she left the bedroom, she used his pen and paper to leave him a note which she placed on her pillow as she gazed at his face just once more.

Sure that she was running out of time, she raced out of the room, down to the elevator and quickly into her guest room. She showered in record time and finished packing her bags and oversized garment bag before setting them outside the guest room door. After a final check of the room, she retraced her steps back to the master suite.

When Laurel re-entered David's bedroom, every fiber of her being wanted to strip her clothes off and return to his side. Instead, she watched him as she waited just inside the door until she heard Henry's footsteps in the hall. Before her courage escaped, she turned and walked out the door just as Henry was about to knock for entrance.

Laurel acted as if this were an every morning occurrence as she whispered, "Good morning Henry. David has a horrible headache this morning. I don't know if he had too much champagne last night or if he's coming down with a cold, but he won't be able to travel today. You and I will have to make the trip by ourselves."

Henry had been blinking his eyes in surprise at her coming through the door from Lord David's private room. With each word she spoke, he had grown more and more pale. "What? I must go in and speak with him; um, well, I would never suit as your escort home. We will have to reschedule the flight."

She was sure he had grown pale from his fear of flying and thinking without David aboard he wouldn't be able to have his shot. Laurel linked her arm into his as she led them down the hall. "Now, now, Henry, relax. I have to get home. I assure you David has every confidence in you being able to take care of matters to get us settled aboard our flight and Anita can take over from there. I have no problem with you taking your shot. Truthfully, I would appreciate the release from embarrassment when I cry all the way home."

Henry heard her words about "confidence in him" as Lord David getting a message to him about the package, that he must be truly ill, and, unable to stop the flight, his need for Henry to take his place. Realizing that there was no escape from accepting his employer's request, Henry's knees began to shake as they walked out to the plane.

Thomas passed Anita on his way up the stairway with the last piece of Laurel's luggage.

Anita waved to Laurel and Henry when she saw them coming through the bushes from the garden. She was familiar with Henry's fear of flight and didn't notice his heightened pallor. "Good morning to you both. I'm glad you're on time. We have a good day for flying."

Thomas, his task complete, came back down the stairway and headed directly to Laurel. Anita walked up the stairway with Henry as Thomas said his goodbyes. "We're all going to miss you something fierce. Always remember, if you ever need anything, no matter where you are, Emily and I are your parents now. All you need to do is call." Tears clouded both Laurel and Thomas' eyes as he grabbed her up in a hug and pressed a paper into her hand. Laurel looked at the paper when he released her and saw Emily's light handwritten note that ended with a phone number. "Thomas, what phone number is this?"

"Emily couldn't stand the thought of not getting to talk to you when she felt like it. We picked up a cell phone while we were in Paris. We'd appreciate your not telling Lord David about it."

Laurel kissed the old man's cheek and then started to board the plane. "Believe me; your secret couldn't be safer." Anita waved to him and then closed the hatch. Henry was sitting in an aisle seat with a box on his lap. Laurel brushed past him to take the window seat, settled herself in with the seatbelt on, and then stared out the window at Thomas and the castle. Tears started falling the minute the plane started to taxi. Laurel looked out the window during and after the takeoff until she couldn't see so much as a tower in the horizon.

Openly crying, Laurel turned, put her head on Henry's shoulder, and felt his trembling. Henry pressed the handkerchief from his coat pocket into her hand as she spoke. "We're in the air Henry. I'll be fine. Go ahead and take your shot."

"I can't do that just yet. Oh, God, where do I start?"

Confused and alarmed, Laurel queried, "Henry, what's the matter with you?"

"Laurel, I'm going to tell you something Lord David had planned to discuss with you as best I can. Do you remember Lord David receiving a package from Lady Shelby?"

"Yes. Why?"

Henry's brow had beads of sweat from his nervousness. "It appears there was a problem, oh my, a situation that occurred with your husband, I mean with the note, oh I don't know how to tell you about what's in this box," he declared.

"Henry, I don't know what the problem is, but I assure you we can solve it. Why don't you take your shot, give me the box, go lie down and I'll solve the problem while you take a nice rest."

He felt so relieved and yet so guilty at being such a coward. "Yes, that's how we'll do it." He plopped the box on her lap and practically leapt from his seat. "Be sure you read Lady Shelby's letter first," he instructed as he headed to the rear of the plane.

Laurel slowly opened the box and removed Shelby's letter. For the next half hour, she went through a five-step emotional roller coaster of shock, anger, doubt, betrayal and resolution. She looked at the last paper with the picture of Henry's peculiar handwriting on the torn note and wiped her tears with the handkerchief. Putting everything just as she found it back into the box, Laurel squared her shoulders and went to the cockpit to talk with Anita.

Knocking on the frame of the curtained cockpit, Laurel called out "Anita, may I come in and talk with you for a moment?"

Anita answered back, "Only if you bring a soda from the refrigerator with you."

Laurel passed the sleeping Henry on her way to the galley and retrieved the soda. Parting the curtain and stepping into the cockpit, she stopped still to look at her first sight of an airplane's control center.

Anita put her hand out for the soda and Laurel opened the can before handing it off to her. "Thanks. You can sit in the co-pilot seat."

"I never thought I'd be doing this," she mumbled as she buckled herself into the seat. "Anita, we've never had much time to talk. Exactly how much do you know about my arrival to Whitethorn?"

"I know that I never saw you walk on board this plane. I also know this is only the second time I've seen that big trunk that's sitting in the back of my plane. When I did see you, I never saw any distress signals so I didn't ask any questions. There are some things I don't want to know. Why are you asking?"

"Because I think you need to know those things now." For the next forty-five minutes, Laurel told Anita the full story.

"Shit! What the hell do we do now?"

"I've thought of a plan, but I need some questions answered to know if it will work."

"Lay them on me."

"Okay, tell me about our flight—how much time do we have?"

"Shortly we will be landing at Heathrow. Our co-pilot, who is also Lord David's body guard and driver when he travels for short trips abroad, will meet us onboard Lord David's personal transatlantic plane before we continue on to San Francisco. You should be walking up your driveway in Keddie at about 5:15 in the morning."

"As a diplomat, do you have to go through security at Heathrow and San Francisco?"

"Of a sort. Clarence, that's the co-pilot, will have a standard luggage trolley sent to us for transfer to the other plane. We will be going into a separate room near the hangar to have our passports checked and walk through a metal scanner before we board for the flight to San Francisco."

Laurel unbuckled her seatbelt and stood up. "Hmmm, a passport check; hold on, I'll be right back," and went to the closet cubicle with the oversized garment bag. The bag, designed for formal wear, was about fourteen inches deep, four feet wide, and five and a half feet high. In an effort to create a "designer look", it was constructed of pink reinforced denim with a mod print and had a plastic liner inside to protect the clothing. Laurel stood sideways next to the bag and pushed on the sides to gauge the fullness of the ten hanging dresses inside the bag. Smiling and thanking her guardian angel for making her do ballet plies with Cat, she returned to Anita. "Okay, I have an idea. Is it possible for you to contact Clarence before we land?"

"Yes, I have a phone right here."

"Perfect; would you please call him and ask him if he would meet us at our plane instead of aboard the next one? Oh, and also ask him if he could have a luggage carrier that has a rod for my garment bag?"

"Sure, what are you going to do?"

"I only weigh about one hundred and twenty pounds. The reinforced fabric on the garment bag should be able to hold that weight without ripping. I am hoping that Clarence is a large man. I plan to do a plies inside the middle of the bag and hang on to a hanger. I want him to carry me out just as he would any garment bag and hang me on the rod of the carrier so I can rest my legs a moment. At the passport check, I want him to continue to treat me like a bag and carry me over his shoulder through the scanner. I'm also hoping he can put a little swing in his step and look overly concerned about Henry. The only way my pink luggage won't draw attention for further scrutiny is if everyone believes Henry and Clarence are gay."

Anita smiled, "You are very smart for an interior designer, and lucky too. Clarence is a very large man and will easily be able to carry you. He's also a very good sport. I've got previous experience moving Henry. There's a wheelchair in the rear of the plane I take him out on. Go back to your seat and get buckled in. I'll call Clarence and get everything set up. You can talk to me again once we're in the air so we know what we're going to do at San Francisco."

Laurel took her seat, buckled up and put her head in her knees when she felt the start of their descent. She didn't want to take any chances with someone seeing her head through the window. The minute the plane came to a stop, Laurel unbuckled the seatbelt and crawled up the aisle to the closet before standing up.

Anita parked the plane in its hangar and opened the hatch for Clarence before joining Laurel at the closet.

Laurel was braced for movement on either side of the aisle in front of the closet. She thought the reason she was unsure the plane had stopped was due to the massive size of the footsteps on the stairway of the man heading towards her. Laurel looked at the huge, olive skinned man before her and couldn't stop from asking, "Are you a sumo wrestler?"

Clarence may have been big, but he had the heart of a child's teddy bear, "I was. You must be my carryon luggage," he said while unzipping the garment bag. He reached in and removed half of the dresses and handed them to Anita. He looked at Laurel's puny frame and took hold of either side of her waist. "Are you ready?"

Laurel barely got out her "yes" before she was lifted easily off of the ground. Clarence placed her so that she would be facing forward to the zipper and waited while she grabbed onto the hanger of the gown closest to her when Anita lifted them over the side of Clarence's arms and put them in front of her. Once Clarence released her, Laurel moved her knees into position and did a slow plies. "Okay, I'm ready."

Anita quickly zipped the bag shut and Clarence whisked the bag up and over his shoulder. Laurel bumped a little against the aisle ceiling as he carried her up the aisle and out onto the luggage carrier. He was very graceful for such a large man. He easily swung the garment bag onto the rod and then appeared to be straightening the bottom of the bag to prevent wrinkling when he actually lifted Laurel's legs up and brought them down onto the platform of the carrier so she could rest. Anita had moved to get the sleeping Henry in the wheelchair while Clarence got Laurel off the plane. She met Clarence at the doorway and he lifted the bottom of the chair while they maneuvered Henry down the stairs. Clarence gently caressed Henry's cheek to appear to be checking on his welfare. Anita waited with Henry by the carrier while Clarence retrieved the remainder of Laurel's luggage.

Clarence and Anita exchanged a glance and assembled the motley crew together. Strolling casually, they made their way to the passport check in. Clarence removed the garment bag from the rod and nodded to an airline worker as he took the luggage carrier from him and proceeded to a scanner before putting it in the bottom of their waiting plane. Anita ushered Henry, still asleep in the wheelchair and after Clarence gave him a kiss on his sleeping cheek, through the scanner. She passed their passports over for inspection and then continued onto their plane when they were handed back to her. Clarence had a slight hitch when he couldn't go through the scanner with the garment bag on his shoulder due to his height. Just as the security guard offered to take it from him, Clarence swung the bag off his shoulder and into a football hold closely against his waistline. "I didn't want to trouble you," he said effeminately as he walked through the scanner and received approval to board the plane.

Laurel was a little dizzy from all of the bouncing and swinging inside the dark bag. She felt herself hanging once again and heard Clarence tell Anita the hatch was secure a moment before the zipper opened and she was released from the temporary cocoon. "It worked!" she beamed. Clarence took hold of her waist again and lifted her out of the bag.

He smiled into her face as he pushed down on her shoulders for her to crawl up the aisle. "Can you get into a seat and keep your head down until we take off?"

"Yes—I've already had practice at that," and off she went.

Once they were airborne, Laurel walked her way up the aisle to the cockpit. Clarence had left the door open for her and barely turned his head at her entrance. "You can sit in the navigator seat behind me."

She looked around the door and found the seat he had indicated. "Thank you."

He quickly raised his hand to signal her to be quiet as Anita started talking on her headset. Laurel was fascinated to watch all the buttons and knobs being pushed and pulled and hear "airport" talk from Anita.

Anita finished her duties, flipped a switch, and glanced back at Laurel, "We can talk now."

"Amazing; are we going to do the same thing at San Francisco?"

Anita was happy to tell her they didn't have to. "No, not quite; our limousine with the diplomatic plates will be waiting at our arrival. Airport crewmen will place our luggage into the car, you'll go out over Clarence's shoulder and then Clarence will drive us out a designated exit."

Laurel was feeling a little claustrophobic at the thought of being inside a garment bag and also inside the trunk of a car. Her voice a little weak, "are you going to put me in the trunk all the way to Keddie?"

Anita and Clarence exchanged grins before she answered her, "as much as you deserve that for all the trouble you've put us through, no. Clarence will put you over a seat inside the limo. We'll stop somewhere once we're out of the airport and get you out."

"Oh, I am so relieved, thank you."

"Don't breathe too deeply yet. We've never had a problem after our security clearance at Heathrow, but with heightened security, we don't know without a doubt that we won't have new security checks at San Francisco. They don't send out announcements, you know."

Laurel felt like the breath had been sucked right out of her. "What do we do?"

"Be prepared to act like luggage and go with the flow. We have no other choice. We normally take an eight hour rest period at the Hilton before flying back. To make sure we get out of here safely, we are going to cut that to four. Does your plan once we get you home allow that much time before the world hears your story?"

"Damn! If I wasn't trying to protect David's friggin' butt, I could have just gone up to anyone at Heathrow airport, identified myself and let the chips fall where they may. But oh no, I have to play secret agent." Letting out a sigh of exasperation, she continued with her litany, "Yes, I plan to talk with my husband privately before anyone else. I'll make sure I watch the time."

Clarence was very fond of his employer and stopped Laurel as she was leaving the cockpit, "We all have to play friggin' secret agents and we're going to do a damn fine job—got it?"

One look at Clarence's face and Laurel knew he wasn't threatening her; he was just worried for all of them. "I got it. Anita, can I use the phones for awhile?"

"You have at least ten hours. Be my guest."

"How do I make a call to the United States?"

"There's a card next to the phone. Just follow the directions."

"Thanks."

It had been so long since Laurel used a telephone it felt strange to be dialing one now—especially in an airplane.

As Laurel was placing her call, hundreds of miles away a groggy Lord David awoke in his bed and saw what he thought would be a love note from Laurel on the pillow next to him. On Laurel's end of the phone, she heard her nephew's excited "Aunt Laurel!" and not so much as a decibel of her lover's anguished cry.

CHAPTER 30

Laurel had to give Clarence directions to her home. He wasn't David's driver on his previous visit since it was meant as a long-term stay. She had him park the limousine three houses down from her front door. The lights were on inside and she didn't want Greg to come to the front door at the sound of a car and spot Clarence. She looked around the neighborhood as Clarence opened the trunk and started to remove pieces of luggage. All was quiet and no one was in sight. She could see how David and Henry were able to take her unobserved.

Clarence placed the last piece of luggage on the sidewalk and pressed the trunk closed. His voice low, he picked up one piece and put it under his arm and then picked up two more pieces—one in each hand before asking "can you take the last bag?"

"Yes," she whispered in return. "Let's set them in the courtyard. I'll stand outside while you bring me the garment bag and then wait until I see you drive around the corner before I go inside."

Laurel reached into the smallest piece of luggage and retrieved her house key while she waited for Clarence to return. She was touched by the large man's wordless hug goodbye before he left her. As soon as she saw the car safely around the corner, she put her key in the lock and opened the door—ready to turn off the alarm if it started to sing.

Shelby's laughter was the only sound Laurel heard when the door opened. She heard Greg's laughter in response coming from the kitchen and knew they hadn't heard the front door. She stood there for a moment, stunned with shock that she had no desire to run to her husband with greeting. She put the garment bag on the bed in the front bedroom and slowly walked through the house to the kitchen.

Greg's back was to the door so it was Shelby who spotted Laurel first. Greg turned to look when he caught the expression on Shelby's face and bolted out of his chair, "Laurel!"

Laurel's body stood braced to meet the thrust of Greg's as he ran to her. Husband and wife met, clung and kissed. Greg held on to her not believing she was actually there as she put a hand on his cheek and looked into his eyes. "Yes, Greg, you aren't dreaming, it's really me." Turning them around to face the shocked Shelby, Laurel pulled on Greg's arm to get him back to the breakfast table. "Shelby, sit down before you upset your baby."

"What? How do you know my name? Where did you come from?"

Pushing Greg into his chair and taking one in the middle between the gawking couple, "It's a long story and my nephew Tyler is going to be here soon." Looking at the clock above the microwave, it read five thirty-five in the morning. "His plane landed in Keddie about twenty minutes ago. I want to wait to tell you all about what happened, but to set your mind at ease, Shelby, I know your name and about your baby because your brother told me about you."

Greg hadn't let go of his wife's hand from the moment he reached her. Pulling on it so she would face him, he looked deep into her eyes as he asked, "You were with her brother?"

The doorbell rang just as she was about to answer him. "Yes Greg, in England. Let me get Tyler in here and I'll tell you the whole story."

Laurel heard Greg's outraged roar as she hollered out to her nephew that the door was open, "What did you say? You were in England?"

Tyler brought in some of the luggage with him. Dropping them in the entry way, he ran to his aunt. "Aunt Laurel! I still can't believe it's really you!"

Laurel received another gargantuan hug and brought her nephew in to join the others at the table. "Shelby, I don't believe you met our nephew, Tyler. Tyler, this is Shelby Abbott, the new owner of this home."

Tyler turned from hugging his uncle hello and shook hands with Shelby. "It's nice to meet you Mrs. Abbott."

"Please, call me Shelby. I feel like I know you from all of your newspaper articles."

Greg turned an exasperated face on his wife, "Is everyone here now so you can tell us what the hell happened to you?"

Laurel couldn't help remembering Greg's ability to change from happy, loving husband to a fed up and angry one in under a minute. At least this time he had one hell of a good reason. "Yes, until about eight o'clock."

"Who's coming at eight o'clock?"

"First Detectives Peters and Thompson with Karen; then at around eight thirty, Veronica Garcia will be arriving with a mobile film crew. Greg, please, I know you, well, all of you actually, have lots of questions. If you'll sit down now and listen, I want to tell you what really happened to me—uninterrupted."

Greg hadn't paid close attention to hear his wife's request to "sit and listen"; all he heard was the ending up to the word 'really'. "What do you mean what "really happened to you"?"

Already back to the familiar, Laurel grabbed his hand and begged with her eyes, "Greg, please, sit and listen."

For the next hour and a half, except for telling exactly how close she and David had become, Laurel told the entire story of the past five weeks. "Shelby, because Henry had left the note on the door and you didn't tell your brother about anything going on here in Keddie, we didn't know until receiving the package with the newspapers that total chaos had erupted. Believe me, when you told him you were "shutting out the world" he never thought you weren't at least checking your newspaper."

"I know." Looking apologetically at everyone, she confessed, "It's my fault they didn't find out as soon as I knew you were missing. I could have called my brother to tell him about Laurel, but I was afraid he would go ballistic and insist on my returning to England so I would be safe at Whitethorn. England is no longer my home and I didn't want to be pressured. That's why I made sure to tell him I was having my utilities transferred and would be too busy in the move to take a cell phone call. I wanted to send him the package so he could see that Greg hadn't murdered you and all was safe."

Laurel put her hand on Greg's. "Honey, I am so sorry you went through all of that mess."

Greg had been watching his wife closely during her story. "It's not your fault. Shelby, I'm sure your brother's a great guy, but the fact is, no matter how this all turned out, he's a goddamned kidnapper."

Shelby started to respond but Laurel cut her off. "Greg, stop it!" Tyler and Shelby stared at Laurel when she raised her voice. Shelby noticed how Laurel's face had gone soft every time she said her brother's name during her story and now she raised her voice in his defense. As she listened to her try to talk some reason into Greg's head, she knew Laurel had fallen in love with David. "Greg, the only reason David took me instead of meeting with me that night was because of the emergency involving his child. The only reason any of this happened was because a man wanted to provide a loving home for his children to grow in. He's not a monster, Greg, he just loves his children."

"Christ! Okay, if it's going to make you that upset, we won't press charges."

"Thank you."

Shelby had to ask about Whitethorn. "You really renovated the entire castle in five weeks?

"Yes. Before you get too impressed, you should know that four workmen from town and their wives were there to help. I don't know what magazine Donovan is going to submit his story to, but I'm sure your brother will send you a copy so you can see what we did. I know that he and the children can't wait for your visit after Morgan is born."

Shelby put her hands around her middle to cradle the baby inside. "I can't wait to see it for myself. It sounds fabulous."

Greg noticed the time and needed to know what Laurel planned next. "I hate to break up this touching trip down memory lane, but I think we have some detectives arriving pretty soon. I want to know what story you're going to tell them, and better yet, why not the truth?"

Shelby sensed that Greg wasn't going to like what was coming, "Tyler, why don't we give your aunt and uncle some time alone while I show you the new nursery?"

Tyler could feel the strong emotional currents running between his aunt and uncle and was glad for an excuse to leave them alone. "I'd like to see it, Shelby, lead the way."

The minute Shelby and Tyler were out of earshot, Laurel turned soft eyes to Greg's face. "Greg, tell me, when you discovered I was gone, what was your first thought?"

"That you were really pissed off about trying for a baby and left me."

"I see, and now that you know what really happened, what are your thoughts for the future."

"Well shit, Laurel, that should be obvious. We need to get settled down south and go see the doctor I was telling you about."

"Just like that, huh, we pick up as if the last five weeks hadn't happened and live happily ever after."

"Aw come on, Laurel, you know what I mean."

"Unfortunately, I do. Greg, these past five weeks have changed everything. I realized something when I watched David with his children on their horses

Anita and Clarence exchanged grins before she answered her, "as much as you deserve that for all the trouble you've put us through, no. Clarence will put you over a seat inside the limo. We'll stop somewhere once we're out of the airport and get you out."

"Oh, I am so relieved, thank you."

"Don't breathe too deeply yet. We've never had a problem after our security clearance at Heathrow, but with heightened security, we don't know without a doubt that we won't have new security checks at San Francisco. They don't send out announcements, you know."

Laurel felt like the breath had been sucked right out of her. "What do we do?"

"Be prepared to act like luggage and go with the flow. We have no other choice. We normally take an eight hour rest period at the Hilton before flying back. To make sure we get out of here safely, we are going to cut that to four. Does your plan once we get you home allow that much time before the world hears your story?"

"Damn! If I wasn't trying to protect David's friggin' butt, I could have just gone up to anyone at Heathrow airport, identified myself and let the chips fall where they may. But oh no, I have to play secret agent." Letting out a sigh of exasperation, she continued with her litany, "Yes, I plan to talk with my husband privately before anyone else. I'll make sure I watch the time."

Clarence was very fond of his employer and stopped Laurel as she was leaving the cockpit, "We all have to play friggin' secret agents and we're going to do a damn fine job—got it?"

One look at Clarence's face and Laurel knew he wasn't threatening her; he was just worried for all of them. "I got it. Anita, can I use the phones for awhile?"

"You have at least ten hours. Be my guest."

"How do I make a call to the United States?"

"There's a card next to the phone. Just follow the directions."

"Thanks."

It had been so long since Laurel used a telephone it felt strange to be dialing one now—especially in an airplane.

As Laurel was placing her call, hundreds of miles away a groggy Lord David awoke in his bed and saw what he thought would be a love note from Laurel on the pillow next to him. On Laurel's end of the phone, she heard her nephew's excited "Aunt Laurel!" and not so much as a decibel of her lover's anguished cry.

as he took the luggage carrier from him and proceeded to a scanner before putting it in the bottom of their waiting plane. Anita ushered Henry, still asleep in the wheelchair and after Clarence gave him a kiss on his sleeping cheek, through the scanner. She passed their passports over for inspection and then continued onto their plane when they were handed back to her. Clarence had a slight hitch when he couldn't go through the scanner with the garment bag on his shoulder due to his height. Just as the security guard offered to take it from him, Clarence swung the bag off his shoulder and into a football hold closely against his waistline. "I didn't want to trouble you," he said effeminately as he walked through the scanner and received approval to board the plane.

Laurel was a little dizzy from all of the bouncing and swinging inside the dark bag. She felt herself hanging once again and heard Clarence tell Anita the hatch was secure a moment before the zipper opened and she was released from the temporary cocoon. "It worked!" she beamed. Clarence took hold of her waist again and lifted her out of the bag.

He smiled into her face as he pushed down on her shoulders for her to crawl up the aisle. "Can you get into a seat and keep your head down until we take off?"

"Yes—I've already had practice at that," and off she went.

Once they were airborne, Laurel walked her way up the aisle to the cockpit. Clarence had left the door open for her and barely turned his head at her entrance. "You can sit in the navigator seat behind me."

She looked around the door and found the seat he had indicated. "Thank you."

He quickly raised his hand to signal her to be quiet as Anita started talking on her headset. Laurel was fascinated to watch all the buttons and knobs being pushed and pulled and hear "airport" talk from Anita.

Anita finished her duties, flipped a switch, and glanced back at Laurel, "We can talk now."

"Amazing; are we going to do the same thing at San Francisco?"

Anita was happy to tell her they didn't have to. "No, not quite; our limousine with the diplomatic plates will be waiting at our arrival. Airport crewmen will place our luggage into the car, you'll go out over Clarence's shoulder and then Clarence will drive us out a designated exit."

Laurel was feeling a little claustrophobic at the thought of being inside a garment bag and also inside the trunk of a car. Her voice a little weak, "are you going to put me in the trunk all the way to Keddie?"

one day. This man would do anything, did do anything, for the love he felt for his children. Greg, you would be exactly like that with your child. You need to have a child of yours to father; it's a driving force in your soul. I may not have been blessed with children, but God blessed me with an artistic gift. Creating art is the very heart of my soul and I need to feed that gift, Greg, not as a hobby but as a daily part of who I am."

"What are you telling me Laurel?"

"I'm telling you that we would destroy each other and what we've had if we stayed together. I know that I've loved you, but lacking confidence in my abilities, I have been suppressing an artistic career to be the wife I thought you wanted. Ultimately, both of us have been cheated of the higher level of love that marriage should be."

"Laurel, you don't mean that. We can't divorce; we're catholic for God's sake. If you don't want to try having a baby of our own, we can adopt."

"Greg, please, I've gone over and over this in my mind. You've gotten close to Shelby, I can tell. Did she tell you about her and her husband?"

"Yes, she did."

"Tell me honestly, Greg, do you think we have a love even close to what theirs was?"

"No, but she may have been exaggerating after his death."

"She wasn't. Her brother told me they were always soul mates."

"What does that have to do with us?"

"If we stayed together and did things your way, both of us would lose. You really want to have a child of your own, and I want you to have that. Both of us deserve to live our lives finding what really makes us happy and fulfilling who we were meant to be. We can't use our religion as a reason to deny the truth, Greg. We are typical sinners, actually. When we wanted to try artificial insemination, we ignored the fact that our religion told us it was wrong. Greg, we've questioned the church on several other topics over the years. I believe we have a loving God and that no matter what religion we are, we are human and need only to follow His teachings as best we can and seek his forgiveness when we fail. I don't want to spend another day not using God's wonderful gift. I don't want us to end up hating each other either. You need to find the right partner, Greg, and that's why I'm setting you free."

Greg sat back in his chair, totally defeated. He thought about all Laurel had said for a moment and then leaned forward and put his clasped hands on top of the table. "Okay. I get it. What's your plan?"

Laurel knew the detectives and Karen would be there any moment. "I don't want you to tell the detectives and Karen anything when they get here. After the initial shock, I'm going to tell them about Veronica Garcia coming here to tape a live show with Tyler. I am going to read a prepared statement I've written on the show and then briefly answer a couple quick questions to end the public's attention on us. As soon as Veronica leaves, I'm sure the detectives are going to have some questions for me. I am going to answer any questions to keep a father out of trouble with the law as best I can. Tyler is going to be going back to the studio with Veronica to do a follow up piece to be telecast in Philadelphia. After the detectives and Tyler have left, I want to talk alone with Karen."

"What are you going to tell Karen?"

"The truth, she'd know if I was lying."

"And then?"

"Then, I'm going to take a trip, to Italy. I don't need a visa for up to ninety days. I know Karen missed her trip to India and I imagine she'll go there immediately. I'm hoping she'll join me in Italy in a few weeks. I have a lot I need to sort out in my mind and I could use a good friend. I would appreciate it if you would file the necessary paperwork to start the divorce for us."

"I see you've thought this through well."

"I had a lot of time on the plane." The doorbell rang and Laurel knew the detectives and Karen had arrived. "Well, Greg? Will you do it?"

Shelby and Tyler had come out of the sitting area next to the nursery where they had been waiting to answer the door. Greg watched them go by and then grabbed his wife in a fierce hug and talked close to her ear, "Yes, I'll do it. I know you're right, but it hurts like hell. Promise me we aren't going to end up hating each other."

Tears were running down Laurel's cheek as she leaned back to look at him as she answered, "I promise."

Greg released Laurel and the couple turned just as Karen threw herself at Laurel "You're home! You're okay!"

Laurel held her friend tight and looked over her shoulder at the detectives as she answered, "Shhh yes, everything is fine. Calm down." Laurel reached out to the detectives, "Are you Detective Peters or Detective Johnson" she asked the first one to reach her hand.

Neither of them thought it was unusual to see tears. They assumed they were from happiness. "I'm Phil Peters," he said shaking her hand, "and this is Matt Johnson."

Laurel shook Matt's hand. "It's nice to meet you both. I know there's a pot of coffee in the kitchen, why don't we all take a cup and sit down in the living room where there's more room to talk?"

Everyone but Shelby thought coffee was a great idea. Shelby poured herself a glass of milk and followed everyone into the living room. Phil turned around at her entrance to ask "I'm sorry, I don't know your name or why you're here."

"I'm Shelby Abbott, the new owner of this home. I moved in just a few days ago."

"I see." Phil looked at his partner, "Matt, we better pick some comfortable seats. I think we're in for quite a story."

Laurel silenced Greg, Tyler and Shelby with her eyes. "Please, everyone find a seat and make yourselves comfortable. I know you have a lot of questions, but I would appreciate your holding them for a few minutes. You see, I only found out yesterday about the investigation of my whereabouts. I feel horrible that Keddie has been alarmed by another astronomical mystery. For that reason, I have asked Veronica Garcia from *Eye on Keddie* to join us. She and Tyler will do a live taping to clear up the public's fears."

Matt pointed over his shoulder to the entry way. "Is the story going to explain the luggage outside and in the doorway?"

Laurel jumped up immediately. "Oh my God; Tyler, help me get the luggage into the front bedroom will you?"

"Sure." Tyler and Laurel hurried and put the luggage in the front bedroom and closed the door before returning to their seats in the living room. The detectives both noticed that Greg and Shelby were completely relaxed, although Greg looked a little rough around the edges.

Phil took a sip of his coffee as Laurel started to speak again. "Believe it or not, yes, it will explain the luggage." Looking at both detectives, she picked her coffee cup up off the table in front of her and held it to warm her hands, "I am sure both of you are going to have very specific questions you need answered to close your investigation. May I ask that you hold them until after the news taping and Ms. Garcia and any of her crew has left?"

Matt deferred to Phil. "Very well."

The front doorbell rang again upon Veronica Garcia and her cameraman's arrival. Tyler got up to let her in. "Tyler, hello, it is so nice to see you again—and with happy news!"

"You too, Veronica; come on in and I'll introduce you to my aunt."

Veronica entered the packed living room behind Tyler and stood directly in front of Laurel. The newswoman thought Laurel was even more beautiful in person. "Mrs. Andrews, I am thrilled to meet you and thank you for trusting me with your story."

"Please, call me Laurel. After reading the *US News Report* story following your show, I couldn't see letting anyone else other than you and Tyler have an exclusive release."

Shelby signaled Phil Peters to help her get up. "Excuse me, Veronica, I'm Shelby Abbott and I would really prefer to have my name and position in this household left out of the story. You see, I'm the new owner of this house and I don't want to have that publicized at this time."

Looking at Shelby's swollen stomach, Veronica could understand why, "I understand. Do you want to wait out of sight in a back room for awhile?"

"Yes, please. I have some reading I need to do."

Veronica checked the time, "Okay, everyone we go live in about ten minutes." She noticed her cameraman had already set himself up across from two couches in a corner of the living room. "That's a great spot, Eddie. Detectives Peters and Thompson, why don't you stay where you are, and I'll sit on the end in the corner between the two couches. And, let's see, Laurel if you'll sit on the other couch closest to the end across from me, Greg next to her, and Karen how about you sit on the far end. Tyler, do you think you can squeeze in next to your aunt so you and I are together for the interview?"

"It will be tight, but I think we can do it."

"Eddie how does this look in the camera—will this work?"

"We're good, Veronica." A phone in Eddie's pocket rang and the group heard him say "okay, and five, four, three, two one, and Veronica we are live."

With that, bright lights lit up the room and Veronica looked directly in the camera showing only her upper body as she started the program, "Good morning Keddie! I'm your hostess, Veronica Garcia, and today, *Eye on Keddie* is coming to you live from the home of Greg and Laurel Andrews." With that, the camera panned out to show Tyler sitting opposite from her. "Some of you may remember Tyler Grant and our story on the kidnapping of his aunt, Laurel Andrews. Well, today, we are here, live, to announce that she has been safely returned home, and in an exclusive interview, find out what happened." With that the camera backed up to include the entire seating arrangement in the view. "Tyler it's good to have you here again—and with such good news!"

"Great news, Veronica."

"Let's introduce everyone to our viewers. On my left, I'm sure you remember Detectives Peters and Johnson." The men nodded as she said their names.

"And starting with the lovely lady at the opposite end of Tyler, we have Karen Vincent, Greg Andrews and the lady of the hour, Laurel Andrews."

Laurel had regained her focus while Veronica was setting up for the show. Taking Greg's hand, she waited for the interview to begin.

Tyler picked up Laurel's other hand and indicated to Veronica that he would take over. "Aunt Laurel, all of the United States has been searching for you and had presumed you were murdered. Would you please tell us what happened?"

"Of course, Tyler, but first, I must apologize to everyone watching for being the cause of so much distress and I thank you all, from the bottom of my heart, for your efforts and good wishes. While I was never in any danger, you must understand that my husband, just like all of you, was not aware of that and you helped him tremendously."

Releasing one of her hands, Laurel pulled her folded statement she wrote on the flight from her jacket pocket and then read a deftly prepared, completely truthful story. "Five weeks ago, my husband and I did have a fight the evening before the morning of my disappearance. Because I wasn't speaking to him, I left on my morning run while he was in the shower knowing he would leave for work before my return. Just as I neared home, a van pulled up with a new acquaintance of mine, Lord David Whitethorn, and his assistant here on a visit from England. Lord Whitethorn was interested in having me renovate Whitethorn Castle after seeing my home on a house tour. Lord Whitethorn was quite distressed as he had received a phone call advising him of his daughter having had an accident and his need to return home immediately. I had agreed to the renovation, and assured that Lord David's staff would see to my needs, we left immediately for his personal plane that was waiting at the airport. His assistant left a note for my husband on our door. Lord Whitethorn has been in the United States many times since former President Clinton gave him diplomatic status to enable a partnership utilizing Lord Whitethorn's unique power saving architecture in several projects throughout our country. Lord Whitethorn is a single parent of two children and his family estate has been secured on a large piece of land away from television and the public to provide his children a life free from his celebrity. Over the course of the next few weeks with the help of a team of workmen, the interior of the castle was completely renovated to my design. It wasn't until a box arrived containing several weeks worth of papers from Lord Whitethorn's sister, who had been in seclusion following her husband's death, that we found out the note had been taken and the mistake concerning my disappearance. The well known photo-journalist, Donovan Metcalf, had just completed a story on the renovation when I received the news and headed home to America immediately."

Tyler was pleased to see Veronica completely captivated by his aunt's tale. "So, if Scott Gregory hadn't swiped the note off of your door, your husband would have known you were suddenly called away on business."

"That's correct."

Shaking her pretty head and looking at the detectives, Veronica gave Phil Peters the floor. "Amazing, isn't it Detective Peters?"

"Yes, it is."

"Tell us, what, if anything happens now to Scott Gregory?"

"That will be for the court to decide. He is still in custody for the ongoing fraud investigation. I'm not sure that he could be charged as an accessory since it appears the crime of kidnapping didn't happen. I do feel he should be responsible for some kind of reimbursement to the City of Keddie for the man hours involved in an unnecessary investigation."

Turning to look back at Greg, she took a quick poll on his feelings before they were out of time. "Greg, what about you; I'm sure you're relieved to have your wife home safely, but you were put through an absolutely horrendous ordeal. Do you have any thoughts about filing a civil suit against Scott Gregory?"

Greg rubbed his chin with his hand before answering, "Veronica, I don't think any lawsuit is going to have a punishment suitable for payment of five weeks of my life, do you?"

"Probably not," she answered. Seeing Eddie's signal to wind it up, she thanked everyone before closing. "Tyler, Detectives, Karen, Greg and especially you, Laurel, thank you for sharing your story with us this morning. We're out of time. This is Veronica Garcia with *Eye on Keddie* wishing everyone a great day." The camera showed the group talking animatedly as the credits rolled.

"And, we're off," Eddie stated.

Veronica, Tyler and Eddie left quickly to head to the station to film the broadcast for Philadelphia. Laurel took Karen's hand and pulled her to the side after they stood up. "Wait for me for a few minutes in with Shelby, okay?"

Seeing the Detectives waiting for Laurel's attention, Karen knew there wasn't a choice in the matter. "Sure. Try to hurry so we can talk, okay?"

Laurel turned back to the two detectives as Greg stood next to her side. She sensed that Matt Johnson was the more aggressive of the two and was surprised when he kept quiet while Phil Peters took over the questioning.

"Laurel, first let me say how happy we are that you are safe and sound. I'm not sure exactly what went down that you didn't just wait to call your husband and fly to England the next day, and I don't want to know. I'm going to assume you are extremely stubborn and wanted to take the opportunity to cause your husband some grief after your fight. This would have never come to our attention if Scott hadn't taken that piece of paper off of your door. One thing I do know is that your passport was still here and you better prepare yourself for a possible visit from Homeland Security if they find that out."

"Detective Peters, Lord Whitethorn has done a tremendous service to our country in taking steps to help preserve energy. I also know the story Donovan Metcalf did is going to create not only a lot of goodwill between England and America, but provide good press in a world that is scrutinizing our every move. I'm going to hope that the detail of my passport never appears in any of your reports."

Matt Johnson finally spoke up, "Phil, what are you talking about? I don't remember anything about any passport."

CHAPTER 31

Three weeks after her arrival in Rome, Laurel was surprised to awaken to soft knocking on her door. She had lodged herself in one of Italy's "houses of hospitality"—a convent that had rooms rented to visitors as a way to make money. This one had been heaven sent. Not only did she have a room with a private bath, she had become friends with one of the nuns who spoke English, Sister Kathleen, and their early morning walks had been very therapeutic. Glancing at the clock on her bedside table, she was shocked that she had slept through her alarm again. Hopping out of bed, she called out, "Come in."

Sister Kathleen's smiling face greeted Laurel on her way to put on her robe. "Good morning, sleepyhead, am I early?"

"No, Sister Kathleen, I overslept again. I don't know what's the matter with me; I must have been more tired than I thought from all of the stress."

Sister Kathleen knew she would have to wait while Laurel dressed, Taking a seat on a chair, she nodded at Laurel, "Yes, well stress can certainly take a toll on the body. Are you excited to see your friend from America today?"

"Yes. Karen is going to be very grateful to you."

"Why would your friend be grateful to me?"

"Because you have listened to me over and over again as I worked through the problems of the world so she won't have to."

The nun shook a hand at Laurel, "Oh, you! From what you've told me about Karen, I know she would have wanted to be here for you. If I have been any help to you, I'm glad. Maybe now you and Karen can travel and enjoy Italy the way two good friends should."

Laurel headed towards the bathroom, "Maybe. Give me five minutes and I'll be ready to go." Pointing to her cell phone on the bedside table, she posed a request, "Will you listen for my phone in case Emily calls?"

"You know I will, now, get moving!"

Moments later, the ladies left for their walk along the convent grounds. Sister Kathleen planned to walk a little longer than usual this morning to satisfy herself that Laurel was ready in both mind and body to move forward in her life. "I've prepared the room next to yours for Karen."

"Thank you Sister, I hope you didn't have too much trouble arranging that. I know how busy the convent can be."

"It's almost winter Laurel. We won't be as busy again before spring. So, tell me, between your talks with Emily, our morning walks, and solitary contemplation while you've visited Rome's attractions, have you been able to sort out everything in your mind?"

"For my feelings, yes, its David's feelings I can't be sure of. Sister Kathleen, I know this has been horrible for you to try to give me guidance since I've done some activities directly against the church's teachings and am about to be divorced. You'll never know how much your kindness has meant to me. You never once made me feel as if you were judging me."

"It's not for me to judge you my dear. Why is it that everyone thinks all nuns are angels and have never done anything against God's teachings? I'll have you know, I was a very wild teenager."

Laurel looked at her with surprised eyes, "You? I would never have guessed that!"

"Well, it's true. I won't give you specifics since I'm saving them for our maker, but I will tell you I'm no closer to a saint than you are. Can you tell me what you've heard from Emily?"

Sister Kathleen thought the crestfallen look on Laurel's face at her question spoke volumes. "Emily says she misses me terribly and that the children are having a hard time adjusting. She said the sweaters and letters I've sent helped cheer them up, but they don't understand why I can't come and visit them again to play with them. They don't really understand the difference between visiting and my working on their castle. My husband wasn't real to them either—they never met him. She also said that David has become very withdrawn—even more so than when Lady Elizabeth left him years before. She said they are living in a very beautiful, but very somber household."

"And David still doesn't know she has been telephoning you regularly?"

"Good Lord, no, he would not be happy to find out about that. Emily said that after I left, David got a call from his sister and found out about how I got back into America and my decision to divorce Greg. He practically went through the phone lines trying to get his sister to tell him where I had gone, but Shelby kept her promise to me and never told him about my trip to Italy. If he found out that Emily knew where I was all of this time, heads would roll."

"Shouldn't that tell you how much he loves you?"

"If he had met and dated other women in the past few years for comparison, yes. However, I still don't know that his feelings didn't evolve because of the excitement of the remodeling and the fact that I was the only woman he had been near in such a close capacity for so many years that he was merely carried away."

"Yet you are sure that you are in love with him and not that you were caught up in the fantasy of your surroundings?"

"Oh God, yes, I'm dying a little everyday when I travel through the city. I saw the Colosseum and wanted to hear him tell me about the architecture. I visited the Vatican and its museum, the gardens and the Sistine Chapel and ached to have my hand in his as we explored every nook and cranny. I threw a coin in the Fontana di Trevi yesterday and wished for him to magically appear next to me. I have never felt my mind and soul as alive as it did the five weeks I was at Whitethorn Castle with David."

"Well, I think you are wrong about his feelings for you. This is a mature man who has traveled and handled tremendous responsibility. I think he is very aware that you are his perfect compliment and that he loves you, and only you, very much. I hope when your friend Karen gets here she will be able to convince you of that so you will return where I feel you really belong. Given the circumstances of your leaving him, I'm not sure even he would wait for you forever."

The ladies were circling the gardens near the end of their walk, "I hope I make up my mind soon too. I'm exhausted from all of the thinking." As they neared the stairway to her room, she stopped and took Sister Kathleen's hand in hers, "Again, my dear friend, thank you for all you've done. I'll see you later after Karen arrives and I've cleaned up."

Sister Kathleen watched her as she made her way up the stairs. She was seriously concerned she was ill; she could tell Laurel was tired from their walk and could easily go to sleep again. She was a young woman, she should be awake and excited about her friend's impending arrival—stressed or not.

Laurel did take a nap for an hour before showering. She went downstairs to the main room two hours later to wait for Karen. The taxi pulled up fifteen minutes later and Karen emerged from the car with a smile of appreciation on her face as she took in the beautiful convent. Karen had stayed here before and recommended it to Laurel.

Laurel rushed out to the street the minute the taxi pulled up and she saw Karen. Opening her arms and smiling wide, she welcomed her friend, "Karen, boy am I glad to see you!"

Returning Laurel's hug, Karen had noticed the dark circles under her friend's eyes. "That goes for me too. Are you okay? You look really tired."

"I'm okay. I think the stress is just taking its toll. Come on, there's someone I want you to meet inside and then we can get you settled. You're in the room next to mine."

Sister Kathleen had watched the two women get reacquainted from inside to give them their privacy. After seeing the two friends together, she no longer had any worries for her new friend. These women may not have been born from the same mother, but they were sisters all the same. Laurel pulled Karen along and stopped directly in front of the nun. "Sister Kathleen, I'd like you to meet my best friend and a wonderful writer, Karen Vincent. Karen, this is my new friend and therapist, Sister Kathleen."

Sister Kathleen was chuckling as she shook Karen's hand. "It's wonderful to meet you Karen. I've heard so much about you and the convent is very happy that you gave us your recommendation for lodging in your book, business has been wonderful."

"It's nice to meet you too. I'm glad you've had a benefit from my previous stay. I'm surprised I don't remember you from my last visit. A nun that speaks English would have been a big help."

"I am sure I would have been. I just transferred to this convent about six months ago. Why don't we get you settled in your room and then we can talk a little more over lunch, if you two don't mind my joining you."

Both women spoke at once "that would be great!"

"Thank you. I am excited to hear where Karen has planned for you to visit in our country, Laurel. Follow me ladies."

Sister Kathleen led them out to the gardens and circled the perimeter to take a stairway at the opposite side leading up to their rooms. Opening the door of the room next to Laurel's, Sister Kathleen stood aside and handed Karen the key as she passed over the threshold. She was very pleased to hear Karen exclaim, "It's every bit as beautiful as I remember. Thank you, Sister."

"You're welcome, Karen. I'll leave you two ladies now. Shall we meet at noon to have our lunch?"

Laurel answered for them both, "that would be perfect, Sister Kathleen. After lunch, I'm sure Karen could use the rest time after her trip and I seem to be part Italian the way I've rested every day."

Karen looked her friend up and down the minute they were alone. Laurel not only looked tired, she could tell Laurel had lost weight. "Laurel, are you sure you're alright? You've lost some weight."

"Karen, stop it, I'm fine. I'm sure it's just stress. Now that you're here, we'll get on with our traveling and it will take my mind off of the rest of my worries. Sister Kathleen has brought me a long way."

"I'm glad she was here for you. I'm also sorry I wasn't. If this is an improvement, I should have been here sooner."

"No you shouldn't have. I was in very good hands and you put your career on hold for five weeks as it was. Now, enough; I just want to help you get settled so you can tell me where we're going first."

"Oh no you don't, we can talk about that with Sister Kathleen at lunch. I want you to tell me what you've decided about David."

"Good God, are you sure you didn't talk with the Sister before you arrived?"

"NO! Now quit stalling and start talking."

"Okay, I know that it's only been a little over two months since my life turned upside down, and a month since Greg filed the papers for the divorce, but, in my heart, I know what I feel when I'm with David is love—and a perfect love for me, at that. With Sister Kathleen's help, I've been able to sort out my guilt over my adultery with David and I know that I wasn't carried along by the fantasy of my environment. Quite simply, I love the man and I sinned against God. I've gone to church and asked for forgiveness for both the adultery and my impending divorce. Sister Kathleen told me there has been a lot of talk within the Catholic Church about allowing divorcees the opportunity to continue within the faith. Even though Greg agreed to seek an annulment within the church, it was a great comfort to know that I still had an open door if I wanted it. David is my other half, Karen, I can feel it. We don't need to speak when we're together, our minds are circuited the same. His love of art perfectly meshes and feeds mine. I feel whole when I'm with him. I've missed him so much, I think that's why my appetite has been off and I'm so tired. I'm depressed."

"I see, and the reason you haven't called the man and told him this would be?"

"Damn it, Karen, you know what I told you about his honor and strong family values. He married before to keep a promise to his father. I don't want him to marry me because he feels guilt over my divorce and trying to do the "honorable thing". I want him to be sure he loves me and that he wasn't caught up in the excitement of the party resulting in misleading emotions."

"Laurel, do you remember what you told me a few years ago when I hadn't met my Prince Charming and I was staying at home in between trips abroad?"

"Not exactly; why?"

"You said that all men, Prince Charming included, were incapable of using ESP since they didn't have that particular gene and that if I thought my prince was magically going to show up at my front door, sensing the woman of his dreams was inside, was pure insanity. You insisted I not only had to go out my door, but that when I was on trips, I actually had to talk with any princes that happened to cross my path."

"Oh, yes, I do remember that."

"Then how do you expect David to know you love him and give him the opportunity to tell you if he feels the same if you don't talk to him?"

"I don't know. I only know he has to find his own heart's feelings just as I had to find mine."

Hearing bells signifying the noon hour, Karen gave up. "Let's go down to lunch. I can tell I'm going to need some of Sister Kathleen's therapy."

Sister Kathleen was waiting for them at the entrance to the dining hall, "There you are. I've saved us a table over in the corner."

Once seated, nuns moved silently through the room serving a delicious salad and pasta meal. Karen was happy to share her and Laurel's itinerary at the nun's request. "We'll be leaving for Tuscany tomorrow. I especially want Laurel to see the Uffizi Gallery in Florence. I know she'll go crazy over the works of Leonardo and Michelangelo. Then I want to take her to the Tower of Pisa before visiting Lucca and Siena. After that, we simply must tour Milan and Venice. Before we start on our trip, though, I want to make a stop at the English embassy and fill out papers for a visa in case she comes to her senses and wants to make a stop in England. I wouldn't mind seeing this castle she decorated in person." At Laurel's shocked expression, Karen put a hand out on top of hers, "Don't worry, Laurel, we don't have to use them if you don't want to. It can take six weeks to get a visa. We don't have a diplomat to pull any strings for us either. I don't want you to miss out on the best thing that ever blessed your life if you decide to take a chance."

Sister Kathleen thought that was an excellent idea and admired Karen's thoughtfulness. "She's made a good point, Laurel."

Tired again, Laurel pushed her half eaten plate away and gave in to the combined force of the two women. "Okay, you win. Let's take care of the embassy first thing in the morning, after we pick up our rental car."

The three finished their lunch and then Laurel and Karen left for the midday rest in their rooms after agreeing to say their goodbyes to Sister Kathleen before dinner. They were planning on going out and wouldn't be back until the ten thirty curfew. Sister Kathleen would be at prayers when they left in the morning.

The next morning, Karen was easily prepared to leave since she didn't bother unpacking anything but her overnight necessities. Closing her personal items in her little suitcase, she popped over to her friend's room to see how close she was to being able to leave.

Karen took one look at Laurel's green complexion and was seriously alarmed. "You're sick! We've got to get you to a doctor."

"I'll be fine in a minute. I didn't want to say anything to you or Sister Kathleen, but I've been sick for the past couple of days. After I'm up for awhile, I'm fine. It's just the stress, Karen, my immunity is low and I've picked up a bug."

"Uh huh, sure. Let's see, you've lost weight, you're sick in the morning and you're tired all the time. Laurel, if the doctors hadn't told you it would be a miracle for you to conceive naturally, what would be your first thought about your condition?"

Laurel's eyes opened wide and she placed her hands across her stomach, "Oh God, Karen, that's impossible," she gushed in denial. "No, I'm sure it's just the stress. Now, help me pack my things up and let's get going."

Karen knew her friend well enough to know it was useless to argue with her. Just as Laurel started towards the bathroom and Karen started packing things away, Laurel's cell phone rang. Laurel picked it up on her way, "Oh, Emily, this is a surprise. Is something wrong?"

Emily was trying to help Gwen while the children were with Roger at their studies. "I know I just spoke with you yesterday, but Gwen is having a problem with Cat and Tim. They miss you so much and are really down in the dumps. Roger was trying to help and suggested that they pretend they were with you in Italy by having a pizza lunch before asking me if I had kept the recipe. The children were so excited that I had to call you the moment Gwen came to tell me the lunch plans because, as you know, I did not keep that particular recipe."

God how she missed Cat and Tim! "No problem, Emily, write this down." After Laurel told her how to prepare the pizza, she asked Emily how David hadn't figured out her whereabouts if his children and everyone else knew where she was.

"I told you, Laurel, he has been completely withdrawn. He doesn't really talk to them; he goes through the motions, but he's not really paying attention. Gwen, Roger and I are actually helping the children the same way we did when their mother left. Lord David was also gone for a week on business and shut himself up again when he returned home."

Karen could see the total devastation Laurel was feeling as she watched her face as she was listening to Emily. Laurel spoke very quietly after Emily finished, "Emily, I am so sorry. You know I left David a note asking him to give me time to sort out my feelings. I had no idea it would result in him behaving this way. Will you ever forgive me?"

"What are you talking about? You know I love you and I want you to take all the time you need. I know you'll figure it all out eventually, and so will Lord David."

"Thank you. Karen is here and we're about to leave. Give my love to everyone and I'll talk to you next week."

"Goodbye darling."

Two hours later, they were on their way to Tuscany after filling out the forms for a visa at the English embassy.

Karen had reserved lodging in advance for every leg of their trip. Laurel fell asleep almost as soon as they started their drive and didn't awaken until they were at their hotel in Florence three hours later. The next few days were exactly the same; Laurel threw up in the morning and then fought to stay awake at some of the world's most incredible sights until Karen couldn't stand it a moment longer. "Laurel, I don't think this is stress and if you aren't pregnant, you have a serious bug. I made an appointment for you to see a doctor this morning and I won't take no for an answer."

Laurel was relieved Karen had made the appointment. She was sure she wasn't pregnant and scared she had something very serious. "I'm not going to argue with you, I'm scared too."

A few hours later, Laurel, with Karen at her side, was sitting stunned and dazed in front of a very nice, very small, Italian doctor listening to him tell her in broken English, "Congratulations, Senora, I am happy to tell you there is no disease, you are going to have a bambino!"

Laurel burst into tears. Karen had to get the doctor's orders for her and then help her out to their car she was so shaken up. Once she had her settled, she kept silent for their drive back to the hotel. She practically carried Laurel up to their room. Once there, she put her in a chair she had turned to face her and demanded her attention. "Okay, Laurel, this changes everything. We have got to contact Lord David and tell him you're pregnant."

"The Hell we do! He would insist on marrying me as soon as the divorce was final out of honor. I am not going to trap him into marriage—I can't do that to him after what he went through with Elizabeth. I need to know he wants to marry me because he loves me and isn't complete without me, not because he feels he has to for the sake of our child."

"But Laurel, you have to think of your child. And, how are you ever going to find out what we've all been trying to tell you, if you don't contact the man?"

"I think if he is really in love with me, he'll find me and let me know." Karen tried to speak up, but Laurel put her hands up and stopped her, "Stop! My mind is made up. You weren't there to see his face or feel his pain when he told me about Elizabeth. We are going to finish touring Italy and then I'm going to fly home and that's it. The article about the castle should come out before we get back to the States so I shouldn't have much trouble starting my own business. I have more than enough money to live on whether I work or not."

Karen knew that look after years of friendship and appeared to give in. "Alright, we'll do it your way. We're going to take it nice and easy, though, I don't want you to take any chances with your little miracle, understood?"

Early in the morning a few days later, Karen was waiting for Laurel to finish with her morning sickness in the bathroom so they could tour some art galleries in Lucca when Laurel's cell phone rang. Karen guessed who was calling even before she read the display. She had promised not to tell Lord David about the baby, but she hadn't promised not to tell anyone else. Lifting the cell phone cover, she quietly spoke into the phone, "Hello, Emily? This is Karen, Laurel's friend. We have to talk."

Almost forty-five minutes later, Laurel exited the bathroom dressed and ready to leave, failing to notice her cell phone was on a different table from where she'd left it. "Sorry, Karen, I'll be glad when the morning sickness part passes."

"Well, the doctor thought that would be soon, so hang in there. I put the luggage in the car except for your overnight bag, so we're set to go ahead and get started for the galleries and then head to Siena. I was wondering, since we're cutting our trip short to head home, would you mind if we went back through Rome? I never leave without tossing a coin in Trevi."

"Of course not, in fact, I think I could use a trip back there myself. A little luck in the wishing department wouldn't hurt."

"It's settled then. When we get to Siena tonight, I'll phone ahead to the convent to make reservations for an overnight stay in Rome."

"I don't know what I would have done without you Karen. How do you feel about being an aunt?"

"Ecstatic. Now let's get going so you can sleep again."

Three days later they were warmly greeted by Sister Kathleen at the convent. Karen had told the Sister about Laurel's pregnancy and asked her not to reveal her knowledge. She simply wanted to relieve her mind about any illness since she and Laurel had grown so close. "Welcome back! I am delighted to see you again. I was surprised to hear you changed your mind and will be returning home early, Laurel. What happened?"

Laurel just couldn't tell the nun about her pregnancy. She was technically still married and not pregnant by her husband. "Oh, I guess I just decided I missed home."

"Home is always where everything begins and ends, isn't it? Do you want me to put your bags in your rooms for you? Karen told me when she phoned in your reservation that you are going back to Fontana di Trevi."

"Would you mind? I really can't wait to see the fountain and make a wish."

"No, it is no trouble at all. You two go on and I'll see you later."

The fountain gave Laurel the same sense of peace and hope she felt the first time she saw it. She was so glad Karen wanted to come here—it was just what she needed. She was a little worried a few minutes after she arrived when she thought she saw Karen talking with Roger, but shaking her head and citing pregnancy brain damage, she decided he was just someone who looked a lot like Roger. A nano-second later, a coin appeared over the top of her head as she noticed Anita, Gwen, Emily, Thomas, Henry, Cat and Tim standing around the fountain and a deep voice behind her made his wish, "Please let the love of my life turn around and tell me she'll share the rest of her days together with me."

Laurel spun so fast at the sound of David's voice she was dizzy. Throwing herself into his embrace, she knew Karen had set her up and that he knew about the baby. Just before she gave into the kiss she'd been holding for a lifetime, she silently asked God to bless Karen. As everyone gathered around the embraced couple, they finished the kiss and Laurel drew her head back to look at her lover's face, "I told you Whitethorn would need a nursery."

978-0-595-49415-6
0-595-49415-3

Printed in the United States
143061LV00002B/5/P